DARK SPACE UNIVERSE
THE LAST STAND

(2nd Edition)

by Jasper T. Scott

JasperTscott.com

@JasperTscott

TABLE OF CONTENTS

ACKNOWLEDGMENTS

Writing, editing, and publishing this book in just two months was a monumental task. The list of people to thank is necessarily shorter, because there just wasn't enough time for most of my advance readers to get through the book and send me their feedback. With that said, I'm very grateful to all of the people who managed to set aside their busy lives and somehow read through this book in a matter of just a few days. My eternal thanks go to: B. Allen Thobois, Davis Shellabarger, Gary Matthews, Gregg Cordell, Harry Huyler, Ian F. Jedlica, Jacqueline Gartside, Karl Keip, Karol Ross, Lara Gray, Lee Anke, Mary Whitehead, Mary Kastle Michael Raycraft, Peter Rouse, Rafael Gutierrez, and Shane Haylock—you guys are amazing!

Finally, an enormous thank you goes to my volunteer editor, Dave Cantrell, who while sick and bed-ridden managed to read through and edit this book in just one week, giving me all the feedback that only a professional editor could give—and all the while refusing my attempts to pay him for his help. Dave, you are a damn fine editor and a fantastic writer, but you're an even better friend. Thank you for all you do.

To those who dare,
And to those who dream.
To everyone who's stronger than they seem.

"Believe in me / I know you've waited for so long /
Believe in me / Sometimes the weak become the strong."
—STAIND, Believe

DRAMATIS PERSONNAE

Ortane Family

Lucien "Lucy" Ortane
Tyra Ortane
Atara Ortane - their five-year-old daughter
Theola Ortane - their eighteen month-old daughter

Lucien's Family

Ethan Ortane - Crusader/Captain of *Dauntless*
Alara Ortane - Crusader/Co-captain of *Dauntless*
Trinity Ortane

Former Crew of the Intrepid

Garek Helios "The Veteran"
Adalyn Gallia "Addy"
Brakos "Brak" - the Gor

Astralis

Joseph Corretti
Bob "The Android"
Admiral Esalia Wheeler

Gideon

Colonel Drask - First Officer "XO"/Gunnery Chief
Major Calla Ward - First Officer "XO"/Gunnery Chief
Lieutenant Roth Sebal - Comms

Veritus

Lieutenant Cassa Alissar - Engineering

Lieutenant Gorman Argos - Helm / First Officer
Lieutenant Lila Asher - Sensor Operator
Lieutenant Teranik - Comms

New Earth

High Praetor Serenity Talos

Others

Etherus
Abaddon - Arch-enemy of Etherus

PREVIOUSLY IN DARK SPACE UNIVERSE

Please Note

The following synopses contain spoilers from *Dark Space Universe (Book 1)*, and *Dark Space Universe (Book 2): The Enemy Within.*

If you haven't read those books and would rather do so, you can get them here:

Book 1: http://smarturl.it/darkspace7

Book 2: http://smarturl.it/darkspace8

Synopsis of
Dark Space Universe (Book 1)

Etherus, the god and ruler of humanity, warned the three hundred million non-believers aboard *Astralis* of the dangers lurking beyond the Red Line, but he allowed them to leave his kingdom and seek the true nature of the universe by traveling to the cosmic horizon.

Tyra Forster, captain of the *Inquisitor,* along with Lucien Ortane and a crew of trained explorers, known as Paragons, blazed a path for *Astralis,* but they soon ran into the Faros, a hostile race of alien slavers. The Faros relentlessly chased them across multiple star systems until the *Inquisitor* became separated from *Astralis.*

Captain Forster and her crew spent the next eight years

in stasis while their robotic navigator, Pandora, took them to the cosmic horizon and a rendezvous with *Astralis.* Soon after reaching that rendezvous, they learned that Pandora was actually a spy for the Faros, and an alien fleet arrived to enslave them all.

During the ensuing battle, the crew of the *Inquisitor* was forced to abandon ship and flee from *Astralis* in shuttles. All of the shuttles were intercepted or destroyed, except for Lucien's, which was badly damaged, but he managed to set down in a Faro colony with three of his fellow crew.

The Faros' leader, Abaddon, nearly killed them, and would have done so but for the efforts of an escaped Faro slave named Oorgurak. He helped them escape to Freedom Station, a haven for runaway slaves-turned-pirates, known as Marauders.

Lucien and his surviving crew mates assume that *Astralis* must have been captured by the Faro fleet, and they are now hoping to meet a Marauder captain who will help them find and rescue their people. Little do they know, the Faros' agenda isn't as simple as it seems, and their people are in even greater danger than they think....

Synopsis of *Dark Space Universe (Book 2): The Enemy Within*

Aboard Freedom Station, Lucien and the surviving crew from the *Intrepid* run into Katawa, an enigmatic gray alien who claims to be from Etheria. He offers to help them find and rescue *Astralis* if they will first help him find a lost Etherian fleet so that he can use the data in its nav computers to discover the way home to Etheria.

Back on *Astralis,* Lucien's clone and his wife, Tyra, are fighting desperately to fend off a boarding party of Faros. The aliens detonate a bomb over Fallside, one of the four "surface-level" cities of *Astralis,* ripping the city open to space and killing millions of people in a matter of seconds. But that was just the distraction. Their real objective was to reach *Astralis's* leaders and possess them with Abaddon's own consciousness. Several other less important individuals are also possessed, including Lucien and Tyra's daughter, Atara.

The Faros remain undercover, working secretly to accomplish their real objective: to find the lost fleet and the way to Etheria so they can get revenge on Etherus and the Etherians for exiling them.

Aboard Katawa's shuttle, Lucien and his crew mates discover that their gray alien friend is actually working for Abaddon and using them to find the lost Etherian fleet. By the time they find out, Katawa has stranded them on an alien planet full of hostile natives, and all that's left for them to do is to find the lost fleet so that they can use it to escape.

Meanwhile, Abaddon knows that Lucien and his crew will take the lost fleet straight to *Astralis* once they find it, and now that he has control of *Astralis* through its leaders, he plans to commandeer the fleet as soon as it arrives.

But before Abaddon can execute this plan, Tyra discovers what he's done to the leaders of *Astralis* and to her own daughter, Atara. Tyra hatches a plot with Lucien and several others to overthrow the possessed leaders of *Astralis* by infiltrating the Resurrection Center and exposing the thoughts and memories of the possessed. In order to accomplish this, Lucien Ortane makes a deal with a local gangster, Joe Coretti, to get them a bomb that they can use to hold the center ransom. They execute their plan and smuggle the bomb inside, but things don't go as planned, and most of the infiltrators die in the fighting, including Coretti. Ultimately, the leaders of *Astralis* are revealed for what they are, but Coretti's android henchman detonates the bomb anyway, and blows up the center as part of an unknown criminal agenda.

Marines and police forces move to apprehend the leaders of *Astralis.* Just before they do, Chief Councilor Ellis sends a message to the nearest Faro fleet, giving them instructions to wait until the lost fleet arrives to spring their trap. They won't be able to commandeer the lost Etherian fleet anymore, so they'll just have to fight for it. With that message sent, the possessed humans all manage to kill themselves before they can be brought to justice, leaving *Astralis's* leadership in disarray, and no one to interrogate. Tyra becomes the acting chief councilor, and promotes Commander Esalia Wheeler, a bridge officer and co-conspirator, to the rank of admiral.

Lucien's daughter, Atara, and a few other scattered individuals remain infected with Abaddon's consciousness, and now that the Resurrection Center is destroyed, there's no way to restore their minds to the way they were before—or to bring back any of the people who died when Fallside was destroyed. Atara is being interrogated to discover what the Faros' agenda really was. The interrogation proves fruitless, but just as it's concluding, the Lost Fleet arrives, followed immediately by a massive Faro fleet.

Now *Astralis* is surrounded, and the lost Etherian fleet has just four crew to command more than a thousand ships. Somehow they have to keep the Faros from boarding those ships or Abaddon will learn the way to Etheria and the invasion will begin....

CHAPTER 1

Aboard the Lost Etherian Fleet

Faro ships streamed into the system by the hundreds, appearing with brief, blinding-white flashes of light. The enemy fleet jumped in all around the dark, gleaming wedge of *Astralis,* surrounding it in seconds.

Lucien Ortane watched impotently from the command control station aboard the *Gideon,* the largest of the one thousand and fifty-seven warships in the lost Etherian Fleet.

"They used us as bait to get to *Astralis*—again!" Addy said.

"I don't think so," Garek replied. "Abaddon is after the lost fleet, not *Astralis.*"

"Then why did they only show up now? Why not ambush us sooner?" Addy demanded, turning from her station to look at Lucien.

Her bald scalp shone blue with reflected light from the holo displays at the helm. Even after two months, their hair still hadn't begun to grow back. Katawa had forced them to shave it all off and bathe in depilatory gel so they could disguise themselves as Faros and go hunting for the lost fleet. Little did they know those disguises were just elaborate window dressing and Katawa was secretly working for Abaddon. They'd been manipulated into stealing the lost fleet out from under the noses of its extra-dimensional guardians, the Polypuses, and now the Polypuses' dire warnings about what would happen if the Faros found the fleet were about to come to pass.

"It's the other way around," Lucien decided. "They used *Astralis* as bait to get to *us.* The Polypuses were right. Now, because we didn't take the fleet straight back to Etheria, Abaddon is going to get his hands on it and learn the way to Etheria. Then the visions we saw of him invading and conquering Etheria and New Earth are going to happen. We need to jump away *now,* before it's too late."

"It's *already* too late," Addy said. The Faros have us surrounded with overlapping jamming fields. We can't jump out. The risk of scattering is over ninety percent. There's a nine out of ten chance that we'll disintegrate if we jump away now."

"Maybe that's for the best," Lucien said quietly.

"Think again, kid," Garek said. "A ninety percent chance of scattering with over a thousand vessels means that at least a hundred of them will survive. Abaddon will still find them and discover the way to Etheria. Getting ourselves killed isn't going to help anyone. Besides, *Astralis* needs us now. If we leave them here, the Faros will enslave them for sure."

"So we fight," Brak put in, turning from his control station to bare his dagger-sharp black teeth at them in a fearsome grin.

Lucien shook his head. "How? We've got just four crew for a thousand ships that are ordinarily crewed by a few thousand people each!"

"They're all set to automatically follow us," Addy said.

"Maybe we can find a way to automate their defenses from here?"

"*Astralis* is launching fighters and galleons," Garek announced. "And the Faros are opening fire on them from extreme range—or maybe that's close range for their weapons systems."

Lucien hurriedly paged through the various displays available from his station, hunting for the gunnery panel.

"Faro shuttles are launching!" Addy said. "They're headed our way!"

Lucien found the gunnery panel and scanned the options for automation settings. He found a column labeled *Fire Mode* at the top of the list of weapons on board; then he selected that column and set all of the weapons from *manual fire* to *auto fire*. He looked up at the holo dome covering the *Gideon's* bridge.

Space was dark; clumps of enemy starships gleamed a dull gray, and new ones continued jumping in with periodic flashes of light. The ships in the lost fleet shone a bright silver, and the giant wedge that was *Astralis* gleamed darkly in the system's sun, its solar-energy collecting side facing *up* and slightly to one side.

Lucien expected to see simulated laser beams flash out from their ship, and missiles streaking into the void—or at least to hear the muffled reports of cannons and launchers rumbling through the deck, but all was silent, and the only flashes of weapons fire he saw were the distant, needle-thin flickers of light from the enemy fleet as it fired on *Astralis* and its garrison.

"Those Faro shuttles are getting closer..." Addy warned.

"I don't get it! I set the ship's weapons to auto-fire!" Lucien said.

"You forgot to set a target," Garek explained. "Hang on, I'll do it...." They'd each passed the time while calculating jumps to *Astralis* by familiarizing themselves with the capabilities of one of the ship's primary control systems. Garek had chosen gunnery, Lucien the command station, Brak engineering, while Addy handled the helm, comms, and sensors.

"Got it!" Garek said.

Lucien heard the muffled reports of weapons fire and looked up to see the black of space suddenly turn as bright as day. Green laser beams snapped out in all directions, and bright blue balls of energy tracked through the void at a much lazier pace—*Etherian missiles?* Lucien wondered. After just a second, explosions began poking fiery holes in the darkness between the stars, as if all of space was a thick curtain holding back a blinding wall of light. The explosions faded and blossomed anew, creating shifting patterns that danced behind Lucien's eyelids every time he blinked. "We're kicking the Faros' asses..." he marveled.

Faro shielding and weapons technology was leagues ahead of what humanity had developed, but Etherian tech was far better still.

"Don't get too excited," Addy said. "We're just one ship against hundreds. If we can't find a way to control the rest of the fleet from here, we're still going to lose."

"I think I've got it," Garek said.

Just as he said that, green lasers and blue missiles snapped out from the rest of their fleet. Green lasers and streaking blue missiles filled the void, drawing bright, flowering orange explosions wherever they converged.

Unable to make any sense of the battle from such a limited perspective, Lucien looked back to his displays and paged through them until he found something called the *tactical map*. He selected it, and a two-dimensional grid appeared, sprawled out in front of him like a chess board. Three-dimensional red and green-shaded miniatures hovered above and below the grid, with straight lines connecting them to it and providing a sense of depth.

Lucien found he could rotate the entire display by moving his hands around it as if he were grasping an invisible ball and turning it in his hands. Simulated laser beams and the tiny glowing balls of missiles flashed between the friendly and enemy ships, causing their miniature 3D icons to flicker as they took fire.

Bright blue circles around the ships denoted their shield strength, along with a percent value. Most of those blue circles were still bright and showing percentages in the high nineties, but a few of the enemy ships were surrounded by much dimmer blue circles, with shield values already dropping into the forties and thirties.

A *contacts summary* to one side of the display gave the numbers of vessels in the two fleets—the lost fleet, labeled *Gideon's Army*, still showed all one thousand and fifty-seven ships they'd started with, while the enemy fleet, labeled the *5016th Faro Fleet*, numbered six hundred and ten—

Six hundred and nine, Lucien corrected, as one of the enemy capital ships cracked apart in a fiery burst of jagged debris.

Sub-groupings within each fleet detailed the number of fighters, shuttles, and other smaller craft. The Faros had deployed thousands of fighters and hundreds of shuttles and other support ships, but the lost fleet showed no such sub-groupings.

Lucien touched each of the enemy sub-groups, highlighting and enlarging them on the display. Swarms of previously invisible red specks appeared. Like a wave of locusts, they swarmed through the lost Etherian fleet. Those fighters opened fire, and suddenly the entire Etherian fleet was flickering on the grid, with shield values slowly dropping.

The Faro fighters quickly broke up into smaller groups, focusing fire on just a handful of ships for greater effect. Then the enemy capital ships began focusing fire on those vessels, too, and their shields began dropping faster. The targeted vessels automatically redirected their fire to the fighters swarming them, revealing that Garek must have found some kind of *auto-targeting* option to accompany the *auto-fire* mode.

Enemy fighters exploded by the dozens, but there were too many of them, and the ships they'd targeted were losing their shields too fast. One of them was down to just fifty-two percent.

Lucien ground his teeth. "If they can drop the shields on just one of our ships, they'll board it with shuttles and use the nav systems to find Etheria. We can't let that happen."

"We could target those ships and destroy them before they're boarded," Addy suggested.

"And waste our firepower by redirecting it on ourselves?" Garek demanded. "Forget Etheria! We've got our own problems! Let's just focus on getting out of here in one piece."

Lucien scowled, watching enemy fighters swarm them

in coordinated attack runs—first one way, and then back the other, like schooling fish. He glanced back at the *contacts summary.* The number of capital ships in the *5016th Faro Fleet* was down to five hundred and ninety two... ninety-one... eighty-nine, while the Etherian Fleet still numbered one thousand and fifty-seven. Below that, a new group had appeared, labeled *Astralis.* A sub-grouping below it showed more than two thousand friendly fighters and over a hundred star galleons—what was left of their garrison. When Lucien selected those sub-groups, he found those ships were all surrounding *Astralis* in a defensive formation, but that garrison was wasted on them. The Faros weren't after *Astralis.*

"Addy, get *Astralis* on the comms. Tell them to fly into our midst so we can pool our defenses."

"On it," Addy said.

"Good idea," Garek replied. "Meanwhile, see if you can find some way to order our ships around so we can move the ones with the weakest shields into cover positions behind the others. They're not responding to orders from the gunnery station, but they might answer to the helm."

"Addy, forget the comms," Lucien said. "I'll contact *Astralis.* You just focus on moving those ships!"

"Aye, aye, Captain," Addy replied.

Lucien frowned at the slightly sarcastic tone in her voice, but he decided not to make an issue out of it. The chain of command had broken down between the four of them months ago. As the former XO of the star galleon that they'd served on together, Lucien was the ranking officer among them, but they seemed to have forgotten that fact. *Time to remind them.*

"Garek, you focus on optimizing our firepower.

Primary targets are any shuttles about to board one of our ships, followed by fighters, and then enemy capital ships."

"Forget the shuttles. They can't hurt us," Garek said.

"Yeah? What happens after they board our ships and start turning our own guns against us?"

"They won't do that," Garek replied. "They want to use the lost fleet to find Etheria. Using captured ships to fire on us would only give us a reason to fire back and destroy them before they can find the nav data they're looking for."

"It's not going to take them long to find that data," Lucien countered. "And as soon as they do that, their goals will change."

"I'll keep the target priorities in mind," Garek replied.

Lucien narrowed his eyes at the back of Garek's bald head, but there wasn't time for a lecture about insubordination.

"What am I to do?" Brak asked.

Good question, Lucien thought. Brak was seated at the ship's engineering station. If the capabilities of the other control stations were anything to go by, he should be able to control the engineering functions of the rest of the fleet from his station. "See if you can manage the power distribution aboard our other ships. Find the ones with failing shields and boost the power to their shields as much as you can," Lucien said.

"Let me see..." Brak replied. "Yes, I can do this."

"Good."

"And what are *you* going to do?" Garek asked.

"I'm going to focus on our overall battle strategy and coordinate our defense with *Astralis*."

"You mean ordering us around," Garek said.

"You have a problem with that?" Lucien demanded.

Garek turned from the gunnery control station. "I have more command experience than you do. With all of our lives hanging in the balance, I say we vote on it."

"This isn't a democracy. We all still have our ranks. I'm a commander and you're a lieutenant."

"I outranked you back in the Etherian Empire," Garek pointed out. "I was a crusader, the equivalent of a captain in the Paragons."

"Until you let personal feelings get in the way of your orders. You slaughtered thousands of aliens just because they hurt your daughter. You'd probably sacrifice this entire fleet if it meant you could save her and *Astralis* now. A good leader doesn't allow personal bias to guide their actions, but you did and you'll do it again."

Addy turned from her station, her green eyes flicking from Lucien to Garek and back again. "Are you two done with your pissing contest?"

Garek glared at her. "He's not fit to command this fleet. He'd gladly throw all of our lives away if it meant keeping Etheria safe. Go ahead, ask him!"

"Lucien?" Addy's gaze bored into him.

Lucien hesitated before giving a reply. "There are three hundred million people on *Astralis* and—"

"Probably more by now," Garek interrupted.

"Regardless, that's nothing compared to the trillions of people in Etheria and on New Earth."

"So whose lives matter more?" Addy challenged. "Theirs or ours?"

Lucien shook his head. "Life is life, and it's all equally valuable, but the greater loss of life will be in Etheria—and on

New Earth—if the Faros can somehow use this fleet to find the way there. We have to stop them, no matter what the cost."

Silence rang on the bridge. Lucien could tell what they were thinking—Garek was thinking about his daughter; Addy was thinking about her own life; and Brak...

He was a wild card, but since he always seemed to put his people first, and all of them were living on New Earth, it was safe to say that he probably agreed with Lucien's goal of keeping them safe from the Faros.

"We're wasting time!" Lucien growled. "Eyes on your stations! If we all do our jobs, then maybe no one will have to die."

Slowly, reluctantly, both Garek and Addy turned back to their stations. Lucien watched them carefully, eyeing the backs of their heads, and thinking: all of them were wearing Paragon-issue exosuits with integrated weapons. If it came to a mutiny, there'd be a firefight, but who would side with whom?

Addy should have been on his side, but their relationship had been in an awkward place ever since he'd rejected her suggestion that they run away together and explore the universe, leaving someone else to worry about waging war with the Faros.

Lucien shook his head to clear it, and directed his attention back to his displays. He found the comms panel and contacted *Astralis*.

"This is Commander Ortane of the Etherian vessel, *Gideon*. I need to speak with *Astralis* actual."

CHAPTER 2

Astralis

"*Astralis* actual speaking. Go ahead, *Gideon,*" Admiral Wheeler—formerly *Commander* Wheeler—answered.

"That's Lucien you're speaking with," Acting Councilor Tyra Ortane said.

Wheeler glanced at the other woman, the one responsible for her promotion.

Commander Lucien Ortane's voice came back to them over the comms. "We need you to move *Astralis* into the middle of our formation. The Faros aren't after you, but we could use the help of your garrison to keep our own ships safe. We don't have any fighters, and yours could go a long way to covering that weakness."

Wheeler frowned. "They're not after us *yet,* you mean. We just finished rooting out all of the undercover Faro agents from the last time they managed to board us, and we're not in a hurry to go through that again, Commander."

"We'll stand a better chance against them if we pool our defenses," Lucien insisted.

"Agreed, but we need to establish a chain of command. From here on out, *Astralis* gives the orders. Are we clear on that, *Commander?*"

There was a brief pause on the other end of the comms.

"I think I can agree to that—for now."

"What do you mean *for now?*" Wheeler demanded.

"The situation is complicated. This fleet is ours by right of salvage and we have an urgent mission to return it to Etheria."

"What? Why?"

"Because the Faros have been trying to find this fleet for more than ten thousand years. If they get access to just one of our vessels, they'll find the way to Etheria, and then they'll send an invasion fleet to conquer them. If Etheria falls, New Earth will be next, and *Astralis* won't be able to run forever."

"Assuming that's all true, and that the enemy's goal really is to commandeer your vessels, protecting Etheria is still a secondary objective. And if your fleet is any indication of the Etherians' defensive capabilities, they may not us to protect them. Rest assured, we'll weigh all of the competing interests when deciding how to use the fleet you've found after we win this battle."

"Sorry. My fleet, my decision."

"You're a commissioned officer of *Astralis!*" Wheeler boomed. "I don't care what you salvaged. You owe us your service, and that includes giving us any and all resources you have at your disposal."

"The law doesn't agree with you, ma'am. Personal property is personal property, whether it's a fleet or the shirt on my back. Regardless, we can discuss this later. I will agree to submit the fleet to your authority until the immediate danger has passed."

"Fine, but we *will* discuss this again later, Commander," Wheeler intoned. "*Astralis* Actual out." She killed the comms from her end and blew out a frustrated breath.

"He's right," Chief Councilor Tyra Ortane whispered. "The law will award the fleet to him and his crew mates."

Wheeler shot her a scowl. "Then why's he wasting his breath by telling me that?"

"Because we could seize the fleet by fiat."

"Then maybe that's exactly what we should do."

"We need to win this fight first."

"Yes," Wheeler agreed. Turning to address the officers on the bridge, she said, "Helm! Take us as deep into that formation of Etherian ships as you can. As soon as we reach their formation, have our fighters peel off and engage enemy fighters."

"Aye, ma'am," the officer at the helm replied.

With that, Wheeler stalked back to the holo table in the center of the bridge to watch the battle unfold. She was peripherally aware of Chief Councilor Ortane following her there. As they arrived at the table, Colonel Elon Drask, Wheeler's newly-appointed XO looked up and saluted. "Admiral," he said.

"At ease. What's it look like out there, Colonel?"

"Those Etherian ships pack a punch, ma'am, and they have yet to lose a single vessel, while the enemy is down by over a hundred already. They were outnumbered to begin with, so we're definitely winning."

Wheeler's eyebrows shot up, but promptly dropped back down as her brow furrowed in thought. "So, the Etherians have been holding out on us...."

"Ma'am?" Colonel Drask replied.

"All this time they've had tech that's leagues ahead of anyone else's, yet they've never used it to fight the Faros.

Why?"

Colonel Drask shrugged and scratched a dark shadow of stubble on one cheek. The other was clean-shaven. He'd been caught in the middle of shaving when the Faros had arrived. Wheeler had been in the ward room, about to grab a much-needed cup of caf, but she'd never had the chance.

"Maybe they don't have the numbers to win a war," Drask suggested. "Or they have nothing to gain by starting one. Their superior technology might have served as a deterrent. That would explain why the Faros have never dared to cross the Red Line before."

"Maybe, but that doesn't explain why they supposedly want this lost fleet to find the way to Etheria. They'll have to cross the Red Line to get there."

"Assuming Etheria is inside the Red Line," Drask pointed out.

"We've all been there, Colonel. If Etherian ships had to risk engaging the Faros every time they shuttled visitors to and from Etheria, then I think we'd have heard about it—or witnessed those attacks by now. Besides, my understanding is that the Red Line was negotiated as part of a territorial treaty with the Faros. If the Etherians make a habit of crossing that line, then the treaty wouldn't have lasted as long as it has. No, Etheria must be somewhere inside of the Red Line."

"That still covers a lot of space," Chief Councilor Ortane put in. "There's over a hundred thousand galaxies inside the Red Line. The Paragons have barely begun exploring them."

Wheeler nodded. "Yes, it is a lot of space to cover, but not an infinite amount. If the Farosien Empire is really as vast as it claims to be, spanning the entire universe beyond the

Red Line, then it should be a simple matter for them to dispatch a hundred thousand ships—one for each galaxy inside the Red Line—so that they can find Etheria for themselves. So why haven't they? Why spend ten thousand years looking for this lost Etherian fleet instead?"

"Maybe they want the element of surprise," Drask said. "A comprehensive search of a hundred thousand galaxies would break the treaty and give away their intentions, and maybe they needed all the time they spent searching to prepare for a war with Etheria."

"Perhaps..." Wheeler replied. "But my gut is telling me that we're missing something important."

"Like what?" Chief Councilor Ortane asked.

Wheeler shook her head. "I suspect we'll need a look at the nav data aboard those Etherian ships to be able to answer that. For now, all we can do is guess." She directed her attention to the battle unfolding on the holo table in front of her.

"Are we still winning?" the chief councilor asked.

Wheeler looked to her, noting the tightness around Tyra's blue eyes and the ashen tone of her porcelain skin. She was still wearing a hospital gown—covered by a doctor's smock that she must have borrowed or stolen on her way out of the hospital where she'd just finished integrating her consciousness with that of her clone, Captain Forster of the *Inquisitor*.

"Winning?" Wheeler echoed. "That depends whether the enemy has reinforcements on the way. My bet is that they do. The question is, will they arrive in time to stop us from jumping away?"

The chief councilor nodded slowly. Her eyes grew

wide and glazed over as she stared into the mesmerizing swirl of battle on the holo table.

She looked afraid. Wheeler couldn't blame her. They'd barely survived their last encounter with the Faros, and then only because Admiral Stavos had jumped them through the enemy's jamming field, risking a stunning fifty percent chance of scattering. Even after surviving that, the enemy had still managed to board them and blow a hole in the artificial sky over Fallside, destroying one of the four picturesque cities on *Astralis's* surface level.

And it hadn't ended there. That had just been the distraction for them to reach *Astralis's* leaders and possess them with the consciousness of their own leader, Abaddon. Admiral Stavos, General Graves, Chief Councilor Ellis, Director Nora Helios of the Resurrection Center, and even the new chief councilor's eldest daughter, Atara Ortane, had all been infected.

All of them were lost now that the Resurrection Center was gone, destroyed by the a bomb smuggled into the center by the crime boss Joseph Coretti.

Now there was no way to resurrect their dead leaders and civilians, and any surviving Faro agents couldn't be restored to their uninfected state.

Wheeler's attention drifted back to the holo table in front of her. Explosions bloomed as enemy ships succumbed to weapons fire from the Etherian Fleet.

Then one of the Etherian ships exploded, cracking apart into dark, drifting chunks. Wheeler frowned into the fading light of that explosion. If the Faros were trying to capture the Etherian ships, why would they destroy one of them?

"What happened to that ship?" Wheeler asked, looking up at her XO, as if Drask somehow knew more than she.

"I don't know..." he replied. "Its shields were failing, but the hull was still in perfect condition. Maybe the Faros scored a lucky hit?"

Wheeler watched a flight of Faro boarding shuttles bank away from the ruins of that ship, heading for another Etherian vessel with failing shields. Just as soon as that ship's shields failed, it also flew apart with a bright flash of light. "They're self-destructing their ships before the Faros can board them," Wheeler said.

"Damn wasteful to self-destruct every ship that loses its shields," Drask said. "If we had Marines on board we could fight off any boarders and keep those ships."

Wheeler shook her head. "We have over a million Marine bots and sergeants aboard *Astralis,* and yet a few hundred Faros still managed to accomplish their mission when they boarded us."

"We weren't prepared for the strength of their personal shields, but we found ways of fighting them in the end," Drask countered. "You better believe we can kill them now that we know what kind of firepower it takes."

Wheeler waved her hand dismissively at the colonel. "I'm glad to hear it, but the discussion is hypothetical until we are actually able to get Marines on board the Etherian fleet."

"We could send out our own boarding shuttles to contest the enemy for the ships they're trying to take."

"And leave ourselves vulnerable to boarders?"

"We can spare the men without compromising our own defense," Drask replied.

"Yes, I suppose we can. All right, get me—"

"Admiral, we're being hailed by the enemy fleet!" the comms officer called out.

Wheeler turned to address the woman. "Now that they're losing, they want to talk?" Wheeler took a breath. "Patch them through to the main forward display, Lieutenant."

"Yes, ma'am," the comms officer replied.

Wheeler turned to Chief Councilor Ortane. "Councilor, I believe you should be the one to answer this."

The other woman nodded slowly, and the glazed look left her eyes. "Agreed."

"This way," Wheeler said, leading her from the holo table to the observation dais at the front and center of the command deck, overlooking the lower two decks of the bridge. Wheeler indicated that the councilor climb a short flight of stairs leading up to the dais, while she remained standing below those stairs and to one side.

Everyone directed their attention to the three-story-high viewscreen at the front of *Astralis's* hexagonal bridge, and moments later, that screen faded from stars and space to show the head and shoulders of a by-now-familiar blue-skinned humanoid with glowing, ice-blue eyes. He wore a luminous golden crown, gray robes, and a chilling smile that was framed by perfectly even white teeth.

This was Abaddon, the king of the Faros—or one of them, anyway. He supposedly had billions of identical clones, all somehow sharing the same consciousness and memories.

"Abaddon," Councilor Ortane said. There was no concealing the ice in her voice. "What do you want?"

Wheeler felt her stomach tense at the abruptness of those words. This was the being who had erased the councilor's eldest daughter's consciousness with his own. Suddenly Wheeler wondered if *she* should be the one standing on that dais to address the enemy leader. *Anger is fog for the brain.*

"Straight to the point," Abaddon said, his smile broadening. "Good. I would hate to waste my breath."

"You're wasting it now."

Abaddon's smile vanished and his glowing blue eyes flashed, but just for a second. He clamped down on that reaction, and his smile returned.

Don't goad him, Wheeler thought. *We're winning* now, *but we don't know what kind of reinforcements he has coming.* With hundreds of capital ships and thousands of fighters still firing on both sides it was no time to be smug. *He must be speaking to us for a reason,* Wheeler thought.

"I would like to negotiate," Abaddon said. "I assume you also speak for the Etherian fleet that is attacking my vessels?"

"You are the aggressor here," Councilor Ortane replied, "but yes, I speak for all of us."

"Good, then here is what I propose: give the Etherian fleet to me, and I will grant all humans everywhere full citizenship in the Farosien Empire. My fight is with Etherus and his chosen people, the Etherians, not with any of you."

Wheeler blinked, momentarily shocked by the offer.

Chief Councilor Ortane replied, "What guarantee do we have that you won't turn on us as soon as you have what you want? If we give you the fleet, we won't be able to defend ourselves anymore. Besides, I'm told that the reason you want the fleet is to use it to find Etheria. You can do that just as easily with access to one ship as you can with access to all of them."

"True, but you can't blame me for trying. The fleet has impressive firepower and shielding. It would be a great asset in my war."

"You can have one ship."

"Of my choosing?"

"No."

"Then I want a hundred."

Councilor Ortane shook her head. "Try again."

Abaddon grinned. "Ten."

"We may be able to accommodate that.... I'll need to consult with the other councilors and my military advisers. In the meantime, I suggest a cease fire."

"Agreed." Abaddon turned to give an order—in Farosien rather than Versal—to someone they couldn't see. A moment later, he turned back to them. "Done."

Chief Councilor Ortane glanced over her shoulder at the holo table where Colonel Drask stood. "Colonel?"

"They've stopped firing, ma'am."

"Good. Admiral Wheeler, please give the order for our forces to stand down."

"Yes, ma'am," Wheeler said. Turning to her comms officer, she gave the command, "Comms, send a priority message on an open channel to all of our forces: cease fire in effect. Weapons hold."

"Aye, Admiral," the comms officer replied.

"Sensors, confirm weapons hold," Wheeler said.

"All ships have stopped firing, ma'am," the sensor officer replied a split second later.

"Good..." Abaddon said, his voice all but purring in Wheeler's ears.

The chief councilor nodded. "There is one other thing. We still have several of your agents on board, humans harboring copies of your consciousness. Some of them are not as thoroughly infected as others. They have your personality, but not your memories."

"Yes, one of them is your daughter, Atara," Abaddon replied, smiling and nodding.

"We also have several dozen Faro prisoners on board," the chief councilor went on, not skipping a beat at the mention of her daughter. Wheeler felt a measure of grudging respect for Tyra at that, and her concerns about who should be handling these negotiations faded away.

"You want to trade," Abaddon said. "I reverse what I did to your people in exchange for you giving me the Faro prisoners."

Chief Councilor Ortane inclined her head in a shallow nod. "It would go a long way to proving your intentions with regards to us and the rest of humanity. Consider it a show of good faith."

"*Faith*—I'm not a fan of that word," Abaddon replied.

"*Good will,* then," Councilor Ortane replied.

"What makes you think I *can* reverse the transfer of consciousness?" Abaddon asked in a sly tone.

"Can you?"

The Faro king's eyes brightened and danced with amusement. "I can, but only for the one's who harbor partial copies of my consciousness, and I'll need to touch them again in order to do so."

"Fly a shuttle out to *Astralis*. I'll send a fighter escort to direct you to one of our hangar bays. Make sure you come alone. If we detect more than one lifeform aboard, we'll destroy the shuttle and the cease fire will be over."

"My my, but aren't you enjoying ordering me about," Abaddon said. A smile remained on his lips, but his glowing eyes glittered coldly.

"Do you or don't you want the access to the Etherian ships?" Chief Councilor Ortane asked. "You could go on trying to board them, but we'll just keep self-destructing them before you can. Even if you have reinforcements coming, that outcome doesn't change. Negotiating with us is the only way for you to get you what you want, but you already know that, otherwise you wouldn't be speaking to us now."

"I accept your terms," Abaddon said, waving his hand to forestall further arguments. "You should see my shuttle approaching soon."

"Good, we'll—"

The image of the Faro king vanished, cutting the chief councilor off midstream. A pregnant silence reigned on the Bridge as stars and space returned to the main forward display.

Abaddon was coming.

CHAPTER 3

Astralis

"I don't trust him," Admiral Wheeler said, breaking the silence on the bridge.

"Neither do I," Chief Councilor Ortane replied as she turned and stepped down from the observation dais.

"He's buying time for his reinforcements to arrive," Wheeler said. "Once he has the upper hand he'll turn around and threaten to destroy *Astralis* if we don't hand over the fleet."

"And in turn we'll threaten to self-destruct the Etherian fleet."

"That still either leaves us all enslaved or dead," Wheeler pointed out. "He knows we wouldn't risk that."

"Wouldn't we?" the chief councilor asked. "He won't risk it. He's spent ten thousand years looking for this lost fleet, why risk losing it by calling our bluff? He doesn't care about *Astralis*. All he wants is that fleet."

"Then why work so hard to infect our leaders and take over *Astralis* from within?" Wheeler asked.

"They were using us as bait to lure the lost fleet here, and if they were still in control of Astralis, they'd have been able to seize that fleet without a fight. *Astralis* was just a means to that end. I think Abaddon was telling the truth when he said that his fight is with Etherus and the Etherians. He doesn't care about humanity."

"Let's say that's true," Wheeler said. "And let's say he honors his promise to grant us all citizenship in his empire. Who's to say that he won't renege on that deal after he's conquered Etheria? We still can't trust him."

"No, perhaps we can't, but if this fleet is any example of the Etherians' defensive and offensive capabilities, then why should we be afraid that Abaddon might find the way to Etheria? You said it yourself: the Etherians can take care of themselves. We, on the other hand... we're stranded in enemy territory, and if we don't give the Faros what they want, I wouldn't put it past them to kill us all out of spite—and later New Earth, too, when they get the chance."

Wheeler blew out a breath. "All right, so we let Etherus and the Etherians look after themselves, and we look after ourselves."

"For now. When we're done here, I suggest we take *Astralis* and the rest of the Etherian fleet and get back to New Earth as fast as we can so we can warn Etherus that Abaddon is coming. At that point we can join forces and fight the Faros together."

"What if Abaddon predicts that we'll ultimately side with Etherus and he decides to destroy us just as soon as he has the ships he's asking for?" Wheeler asked. "Then we won't have a chance to warn Etherus, and he won't have to fight us again later."

"We still have the upper hand in this fight," the chief councilor pointed out. "We'll win if he double-crosses us now."

"Not if the negotiations take long enough that the

Faros' reinforcements arrive."

"There are ways to give Abaddon what he wants while also allowing us to retreat safely, but all the same, we'd better make sure these negotiations are concluded quickly. I'm going to call a virtual session of council to save some time deliberating over Abaddon's offer."

"What if the council rules against Abaddon's deal?" Wheeler asked.

"I'm confident I can convince the other councilors. Meanwhile, I need you to arrange for the exchange of prisoners with Abaddon in one of our hangar bays."

Wheeler nodded. "I'll take care of it, ma'am."

"Good. Let me know which hangar you choose. I'll see you there, Admiral."

"Yes, ma'am." Wheeler watched the chief councilor leave the bridge with apprehension twisting in her gut. Something felt wrong about what they were doing. It seemed like they were calling the shots, like they had the upper hand in these negotiations, but Wheeler couldn't help feeling that it was actually the other way around.

Perhaps it was superstition on her part, but if Etherus was the God he claimed to be, then Abaddon was the Devil—*and we're making a deal with him,* Wheeler thought.

She shook her head and brushed her misgivings aside. "Colonel Drask—" She turned to face him, and he looked up from the holo table with eyebrows raised, waiting for her orders. "Get a platoon of Marines to Hangar Bay Sixty-six."

"Yes, ma'am."

"Comms, get in touch with our security departments and tell them to escort all of the known human-Faro agents to the same hangar bay."

"Yes, ma'am," the comms officer replied.

"Let's see if Abaddon can make good on his promise to release our people."

Murmurs of agreement rose from the officers on the bridge, and Admiral Wheeler went to stand on the observation dais, overlooking the bustle of activity on the lower decks. She watched as officers went about their duties, managing the lesser function of the ship from its secondary control stations. After a moment, Colonel Drask stepped up to the dais beside her. "Admiral," he said.

"Colonel," Wheeler replied. "Something on your mind?"

"I don't believe we should be negotiating with the Faros. We have the upper hand. We should press our advantage and punch a hole in their jamming field so we can escape."

Wheeler frowned. "I'm inclined to agree with you, but it's a political decision, and besides, if we don't negotiate we might never be able to remove Abaddon's consciousness from the people he infected."

"I'm not sure he will do it. He might just pretend to release them. The negotiations are a stalling tactic to give them enough time for reinforcements to arrive."

"Even if that's the case, as the chief councilor pointed out, reinforcements won't help them get what they want. We can still deny them access to the Etherian fleet."

"Perhaps, but *we* won't get what we want either. We'll all end up dead or enslaved to the Faros."

"It's a risky gamble, Colonel, but I believe the chief councilor is right. The Faros won't risk losing what they came for."

"And what happens after they have what they want?" Drask pressed.

Wheeler had been thinking about that. The chief councilor was right about that, too. "There's a way to conduct the exchange safely. We move *Astralis* and the Etherian Fleet beyond the Faros' jamming field and calculate a jump to a destination we have verified as safe. While we're doing that, we leave the ten ships we're giving to the Faros at the edge of their jamming field. As soon as our calculations are complete, we jump away, leaving Abaddon with his prize and us with our freedom."

"That could work," Drask admitted.

Wheeler turned to look at her XO. His gaunt cheeks and sunken eyes made him look skeletal and frail, an odd aspect for a Marine, but what he lacked in physical strength he made up with in mental acuity.

"It *will* work," Wheeler insisted.

"And if Abaddon only pretends to release our people?"

Wheeler shook her head. "We'll use the AI-driven screening tests we developed to uncover the Faro agents in the first place. If the tests come back clean, then chances are they're no longer infected, but if they're still showing signs of infection, Abaddon will become our next prisoner. Speaking of, I'd better get to the hangar bay for the exchange."

"You're going to attend personally, ma'am?" the colonel asked with a dubious shake of his head.

"After what happened the last time Faros boarded us, I want to keep Abaddon where I can see him."

"But what if he gets to *you* this time, ma'am?"

"Then you'll be in command."

"With all due respect, I don't think you should expose

yourself to the risk. This might just be a ploy to get all of our leaders in one place so that the Faros can smuggle a bomb aboard with their shuttle and detonate it in the hangar."

Wheeler nodded. "Abaddon would die, too, but that's a fair point. Have our fighters escort Abaddon to bay one twenty. That's in one of the evacuated sections over Fallside, so even if there is a bomb, there shouldn't be many casualties. Make sure a platoon of marine bots is waiting to escort Abaddon to bay sixty-six."

"The Faros have shown that they can shoot plasma from their bare hands. We won't be able to disarm him completely," Drask warned.

"If Abaddon betrays us in the hangar, he'll forfeit what he came for the same as if he broke the cease fire now. I don't flatter myself to think that I or even the chief councilor are important enough targets to warrant such an elaborate ruse. And if by some chance that is his game, you'll have your men standing by to gun the kakard down."

"Yes, ma'am...."

"You have the conn, Colonel."

"Aye, Admiral. Watch your back."

"I always do," Wheeler replied.

CHAPTER 4

The Lost Etherian Fleet

Lucien Ortane sat on the bridge of the *Gideon* waiting for further orders, but they never came. The Faros had stopped firing on them, and right after that *Astralis* had ordered them to stand down and hold their fire, indicating that a cease fire had been declared.

"I'm going to contact *Astralis* and find out what's going on," he said.

"They're probably busy negotiating," Garek said.

"We already know what the Faros want, and I explained *why* we can't give it to them," Lucien replied. "There's no room for negotiation."

"I guess *Astralis* doesn't see it that way," Addy said.

Lucien ground his teeth. "We don't have to follow their orders. Their firepower is negligible compared to ours. We can win this fight with or without them."

"Hold on there, hotshot," Garek said. "We don't know what's at stake yet. I'm not going against orders until I know more."

"So let's find out more," Lucien replied. He activated the comms panel from his station and sent a message. "This is Commander Ortane of the *Gideon.* I need to speak with *Astralis* Actual immediately. Over."

"*Astralis* Actual here," a man replied. "Go ahead, *Gideon*."

"Who is this? Where's Admiral Wheeler?"

"You're speaking with her XO, Colonel Drask. Admiral Wheeler is not on deck."

"I see," Lucien replied. "We need an update, Colonel. Why has everyone stopped firing?"

"We've declared a cease fire with the enemy while negotiations are conducted."

"What negotiations?" Lucien said. "Has the enemy made any demands?"

"We'll let you know the result as soon as the negotiations are concluded, Commander. Until then you have your orders."

Lucien shook his head. "We're wasting time. We can't negotiate with the Faros. Inform the admiral that we're breaking the cease fire. *Astralis* will have to decide whether or not to join us."

"Are you threatening insubordination, Commander? If you are, I'll send over a platoon of Marines and take your ship myself!"

"You're welcome to try," Lucien replied.

"Are you prepared to fire on friendly forces? Because if you're not, you *will* be boarded, and we *will* take control of your fleet."

"Then I guess you'd better start launching shuttles. Good luck dropping our shields."

"This is not the time to turn on each other, Commander!"

"I agree, so I suggest you convince the admiral to fight with us rather than against us," Lucien replied.

There came a sudden shriek of weapons fire, followed by a *thud.* Lucien looked up in time to see Brak falling to his knees, his muscles spasming and head lolling as the blue fire of a stun blast skittered over him. Garek stood on the other side of the bridge with his arms raised and the integrated cannons of his exosuit deployed. Addy gaped at him from the helm, her eyes wide.

Lucien shot up from his station, hurrying to deploy his own weapons, but Garek was faster, and his weapons were already deployed.

The next stun blast hit Lucien in the face. Everything went white, and he felt himself falling. The brightness faded and he found himself lying on the deck, blinking up at the holo dome. It was blurry with stars. Muffled voices argued all around him.

"What did you do?" *Addy's voice...*

"What I had to." *Garek.*

"Gideon, what's going on?" *Colonel Drask from Astralis.*

"The situation is under control," Garek replied. "We'll follow our orders."

Lucien blinked, trying to clear his blurry vision. How was he still conscious? The stun blast mustn't have hit him as directly as he'd thought. He heard booted feet go clomping by him and caught a flicker of movement in the corner of his eyes. His arm snapped out and he grabbed what he suspected to be Garek's ankle—

"Atthy, thoot fim!" Lucien slurred.

"Lucien?" Addy asked, sound surprised.

Garek's blurry face appeared, looming into view. "Night-night," he said, and fired into Lucien's face with another blinding flash of light.

* * *

Astralis

Lucien Ortane watched as four squads of Marine bots and their human sergeants escorted the Faro king into hangar bay sixty-six. Abaddon's hands were bound behind his back with stun cords, though Lucien suspected he could break those bonds easily enough if he wanted to.

Beside him, Tyra's whole body went suddenly rigid as Abaddon appeared. Lucien could feel the hatred radiating from her. This was the being who had possessed their daughter, Atara. He reached for Tyra's hand and squeezed.

"It's okay. We're going to get her back now," he said, and desperately hoped that was true.

On the other side of Lucien, Brak hissed and flashed dagger-sharp black teeth at the Faro king. He'd made a miraculous recovery from the injuries he'd sustained while trying to apprehend Abaddon-possessed Chief Councilor Ellis, but he was understandably still carrying a grudge about it. Ellis had shot himself in the head with a sidearm set to *overload,* killing himself and very nearly taking the Gor with him.

Standing behind them, also under guard, were all of the remaining human-Faro agents. The surviving ones, anyway.

Lucien glanced behind him and his eyes found Atara. Like Abaddon, her hands were also bound, but it was almost absurd to think of her as a threat. She was only five years old. And yet... that five-year-old body now harbored some version of Abaddon's own twisted mind. Even as Lucien considered that, Atara's green eyes found his, and she smirked at him.

"That's far enough," Tyra said, and the Marines escorting Abaddon stopper where they were.

The alien king offered them a winning smile. "I came alone, as you requested. And you can see that I am bound and unarmed. What are you afraid of?"

Tyra ignored the Faro's goading words and took two long strides to step in front of her entourage. Her hand slipped through Lucien's fingers, and he cringed to see his wife standing out there by herself, exposed.

"It's time for you to prove you can reverse what you did to our people."

Abaddon shrugged. "You'll have to cut my bonds if you expect me to do that."

"Very well." Tyra nodded to his Marine escort. "Turn the Faro ninety degrees, so that he is facing away from us. Restrain his arms and cut his bonds, but do not release him."

The Marine sergeants standing around Abaddon directed the bots holding him to do as Tyra had instructed, and then Tyra turned and to indicate one of the human-Faro agents in the hangar bay. "Escort High Court Judge Cleever to stand in front of the Faro, within reach of his hands."

Marines and security officers shuffled their feet and looked to one another, as if asking whose responsibility it was to escort the judge. Admiral Wheeler settled the question for them before Tyra could say anything.

"You heard the councilor! On the double, Sergeants!"

The Marines took over, with two sergeants grabbing Judge Cleever by her arms and dragging her forward to her meet Abaddon.

She sneered and spat on the face plates of their helmets, struggling in vain against the augmented strength of their exosuits.

"Don't do it," Cleever said to Abaddon once she was standing in front of him. "I'm you. If you kill me, it will be like killing yourself."

Lucien saw an amused smile spring to the alien's lips. "It won't be the first time I've killed myself," he replied. Turning to one of the bots holding his arms, he asked. "May I?"

The bot gave no reply, but the sergeant commanding it said, "Omega Four, please allow the prisoner to use his arm to touch the woman standing in front of him, but do not allow him to make any other movements."

"Copy that, Sergeant," the bot said in a gender neutral voice.

Lucien held his breath, watching as Abaddon raised a glowing palm toward Judge Cleever's face. She looked terrified, and she began struggling in earnest against the Marine Sergeants holding her. She tried to wriggle free, but they were too strong.

As Abaddon's palm drew near, Cleever's face was inexplicably drawn into it, forcing her neck to stretch out to its limit. Her mouth opened in a soundless scream, and her eyes flew wide.

Anxious murmuring filled the air, bouncing from Marine sergeants to police officers and back again. None of them had witnessed this before, but Lucien remembered seeing Abaddon do this to Atara. This was how he'd transferred his consciousness in the first place, so hopefully it was also how he could reverse that transfer.

After just a few minutes, Abaddon withdrew his hand, and Judge Cleever sagged lifelessly in the arms of the Marines holding her.

"Doctor Fushiwa!" Tyra called out. "Check her vitals."

A familiar man in a doctor's smock stepped out of the group and hurried forward with a life signs scanner. He passed the scanner over Judge Cleever with a flickering blue fan of light, studied the result, and then turned to nod in Tyra's direction. "She is fine, but she has lapsed into a coma. That is consistent with what happened after infection."

"Thank you, Doctor," Tyra said. "Please take the patient behind our lines and wait with her there for now."

"Yes, ma'am."

Abaddon turned to Tyra as the Marines and Doctor Fushiwa withdrew with Judge Cleever. The bots holding Abaddon refused to budge, so he was forced to twist his neck to face her rather than his body. "I have kept my word. Now where are the Faro prisoners?"

"Not so fast. There are still others that you need to un-infect, and we still have to confirm that you are able to do so."

Abaddon's upper lip twitched. "And how long will this take?"

"A few hours, no more," Tyra replied.

"And what am I supposed to do while I wait?" Abaddon demanded. "Stand here and look pretty?"

Before Tyra could reply, Admiral Wheeler strode up to her and whispered something in her ear.

"So... this *was* a ruse to buy time for your reinforcements!" Tyra roared. Admiral Wheeler retreated to stand with hands clasped behind her back, and steely eyes glaring at Abaddon. Tyra went on, "I'm told that another one of your fleets has just arrived. They're moving to surround us as we speak."

Abaddon gave a sly smile and shrugged as best he could while restrained by the Marine bots flanking him. "They were on their way here before the negotiations began."

"Call them off now, or the negotiations will be over."

Abaddon's expression turned contemplative. "Very well... they are leaving."

"Just like that?" Tyra demanded.

"Ask your slave woman to check. You should see them moving away now."

"I am not a slave," Admiral Wheeler replied.

Tyra scowled. "Listen to me, you snake. I will happily deny you what you want out of spite, if you give me even the slightest reason to do so. We'll fight you to the death if we have to."

A nervous shuffling of feet answered that ultimatum, but Abaddon didn't seem concerned. "You would sentence your people to die in order to satisfy your need for revenge?"

"Not revenge. The strength of our position lies in our resolve, and in the knowledge that we have something you desperately want. If our resolve falters, then so does our position. The stakes are all or nothing."

"They were never anything less," Abaddon replied. "Has your council issued a response to my... *request?*"

Abaddon put an odd emphasis on that last word, as if to imply that his request for them to cede ten Etherian ships to him wasn't a request at all, but a demand.

"Yes, we have. Assuming we can establish here that your word can be trusted, we have decided to agree to your terms."

"I'm pleased to hear that," Abaddon replied, smiling once more.

"But," Tyra held up a finger. "We need assurances that we'll be allowed to depart in peace after we give you what you want."

Abaddon's smile faded dramatically, and he glowered at Tyra. "Such as?"

"We're going to send out probes to scout ahead and find a safe destination for us to jump to. You will not attempt to stop the probes from leaving. When they return, in approximately two hours, we should have the results of the tests to determine if you have really un-infected our people.

"At that point, you will withdraw your fleet so that your jamming fields no longer encompass our ships, and we will direct the ten Etherian ships you requested to keep them inside of your jamming field. If the screening tests come back clean, the Faro prisoners will be released to you, and your shuttle will be allowed to leave with them on board. We will then jump away and leave you with the ten ships you negotiated for.

"If, however, our people still show signs that they are harboring your consciousness, or if your fleet somehow moves to prevent us from leaving, we will fight you to the death and self-destruct the Etherian Fleet long before you can ever set foot on any of its vessels. Those are *our* terms for a peace treaty, and they are non-negotiable. Do you accept?"

Abaddon's glowing blue eyes glittered. "You would make a good Faro, Tyra Ortane."

"Answer the question."

"I accept your terms. Bring the others to me and I will release their minds."

Tyra turned and nodded to the police and marines standing around the remaining human-Faro agents. "One at a time, please," she indicated.

Lucien watched as Marines dragged the next one, a young man this time, to face Abaddon and be touched by his glowing palm. The others were all forced to stand in line and wait their turn. They struggled against the Marine bots and sergeants holding them while they waited. Some of them pleaded for Abaddon not to kill them when it was their turn, while others remained stolid in the face of their fate.

Abaddon regarded all of them with contempt as he erased his mind from the human hosts. One by one they sagged in the arms of the Marines holding them. To Lucien's eyes, the scene began to take on a quasi-religious tone—a kind of reverse baptism.

Atara was last in line to be touched. She whimpered and begged for her life just as some of the others had, and it was all Lucien could do not to run to her rescue. *She's not my daughter. She's not my daughter. She's not...*

Abaddon ignored Atara's pleas and wrapped his glowing palm around her face just as he had with the others. Atara's mouth opened in a soundless scream, and then after just a minute, she, too, sagged lifelessly in the arms of the Marines holding her.

"Doctor Fushiwa," Tyra began in a throaty whisper. "Would you please escort the infected individuals from the hangar and have them all screened?"

"Of course—everyone, follow me, please," Doctor Fushiwa said as he turned and strode across the hangar bay to the nearest exit. A mix of twenty Marine sergeants and bots followed the doctor, carrying ten comatose Faro agents—

hopefully now *former* agents—between them.

Tyra nodded to Abaddon. "We'll meet back here in two hours, as soon as we have the results of our tests and our scout ships have returned."

"You never answered my question. What am I to do in that time?"

"You've been alive since the beginning of time, correct?"

Abaddon's eyes narrowed, but he said nothing to that.

Tyra offered him a bland smile. "Then I would think that by now two hours is nothing to you. You'll wait here, under guard. If you need to use a restroom, feel free to piss yourself."

A few of the Marine sergeants snickered at that, and Abaddon's glowing blue eyes flared. He smiled thinly. "I encountered your daughter's consciousness while I was erasing mine. She was alone in the dark, crying, and begging for help. She sounded delirious... I believe she must have been crying for help for a long time already. Unfortunately, no one could hear her."

Lucien's whole body shivered with rage. "You frekking kakard!" he roared, but Abaddon didn't even glance at him. His gaze remained locked with Tyra's.

She'd frozen, and her eyes had glazed over. The only sign of a reaction was the way her shoulders quickly rose and fell, and in the balled fists by her sides. For a long moment, she said nothing. When she finally she spoke, it was in a slow and deliberate tone, as if each word took a great effort: "I'll be back in two hours. You'd better hope that by then I haven't found an excuse to end your miserable life."

"Empty threats," Abaddon smiled. "You can't kill me. I

am but one of many."

"No? Then why were the ones you erased begging to be spared?"

"They were only partial copies of me. Pathetic creatures, shadows of my true glory."

"What you call glory, everyone else calls *evil,*" Tyra replied, and turned to leave.

Abaddon laughed resoundingly as she walked away. "Evil? I'm not evil. Evil doesn't exist! Prove to me that you have the freedom to act otherwise than you do, and I will admit that I am evil. As it stands, I am but a cog in a vast and arbitrary machine of action and reaction, cause and effect—the inevitable result of billions of years of natural laws producing entirely predictable results! You can't judge me for what I do any more than you can judge rain for falling or sunlight for shining!"

Tyra reached Lucien's side and took his hand. "Let's go," she whispered.

Lucien frowned, tempted to argue with Abaddon, but words failed him. The existence of free will had been debated by philosophers, scientists, and religious leaders for eons. Quantum indeterminacy had disproved determinism to some extent, but others argued that even random or unmeasurable quantum factors did nothing to promote the existence of true freedom.

Regardless, it wasn't particularly relevant. Actions still had consequences, and those consequences could still be judged as good or evil. Possessing a five-year-old girl fell into the *evil* category.

Lucien squeezed Tyra's hand again. "Don't worry. If he didn't reverse what he did to Atara, I'll kill him myself."

"You'll have to get in line behind me," Tyra said, her voice quivering with fury.

He swallowed past a lump in his throat and nodded. "Fair enough. Mothers first."

CHAPTER 5

Astralis

—TWO HOURS LATER—

Tyra was stuck on the bridge analyzing the scan data from the probes they'd sent out, rather than where she wanted to be, in the hospital with Lucien. She'd told him to call her with Atara's test results, but it wasn't the same as being there to greet Atara when she woke up.

Half an hour ago Lucien had called to let her know that Atara seemed to be back to her old self. She'd been distraught and crying, inconsolable after what she'd been through.

And I wasn't there to hold her.

Tyra knew she'd never forgive herself for that absence, but she also needed to be here for this—to choose a destination for the fleet to run to after they gave the Faros what they wanted.

"What about SCT-45?" Admiral Wheeler asked as she summoned the scan data on the holo table for everyone to see.

"It has forty-five moons and planets," Colonel Drask objected. "Just because we didn't detect anything to indicate the system is inhabited doesn't mean there's nothing there. We haven't had enough time."

"We scanned it from four different angles to make sure

we captured readings from all side of the system's planetary and lunar surfaces," Wheeler pointed out. "There was nothing to indicate a settlement of any kind."

Drask shook his head. "There are still blind spots in the scans. He pointed to small, fuzzy patches on the surfaces of moons directly facing their parent planets. Without getting closer it was impossible to get a good look at those areas.

"The lack of unnatural EM radiation is further confirmation that there's no advanced civilization in the system," Wheeler said.

"Abaddon may have instructed all nearby systems to impose black-out protocols," Drask said.

"And he also got them to ground or cloak all of their ships?" Wheeler looked skeptical. "This is our best bet, and you know it."

"I agree," Tyra put in. "But, I also agree with Drask. At this point, even safe systems may be compromised in ways we can't detect. Let's calculate jumps to all twelve of the systems we scouted."

"Five of those were inhabited by Faros, or by some other potentially hostile force. The probes never returned."

Tyra frowned. "Exclude those five and pick another five at random."

"We don't have time to send more scouts," Drask pointed out.

"Then let's hope we never have to jump to the systems we haven't scouted yet. Organize the systems from most safe to least. At the first sign of the Faros we'll jump to the next safest system on the list."

Colonel Drask nodded. "Comms—" He gave the order, but Tyra couldn't hear it over the suddenly insistent trilling inside her head. The comms icon on her Augmented Reality Contacts (ARCs) flashed, and identified the caller as Lucien Ortane. Tyra took a few steps away from the holo table to answer the call.

"Do you have the test results?"

"We do." There was no concealing the relief in Lucien's voice. "She's clear, Tyra! Our little girl is back!"

Tyra's gaze blurred with heat and her lips formed a trembling smile. She held a hand to her mouth to stifle any sound that might escape.

"Tyra? Did you hear me?" Lucien asked.

She nodded and wiped her eyes. "I did." She tried to say more, but her throat had shut in a painful knot as all of her bottled-up emotions suddenly burst free.

"I'm still waiting to hear about the others," Lucien added.

Another trilling sound started up inside Tyra's head, and the comms icon began flashing on her ARCs again. Doctor Fushiwa was calling. "I think I'm about to find out," she said, finally managing to speak. "Hold on," she said as she took the other call. "What are the results, Doctor?"

"They're all clear, ma'am—in varying states of shock and emotional distress, but they're clear, and they appear to be back to normal."

"So Abaddon kept his word," Tyra said slowly.

"It would appear so..." the doctor trailed off uncertainly. If he had any data to back up his reservations, he didn't share it.

"I don't know if I believe it either," Tyra said. "But I want to."

"At this point we're right to be suspicious," the doctor

replied, "but our suspicions would appear to be baseless."

"Then it's time to formalize our treaty with the Faros. Thank you, Doctor."

"Of course."

Tyra ended the comms connection and shared the news with Lucien. Then she signed off with him as well and turned to address the others. "It's official: our people have been released. The Faros kept their word. Now it's time for us to keep ours. We are going to officially declare peace with the Farosien Empire."

A cheer went up from the crew. People applauded and whistled. Tyra couldn't help smiling. She understood their enthusiasm: theirs was a mission of science and exploration. None of these people wanted to fight a war.

"Admiral Wheeler," Tyra said before the commotion had fully subsided.

"Councilor?"

"Have a platoon of Marines escort the Faro prisoners onto Abaddon's shuttle in hangar bay one twenty—but *do not* wake any of them from stasis. Make sure they stay in their tanks. Have Abaddon escorted back to his shuttle as well."

"Yes, ma'am. Colonel—you heard the councilor," Wheeler said.

"Aye," Drask nodded and began snapping orders to his Marines over the comms.

Wheeler went on, "Garrison Command, have all ships return to our hangars."

"Aye, Admiral."

Tyra rolled her shoulders to get some of the tension out of them, and then said, "Comms, patch me through to Hangar sixty-six so I can speak with Abaddon."

"Yes, ma'am... you're now live in hangar sixty-six."

Tyra took a deep breath and then said, "It would seem you kept your word to release our people."

Abaddon's voice rippled back over the Bridge speakers. "You sound surprised."

"I am, but pleasantly so. We accept your terms for peace. Our ships are going to begin withdrawing now, all except for the ten Etherian ships that we are handing over to you. The Faro prisoners are being escorted aboard your shuttle as we speak, and you will be taken to join them soon. Make sure your fleet does not fire on us as we withdraw."

"Very well," Abaddon replied. "Is that all?"

Tyra ignored his sarcasm. "Yes. *Astralis* out." Tyra killed the connection and turned to Admiral Wheeler. "Begin the the withdrawal."

"Yes, ma'am," Wheeler replied, turning to her crew, she began snapping orders. "Helm! Take us out of range of the enemy's jamming."

"Yes, ma'am," the helm replied.

"Comms, have the rest of the fleet form on us, but make sure the Gideon leaves Abaddon's ten ships behind."

"Aye, Admiral," the comms officer replied.

"Garrison Command, find me a grounded fighter or shuttle and send a pilot over to the *Gideon* with the jump data for the list of systems we've scouted. We won't want to risk sending it over comms."

"Copy that, Admiral," the garrison commander replied.

Tyra waited by the holo table, watching as *Astralis* and the Etherian fleet withdrew. Ten Etherian ships stayed where they were, quickly falling behind the rest, and the Faros' ships remained where they were, too.

"Abaddon's shuttle is away!" the comms announced.

A moment later, *Astralis* and the lost fleet reached the crimson line that marked the edge of the Faros' quantum jamming field. As soon as they were across it, Wheeler called out: "Have we boarded the *Gideon* with the coordinates of the scouted systems yet?"

"Aye, our shuttle landed just a few minutes ago, ma'am."

"Good. Comms—have the Etherian Fleet inform us as soon as they're ready to jump out."

"Yes, ma'am." Another few minutes passed before the comms officer spoke again. "The *Gideon* is standing by to jump!"

"Tell them to execute their jump right after us, and inform them that we're going to be jamming all outbound comms from now on."

"Jamming, ma'am?"

"We don't know that there aren't more Faro agents on board, and we can't be sure that there aren't any tracking devices, either."

"What about the Etherian fleet?"

"They were never boarded, and if there were any tracking devices aboard their ships, the Faros wouldn't have needed to use *Astralis* as bait to find them."

"Aye, Admiral," the comms officer replied. "Message away. Comms jamming is now in effect."

"Helm, execute our jump," Wheeler said.

"Jumping in three... two..."

Tyra looked up from the holo table just as stars vanished from the bridge's ten-meter-high viewscreens in a bright flash of light. When the displays and Tyra's vision cleared, the stars had all shifted to new positions, and a bright blue planet with fluffy white clouds and a solitary green island lay before them.

A split second later, more than a thousand bursts of light peppered their view of that planet. Tyra found herself blinking against the glare. As soon as it faded, she saw a shining sea of silvery hulls appear—some hovering against the deep blue ocean of the planet, others competing with the stars. The Etherian Fleet had arrived.

"Sensors—report!" Wheeler said.

CHAPTER 6

The Lost Etherian Fleet

"I don't see any sign of the Faros on sensors," Garek reported.

"Why would there be?" Lucien demanded from where he sat on one side of the *Gideon's* bridge, under guard by Lieutenant Sevris, the fighter pilot who'd come aboard to give them their jump coordinates.

Lucien's exosuit lay on the opposite side of the bridge from him, too far away to help him reverse this mutiny. Not that it mattered now. "The Faros have what they want," he said. "Why would they bother chasing us now?"

Garek shrugged. "They might not have to chase us if they're already here."

Lucien frowned. "You checked the system with sensors before we jumped, and we already know that Etherian sensors are like an all-seeing eye. Wherever they look, they see, regardless of the range. You should have told *Astralis* that."

"And give them an excuse to rethink their negotiations with the Faros?"

"You're a damned skriff, Garek," Lucien replied. "All of this just to save your daughter."

"And the rest of *Astralis*," he replied. "If we didn't

negotiate, the Faros' next move would have been to threaten to kill them all if we didn't give them what they wanted. At that point we'd have been forced to negotiate, anyway. I just cut out all of the back and forth in-between."

"I wouldn't have negotiated," Lucien replied.

"You'd have let three hundred million people die for the sake of getting this fleet back to Etheria?"

"If it meant saving trillions of other lives—yes."

The pilot guarding Lucien snorted. "Frekking easy for you to say."

"Only easy because he doesn't have any loved ones on board," Garek added.

"Which allows me to be objective in this situation. *You* clearly can't be. And anyway, you really think Abaddon will honor his promise to give us all citizenship in his empire?" Lucien asked. "You've only delayed this war."

"Why would he go back on that deal? I'm sure we'd make a valuable part of his empire."

"Ignoring the fact that it's an empire of evil..." Lucien said.

"Evil is subjective."

"They're slavers!" Lucien replied.

"So were humans for a good chunk of history. Maybe the Faros just need time to grow out of their bad habits."

"They've had billions of years. How much longer do they need? And what about Etherus? And the Etherians? We all have relatives that decided to go to Etheria. You've sealed their fate."

"We don't know that. Etherus has the technological advantage. He could win the war."

"And if he does, what do you think he'll do to us as

citizens of the Farosien Empire that sold him and his people out?" Lucien demanded.

"You're suggesting Etherus would punish us out of spite after he defeats Abaddon?"

"Why not?" Lucien challenged. "We punish people for war crimes all the time."

"Enough! You guys are giving me a headache," Addy said. "For better or worse, we've already made our choice. There's no point agonizing over it anymore. Let's just focus on what we need to do next."

"Agreed," Garek said.

Lucien held his tongue.

"With *Astralis* jamming all of their outbound comms, how are we supposed to coordinate with them from now on?" Addy asked.

Garek nodded to his displays. "They're sending out more shuttles. I'm going to try hailing them."

He did so, and a moment later, they replied.

"Admiral Wheeler here. We're on our way over to take possession of the fleet and evaluate its capabilities."

"Understood, Admiral," Garek replied. "We'll be waiting. I suggest you land in the same hangar that your shuttle pilot chose. It's close to the bridge. I'll have him waiting to escort you up here."

"Thank you, Lieutenant," Admiral Wheeler said. "You made the right choice," she added after a brief pause.

Lucien saw Garek's gaze flick to him, then back to his displays. "Not all of us would agree, ma'am."

"Yes, I heard there was some confusion about the chain of command."

Garek nodded. "Aye, there was."

"*Astralis* thanks you for your timely actions. We'll be aboard soon."

"See you then, Admiral," Garek replied.

* * *

The Lost Etherian Fleet

"This is incredible..." Admiral Wheeler breathed, while gazing at the Gideon's sensor display. "Are you sure this data is all accurate?"

Garek nodded. "We had plenty of opportunity to test the fleet's sensors in the time it took for us to reach *Astralis*."

Tyra blinked. The scientist in her took over and she shook her head in disbelief. "How is this even possible? Quantum signals aren't instant, and as for the range... nothing can see clear across the universe in *real time*."

"Apparently that's not the case," Garek replied. "Maybe it's some kind of trans-dimensional technology. Our entire universe might actually occupy a relatively small space within the higher spatial dimensions around us."

"Maybe..." Tyra replied. "I guess this means the Faros definitely *can* find Etheria with the ships we gave them."

Garek nodded. "Easily."

Tyra glanced at Lucien, where he sat to one side of the control stations on the *Gideon's* bridge. Lieutenant Sevris and an entire squad of Marines were pointing their guns in his face, while another squad stood guarding the stairs leading down to the entrance of the bridge.

Lucien looked different without any hair. All of her former crew did, Tyra though, her eyes flicking between them. She barely recognized Addy. Tyra felt a flash of smug satisfaction at the sight of Lucien's girlfriend without any hair.

She turned back to Admiral Wheeler. The admiral's green eyes were narrowed, and her brow was deeply furrowed.

"It's too late to regret negotiating with the Faros now," Tyra pointed out.

"Who says I regret it? We secured the future of humanity against an unbeatable enemy. We're just lucky we had something to offer them in exchange for peace."

"Then what are you worried about?" Tyra asked.

"If the Etherians' sensors are instantaneous, then their comms must be, too," Wheeler mused.

"They are," Garek confirmed.

"Which means we can warn Etherus," Wheeler concluded. "The question is, should we?"

"We'd risk breaking our treaty with the Faros," Garek said.

Wheeler glanced at him. "They never said anything about not communicating with the Etherians."

"It's implied. We can't take their enemy's side. Warning the Etherians would be the same as a declaration of war."

"Perhaps there's another way."

"Contacting Etherus could give away our position," Garek added. "We don't know how Etherian comms work, so we don't know that they can't be intercepted."

"All good points, Lieutenant," Admiral Wheeler replied. "How long did you say it took you to reach *Astralis*?"

"Two months."

"And you traveled how far in that time?" Wheeler asked.

"About thirty billion light years."

"So for us to physically travel back to New Earth won't take us another eight years. It should take about... ten weeks," Wheeler said.

"Sounds about right," Garek replied.

"*Astralis* won't be able to keep up with that pace," Tyra pointed out. "It would have to stay here."

Wheeler turned to her. "We need to get back to safety as soon as we can. Until we know for sure whether the Faros are planning to honor their peace treaty with us, we'd do well to consolidate our defenses with New Earth and prepare for a possible attack."

Tyra nodded along with that. "And warn Etherus in the process."

Wheeler shrugged and spread her hands. "We're entitled to reunite with our people and tell them everything that happened while we were away. If the ruler of New Earth and Etheria just happens to hear about it in the process, the Faros can't exactly blame us."

"They might decide to blame us, anyway," Tyra said.

"Then they're looking for an excuse to break their treaty with us, and sooner or later they'd have found one," Wheeler replied.

"Agreed," Tyra said. "It'll be a tight squeeze to get all of our people packed aboard these ships with enough supplies to last them ten weeks."

"Yes," Wheeler replied. "It will be. Fortunately, the Etherians built big ships. This vessel is what... ten kilometers from bow to stern?"

"Fourteen," Garek corrected. "And there are at least a dozen other ships of similar size."

"Good. We're going to need all the space we can get," Wheeler replied. "We'd better get started."

"What about..." Tyra's gaze drifted back to Lucien. She hesitated to call him by name, since he didn't look like her husband without any hair, and he technically *wasn't* her husband. He was her husband's clone. Or no... wasn't it the other way around? *This* Lucien was the original. She frowned and shook her head to dispel her confusion. "What about him?" Tyra finished.

"He was in an impossible situation," Addy said, standing up from her control station.

Both Tyra and Wheeler glanced at Addy, but Wheeler spoke first. "He refused to surrender the Etherian fleet when called upon to do so, and he refused to obey his orders. He'll be tried for insubordination."

"Does that mean he won't be integrated with my husband?" Tyra asked hopefully, suddenly worried that her husband would be held accountable for *this* Lucien's actions.

"That's a decision for the judiciary department to rule on, but personally I think it would be unfair to integrate them under the circumstances. I'll be sure to make that assertion during his hearing."

"Thank you," Tyra replied, nodding.

"Meanwhile, you'd better call another emergency session of council to approve the course of action we've suggested here. If they come out against us returning to New Earth, then we're going to need to come up with a new plan, and fast."

Tyra nodded. "I'm ready to leave when you are."

"I'll be staying here to take command of the fleet," Admiral Wheeler replied. "Lieutenant Sevris—"

"Ma'am?" the pilot asked.

"Take the Chief Councilor and the prisoner back to *Astralis.*"

"Yes, ma'am."

Nodding to Tyra, Wheeler said, "Good luck, Councilor."

Tyra inclined her head to that. "Hopefully the next time you see me I'll be leading the first wave of transports."

Lieutenant Sevris walked up beside her, but the Marines hung back, guarding Lucien. "By your leave, Councilor," Sevris said.

Before Tyra could reply, she overheard Garek asking the admiral about his daughter, Nora Helios. She recognized the name of the now-deceased director of the Resurrection Center, and she winced as Admiral Wheeler explained what had happened to her and her backup memories with the destruction of the Res Center.

Garek was dead silent following that explanation, and Tyra turned to see him staring in open-mouthed shock at Admiral Wheeler, his face ashen, and eyes dull.

"I'm sorry for your loss, Lieutenant," Admiral Wheeler said.

"Ma'am?" the pilot standing beside Tyra prompted.

She nodded absently. "Lead the way, Lieutenant."

"Yes, ma'am." He turned on his heel and strode for the exit. As he did so the Marines guarding Lucien pulled him to his feet and marched after Sevris.

Tyra brought up the rear, getting as close to Lucien as the Marines would allow. As they walked down the stairs and through the doors of the bridge, she whispered to him, "I'm going to do everything I can to get you pardoned."

Lucien flashed a rueful smile. "Thanks, but who's going to pardon the rest of us for helping the Faros to slaughter everyone in Etheria?"

"They haven't defeated Etherus yet, and we don't know that they will."

"We don't know that they'll lose, either," Lucien countered.

"If Etherus is the god he claims to be, he should be able to protect his people."

Lucien said nothing to that. Tyra was no great believer in Etherus, but she knew that Lucien was, so there was no escaping her logic.

A true god would need no help or protection that they could offer, and a false god might deserve to be defeated. Except that after what Abaddon had done to her daughter, Tyra couldn't bring herself to think of him or his empire as the better alternative.

If Etherus was defeated, the best they could hope for would be to find a way to live in peace with the Faros. Tyra just hoped that would be possible.

CHAPTER 7

Astralis

—SIX HOURS LATER—

Joe Coretti sat in the throne room of his night club, the Crack of Dawn, listening to the news. The council had ruled unanimously that *Astralis* should be evacuated to the Etherian Fleet. From there they'd travel back to the Red Line and New Earth in just ten weeks weeks rather than the eight years it had taken them to get all the way out here to the cosmic horizon in the first place.

Peace had supposedly been declared with the Faros, and humanity had been granted citizenship in the Farosien Empire, but no one wanted to stick around and test the Faros' promises.

"This changes everything," Joe mused.

"Yes," Bob agreed.

Joe glanced at his android. He supposed that he'd have to stop thinking of Bob as a *thing* that could be owned now that he was an android, too. Resurrecting himself as an android was the only way to come back safely after Bob had blown the Resurrection Center to bits. The authorities were looking for illegal cloning facilities where he might have planned to come back to life, not an off-the-books bot factory.

It had been Joe's plan all along to blow up the Res Center. Breaking in with Lucien to find evidence that *Astralis's* leaders were really undercover Faro agents had just been the icing to sweeten the plot.

His real goal had been to break in and steal all the data from the center; then blow the place and extort people with their own memories. It was the perfect crime, with unfathomable rewards. Before the advent of immortality through transfer of consciousness and cloning, people would pay inordinate sums to doctors to keep their loved ones alive. Now they would pay inordinate sums to Joe Coretti to resurrect their dead.

How many people had died when the Faros exposed Fallside to space? *Millions.* And of those millions, the vast majority had yet to be resurrected. Joe knew that he could extort untold sums of money to bring those people back.

Executing that plan was a little more complicated, of course: he had to bring those people back as androids, not humans, since he couldn't very well create real clones of the dead without the authorities noticing. But where was the harm in creating robotic effigies to sooth the peoples' grieving hearts? Only Joe's clients would know the truth that those effigies were the real deal. He'd planned to install a fail-safe in all of the resurrected androids to wipe their minds if anyone ever tried to report him, which meant no one would risk it, and if even if they did, the evidence would auto-erase itself.

The plan was genius, but now it was utterly foiled.

"How am I supposed to evacuate all the stolen data, my android factory, and all of the materials and supplies I'm going to need to get things started?" Joe shook his head. "I'll have to wait until we get back to New Earth, and then I'll have to start over from zero! All of my businesses are on *Astralis,* and all my money is in its banks!

"That is troubling, boss," Bob said.

"It gets worse! Back on New Earth, Etherus is sure to figure out what I'm up to, and when he does, he'll seize the stolen data and bring everyone back himself. I'll be lucky not to get executed for my trouble! We're done, Bob," Joe said, shaking his head. "We wasted our time."

"We could remain on *Astralis,*" Bob suggested.

Joe shot him an incredulous look. "By ourselves? And do what?"

Bob shrugged. "We'll have the place to ourselves. You'll be king."

Joe snorted. "King Coretti... that does have a nice ring to it, but what's the point of being a ruler if there's no one to rule?"

"We could resurrect everyone in android bodies after the humans have left."

"Now there's a thought..." Joe sat back in his throne-like chair and considered the idea. "It would take a long time to manufacture that many androids."

"We could ramp up production. If you're the uncontested ruler of *Astralis,* you wouldn't have to hide your operations, and you could requisition whatever resources you need."

"You're right. This is brilliant, Bob! You're a frekking genius!"

"Thank you, boss."

A slow smile spread across Joe's lips. "All we have to do is wait until everyone else leaves, and then get to work. We'll start by resurrecting some of our own to create a militia.

If anyone gets out of line—bang! They're dead." Joe nodded to himself, already imagining what he could do as the uncontested ruler of *Astralis*.

"What about your brothers, boss?"

Joe's lips twisted into a frown. "What about them?"

"Shouldn't we let them know what we're doing so they can join us?"

"And share power with them? No thanks. They can run with their tails between their legs. We'll take over their operations when they're gone. Besides, I seem to recall them saying they wanted no part of the plot to blow the Res Center, so why should they share in the spoils?"

"Good point, boss."

Joe rose from his chair and slapped Bob on the back. "It's just you and me, Bob—King Coretti and... General Bob. How about I give you command of the militia?"

"I'd like that," Bob replied. "But what about the Faros?"

"What *about* them?" Joe asked. "We're at peace, remember?"

"What if the treaty breaks down and war is re-declared?"

Joe considered that. "We're not technically human. Maybe we can negotiate our own treaty."

"We have nothing that the Faros want."

"Then we'd better find something. Anyway, that's a future concern. One problem at a time, Bobby. First we consolidate our power and resurrect our subjects. Then we'll figure out how to protect our kingdom."

"Yes, boss."

CHAPTER 8

The Lost Etherian Fleet

—TEN WEEKS LATER—

Lucien stood in line for the shared restroom in the *Gideon's* crew quarters.

"I need to pee!" Atara whined. She shifted her weight from one foot to the other, doing a little dance.

"I know, honey!" Lucien said, shouting to be heard over the noise in the corridor. "We're almost to the front of the line!"

The commotion aboard the *Gideon* was endless—people talking, shouting, moaning, babies crying, children screaming. There had to be at least a thousand people crowded into this corridor alone.

A Marine bot stood to either side of them, scanning the crowd for threats to the Chief Councilor's family, but these people didn't look threatening to Lucien. They all had the same vacant stares, the same despondent expressions.

Conditions on the fleet were bad. Every available space was crowded with people and their belongings. Their beds were made of dirty clothes and garbage. Food was in short supply, and water was even shorter. Sanitation systems were overtaxed, and showers being rationed to once a week. People were hungry, thirsty, dirty, tired, and sore from sleeping on the hard deck.

The good news was it would be over soon. Just a few hours ago Admiral Wheeler had announced over the intercomm that they were calculating their final jump to reach the Red Line. *Soon. We'll reach New Earth soon,* Lucien assured himself.

Abruptly, someone stood up and announced, "We've reached the Red Line!"

Applause answered that statement, but Lucien frowned, wondering why he was hearing about it from a random source rather than from Tyra or Admiral Wheeler.

The man who'd stood up whistled for attention. "I'm not finished!" he said. "We've reached the Red Line, but we can't get across! Etherus has somehow locked us out!"

"That's impossible!" someone scoffed, and Lucien was inclined to agree. How do you physically block off an entire supercluster of galaxies?

But not everyone was in a mood for thinking rationally. A worried murmur spread through the crowd like a wave, rising quickly in pitch. The wave crested, and several others stood up. "How do you know this?" someone demanded.

"I know someone who's serving on the bridge."

The murmuring turned to shouting as everyone started taking this rumor seriously. One by one people jumped to their feet.

Lucien pulled Atara close as he continued puzzling over the information. *Astralis* had crossed the Red Line to leave the Etherian Empire over eight years ago. They hadn't encountered any mysterious jamming fields on their way out.

What kind of barrier would allow travel in one direction but not the other?

"What are we going to do now?" a woman standing in line in front of Lucien asked.

He slowly shook his head. "I wouldn't take the rumor too seriously. It's not possible for Etherus to lock us out of Laniakea."

"Aren't you the Councilor's husband?" she asked, her eyes narrowing as she scanned him from head to toe. "You know something! What aren't you telling us?"

"I know as much as you do, ma'am."

Her face scrunched up into a sneer, and she looked away. "Hey, everyone! The councilor's husband is here!"

Lucien's whole body went cold as at least a hundred people turned to look. He saw their expressions, and he knew what would happen next. He needed to get somewhere with a door he could lock. The restroom was the closest option. He nodded to the Marine bot to his left. "Shepherd Four, clear a path to the front of the line."

"Copy that," the bot replied. "Make way!" it declared.

But no one budged. Someone shoved the bot, and it opened fire. A stun bolt screeched out from Shepherd Four's left arm, sending the man who'd shoved it crumpling to the deck with his limbs jittering and body convulsing.

"Dad, I'm scared!" Atara screamed as people pressed in around them. Lucien swept her up into his arms and scanned the crowd for a way out. There was nothing but a seething mass of bobbing heads. People were shoving him now and beating his Marine bots with their fists and makeshift clubs.

Shepherd Four fired again, and then Five joined in.

Their targets collapsed, wreathed in blue fire, and the people shoving Lucien grew more insistent. Someone punched him in the side of the head and he stumbled sideways with his ear ringing. Darkness gathered at the edges of his vision, but he blinked it away. He clutched Atara close to his chest, but switched to a one-armed grip so he could fumble for his sidearm. As a former police chief it was his job to help keep order on the ship. Suddenly Lucien wished he hadn't left Brak with Theola in his and Tyra's quarters.

The Marine bots closed in around Lucien, guarding him from the front and back, but they couldn't protect his flanks. Someone elbowed Atara in the face and she screamed, clutching her cheek. Lucien gritted his teeth and flicked off the safety on his gun. He switched the weapon from *stun* to *kill,* and fired at the ceiling. "Everyone stop where you are!" he roared, but no one listened.

The crowd pressed closer, squeezing Lucien and Atara between their bot guardians. Lucien felt the hand holding Atara being crushed, his bones grinding between the unyielding metal of one of the bots, and the bones in Atara's hip. She was sobbing uncontrollably, and her cheek was already badly swollen from where she'd been elbowed in the face.

Lucien fired again and again at the ceiling, screaming until he was hoarse.

Finally the crowd noticed the weapon in his hand, but instead of backing off for fear of getting shot, they pressed closer still, grasping hands reaching for his gun. He held it high, out of reach, but a tall man shoved through the crowd and grabbed the weapon. Lucien wrestled briefly with him.

And then the trigger depressed by accident, and a flash

of crimson light blinded them. Lucien blinked away the sudden glare and watched in horror as the man collapsed, his mouth open in a scream, his hands clutching a smoking hole in his chest. He disappeared under a sea of trampling feet. If the laser bolt to his chest hadn't killed him, the crowd certainly would.

Others rushed in to take his place, and soon Lucien was wrestling with three different sets of hands. His guard bots fired a steady stream of stun blasts into the crowd, and people collapsed around Lucien in waves, unconscious but alive. A woman finally managed to steal Lucien's weapon away, in the process bending his trigger finger back until one of the bones snapped.

He cried out in pain and withdrew his injured hand. The woman who'd stolen his weapon turned it on the bots. She shot one of them three times in quick succession, and it fell to the deck with a noisy clatter. The crowd swarmed over the fallen machine, kicking it as it struggled to rise. Lucien curled his body around Atara to keep her safe while the remaining guard bot turned and did likewise for him. Lucien felt the bot shudder in time to four screeching reports from his stolen sidearm, and then it collapsed, too, leaving Lucien's back exposed.

The crowd swarmed him, beating him with their fists until he fell down. He made sure to fall on top of Atara, so he could shield her from the crowd. She squirmed and cried under him, but he held fast, hoping no one would notice her there.

Then the steel toes of someone's mag boots found Lucien's head, and everything went dark.

CHAPTER 9

The Lost Etherian Fleet

"I'm getting reports of riots throughout the ship," Tyra said from where she sat manning the *Gideon's* comms station. At first, the control stations had been inscrutable to her, since they were programmed in Etherian, but after just a few minutes, the ship's systems had somehow sensed (and maybe even learned) the language of their new operators, summarily translating themselves into Versal. "Somehow they found out that we can't cross the Red Line," Tyra explained, still listening to the reports of unrest.

"Send in the Marines and get our doctors to treat the wounded," Admiral Wheeler said.

"Aye," Colonel Drask said from the sensor control station.

Admiral Wheeler shook her head. "Who the frek told them that we can't cross the Red Line?"

"Someone must have leaked the information from one of the other ships," Colonel Drask said from the sensor control station.

Wheeler scowled. "Councilor, you'd better get on the comms fast to explain the situation."

In lieu of a reply, Tyra did exactly that. "Citizens of *Astralis,* this is your Chief Councilor speaking. There's a rumor that we have already reached the Red Line, but that we are mysteriously unable to cross it. Those reports are false.

"We have reached the Red Line, but there *is* a way to cross it. We've already sent out probes to make sure that the way is safe. Please be patient and remain calm while we wait for our probes to return. I assure you, this is only a temporary delay, and we will arrive at New Earth very soon. Thank you."

"You should have lied," Wheeler said.

"What?" Tyra asked.

"You should have told them that the way *is* safe and that we're already crossing the Red Line."

"And risk an even bigger riot if the way isn't safe and the people find out that we've been lying to them?" Tyra challenged. "No, they needed to hear the truth. Besides, I didn't tell them everything. Only what they needed to know."

"Just as well. If they knew that the only way in was through a wormhole that may or may not even be traversable, we'd have a mutiny on our hands."

"How long before our probes get back?" Tyra asked.

"They should *already* be back," Wheeler replied.

"Great," Garek put in from the gunnery control station.

Tyra glanced at him, then back to Wheeler, and the admiral nodded to her. "You're sure we can't establish a comms connection through the wormhole? Try again to get a ping from one of the probes."

Tyra checked the comms panel once more and shook her head. "Nothing."

Wheeler sighed. "It's no wonder no one tried to contact us after we left the Etherian Empire. They couldn't get a signal out. What I don't get, though, is how we were able to leave in the first place. We didn't have to cross a wormhole."

"No, we didn't," Tyra replied.

"I've got something on sensors!" Colonel Drask said.

"Is it the probe?" Wheeler asked.

All eyes turned to him, and he nodded. "Yes, ma'am. One of them. Receiving scan data now..."

"So where are the other nine?" Wheeler asked, while checking the ship's sensors for herself. "We sent them all out together. Why did only *one* of them return?"

"You think something destroyed them?" Tyra asked.

"Like what?" Wheeler countered.

"Like the wormhole," Drask replied. "The log data from the probe that made it shows the other ones being ripped apart by tidal forces. The traversable throat is very narrow... just two kilometers by the looks of it."

"How wide is the *Gideon*?" Tyra asked.

"One point nine kilometers," Addy replied from the helm. "We should make it, but just barely."

"Interesting that our largest ship has almost the same width as the wormhole," Wheeler mused. "I wonder if that's by design or coincidence?"

"My money's on design," Drask said.

"I agree," Wheeler replied. "Colonel—send the Councilor the scan data from the probe."

"Aye, transmitting to your station, Councilor."

"Got it," Tyra replied.

"Good," Wheeler said. "Councilor, please send the data to the rest of the fleet and tell them to follow the probe's path through the wormhole exactly. We don't want any of our ships getting ripped apart the way that those other probes did. We'll lead the way. Everyone else needs to fly through single file behind us."

"I'll let them know," Tyra said.

"Lieutenant Gallia—"

"Ma'am?" Addy replied.

"Take us through, and try not to scratch the paint."

"Copy that, Admiral."

* * *

The Lost Etherian Fleet

—ONE HOUR LATER—

"We're passing through the throat of the wormhole now..." Addy said.

The *Gideon* groaned ominously as tidal forces gripped it, with gravity attracting the bow more powerfully than the stern, and trying to rip the ship in half. It didn't help at all that the *Gideon* was fourteen kilometers long.

Tyra's eyes flicked up to the unobstructed view from the holo dome that crowned the bridge. Stars and space warped strangely around them, twisting in surreal ways. Then came a blinding flash of light.

"We're through!" Addy called out.

"Comms! Sensors! Report," Wheeler said.

"One second..." Tyra replied, blinking quickly to clear her eyes. "Outbound comms are working again," she said. "We should be able to contact New Earth now."

"Good, send them a message to let them know we've arrived. Warn them to expect an Etherian fleet rather than *Astralis.*"

Before Tyra could acknowledge that command, an

incoming comm call began trilling in her ears, and the comms icon began to flash on her ARCs. It was from Brak. Tyra frowned, wondering what that was about. Brak almost never called her. If he had something to say he usually said it through Lucien.

"Councilor?" Wheeler prompted.

"Hang on." Trya replied. Her heart pounded in her chest as she remembered the riots. Surely Lucien had had the sense to lock the door to their quarters when he heard the commotion outside. She answered the comms and said, "Brak, is something wrong?"

The Gor sitting stolidly on the bridge at the ship's engineering station turned to look over his shoulder at the sound of his name, but she was talking to his clone—not him.

"It is Lucien. And Atara," Brak replied. People attack them when riots break out."

Tyra's breath froze in her lungs, her worst fears suddenly coming true. "Are they okay?" Her brain buzzed with terror. There were no backups of anyone's consciousness anymore. If something had happened to either Atara or Lucien, there'd be no way to bring them back.

"They are alive," Brak said.

Tyra's heart leapt in her chest, but she didn't allow herself to feel relief just yet. If Lucien was okay, then he would have been the one calling her. "But?" she pressed.

"Lucien is in a coma. He is badly beaten. Atara is also hurt and she loses consciousness, too, but she is waking up now. The doctors think she is to be fine. They are lucky. Many others are dead."

"What about Lucien? Are there medics attending him? Have they tried to wake him?"

"Let me ask..." A moment later, Brak replied, "They cannot wake him until the swelling subsides. They are downloading his consciousness to a portable device in case he does not recover."

Tyra couldn't believe it. "How did this happen? You were supposed to stay with them in our quarters!"

"Lucien tells me to watch Theola while he goes to the restroom with Atara. Riots start soon after he leaves," Brak replied.

Tyra cursed under her breath. "Where are you?"

"The end of the corridor outside your quarters."

"I'll be right there," Tyra said. She ended the call and turned to explain the situation to Admiral Wheeler.

Silence reigned in the wake of the news about Lucien and the *many dead* that Brak had mentioned. That drove home just how serious the riots had been. Sitting up here on the bridge under heavy guard by several squads of Marines, they'd been insulated from the chaos.

"You'd better make another announcement," Wheeler said quietly. "Tell people that we're safely across the Red Line and we're on our way to New Earth."

Tyra nodded stiffly and told everyone exactly that in a ship-wide announcement. When she finished, she rose from her control station and said, "I need to go see my family."

"Of course," Wheeler replied. "Drask, you have the comms while the councilor is gone—and send a squad of marines with her. We don't want any more incidents."

"Aye, ma'am. Sergeant Kilian—" Drask nodded to the Marine Sergeant guarding the flight of stairs leading down to the entrance of the bridge. "Take your squad and escort the Councilor," Colonel Drask said.

"Yes, sir," the sergeant replied.

As Tyra started for the doors of the bridge, another flash of light blinded her and stopped her in her tracks.

"What the frek?" Colonel Drask said.

"Welcome back," a new voice added.

Tyra *knew* that voice. She spun around to face the speaker and saw a tall, familiar being standing at the front of the bridge. He had pale, luminous skin and long white hair framing an elongated face. His eyes blazed and danced like twin suns as they swept from one person to the next, forcing them to avert their eyes from the sheer intensity of his gaze. There was no mistaking this being's identity—it was Etherus. But how did he get here?

Tyra's logical mind took hold, and she reasoned that he must have used a quantum junction to jump aboard their ship. Maybe they'd forgotten to engage the *Gideon's* jamming field, or maybe Etherus had ways of jumping through the jamming fields of his own ships.

"You betrayed me," Etherus said.

Tyra forced herself to stare into his blinding eyes. "We had no choice." There was no point in denying it, but Tyra couldn't help but wonder how Etherus knew what they'd done. Had someone found a way to warn him already, or had the Faros already begun their attack?

There was also the dubious third option that the faithful were right when they claimed that Etherus knows people's innermost thoughts.

"There is always a choice," Etherus replied. "Unfortunately, you only thought you were betraying me, when in reality you were betraying yourselves. You didn't pave the way for the Faros to conquer Etheria; you've paved the way for them to conquer humanity."

CHAPTER 10

The Lost Etherian Fleet

"What do you mean we've paved the way for the Faros to conquer humanity? We're at peace with them," Tyra said.

"You won't be for long," Etherus replied. "Even if you could trust Abaddon, he will turn on you out of spite when he realizes that he still can't reach Etheria."

"Why can't he?" Admiral Wheeler asked. "Is it because of the barrier we encountered when we tried to cross the Red Line?"

"You found a way to cross it, did you not?" Etherus replied.

"We had to go through a wormhole to get here," Wheeler replied. "And according to the nav systems on your ships, that wormhole is the only way in."

"If you found the way by accessing the fleet's navigation systems, then the Faros will find it, too."

"How do you know about our negotiations with the Faros? Who's been in contact with you?" Wheeler asked.

"What makes you think I need someone to tell me?" Etherus replied, turning to Wheeler and forcing her to squint against the brightness of his gaze. "The barrier you encountered is a jump interdiction field. I deactivated the interdiction field when *Astralis* left and reactivated it in your wake, but as you have found, there is a way through that cannot be blocked."

Tyra shook her head. "So why is Etheria safe? We located it with your ships' nav systems. It lies through the center of the torus, and at the center of Laniakea. It's in the universe on the other side of this one, and clearly there's a way to get to it, or else we'd have no contact with Etheria."

Etherus inclined his head to that. "Your assumptions seem reasonable, but there are things you still don't know. The universe on the other side, as you call it, is fundamentally unreachable, because it is made out of antimatter."

Tyra gasped. "Anti... how is that possible?"

"When the universe began, matter spewed from one end of a white hole, while antimatter streamed out from the other. Both universes quickly spread and developed into what you know now. This has been going on since the dawn of time, and the two sides of the universes are expanding and accelerating toward each other, drawn across the great divide by the mutual pull of each other's gravity. You refer to the phenomena behind this effect of accelerated expansion as *Dark Energy*.

"Eventually the two universes will meet at the rim of the torus where they will obliterate one another and start all over again in a new cycle, but that is still a long time from happening. Not even light has reached from one side of the universe to the other yet, and the rim of the torus is still dominated by a vast band of emptiness."

Tyra's mind spun. "If that's true, it solves the parity problem..." she said slowly.

"The what?" Admiral Wheeler asked.

"We've always known that antimatter and matter should have been created in equal quantities," Tyra explained. "But we've never been able to find the missing antimatter."

"Isn't antimatter supposed to be extremely volatile?" Colonel Drask asked. "How can there be an entire universe made of the stuff without it self-destructing?"

Tyra shook her head. "It's only volatile if it comes into contact with matter. By itself it's exactly the same as regular matter, with all the same properties. The only real difference is that the charges of all of the sub-atomic particles in antimatter are reversed."

Etherus nodded along with that explanation, but Colonel Drask still looked confused.

"Does antimatter have anti-gravity?" Wheeler asked.

"No," Tyra replied. "If it did, the other universe would not form stars and planets. The antimatter side would be sterile and effectively invisible." She turned back to Etherus. "But it's not—the antimatter universe is just like ours, isn't it?"

"Yes," Etherus replied.

"So Etheria is... *fundamentally* unreachable," Wheeler said, shaking her head.

Tyra nodded. "Matter beings and ships can't cross from one universe to the other..." She trailed off as she realized that couldn't be true. She'd been to Etheria herself, as had billions of other humans. There had to be a safe way to travel there. Etherian ships always ferried them back and forth—maybe they had some kind of defensive shields? But if the Etherians themselves and even the atmosphere they breathed were made of antimatter, then breathing that air with them or even shaking hands with one of them would be enough to cause a massive explosion. Something wasn't adding up.

"The Etherians started out in our universe, in a satellite galaxy of the Milky Way," Admiral Wheeler said. "If no one can travel safely from one universe to the other, then how did you take them to a new galaxy in the antimatter universe after the Great War left their original galaxy uninhabitable? And how are we able to visit Etheria?"

Etherus replied, "Matter or antimatter cannot be transmitted from one side to the other without catastrophic results, but data can travel freely from one side to another in the form of quantum signals or electro-magnetic radiation. There is no such thing as an anti-photon.

"When I took the Etherians to their new galaxy, they left their bodies behind in this side of the universe for them to use when they return. They also left all of their ships and belongings behind, though there weren't many ships left after the war.

"I transmitted their consciousness to the other side, and the data was received, downloaded, and subsequently transferred to cloned bodies made of antimatter that were prepared for them by sentient beings in the antimatter side of the universe. The Since then, Etherians have made the same provisions for humans who wish to visit Etheria. Your minds are transferred to identical bodies waiting for you on the other side."

"So why bother sending ships for us and pretending to physically transport us to Etheria?" Wheeler asked.

"Because protecting your physical bodies becomes our responsibility while your conscious minds are away in

Etheria, and we need to ensure your safe return. The only way we can do that is to keep you on board our ships while you're away."

"And because you wanted to keep all of this a mystery," Tyra said. "You're only telling us now because you want us to understand that we actually frekked ourselves over when we betrayed you and the Etherians. You're just rubbing the irony in our faces. This is one big, fat *I told you so.*"

Etherus turned to her with a disappointed look, and the blinding light radiating from his eyes dimmed slightly. "Do you think so little of me, Tyra?"

She decided not to reply to that.

"I'm telling you all of this now, because you need to understand what is at stake. You need to take the Faro threat seriously and take appropriate action now, before all of humanity is enslaved."

"What action?" Admiral Wheeler asked. "You know how badly the Faros outnumber us. This is not a battle that we can win."

"The wormhole gives you an advantage. Ships can only fly through one at a time, which will allow you to surround and overwhelm them as they come through, but you're right: the Faros have trillions of warships, and you cannot stop them all."

Tyra's blood turned to ice. *"Trillions?"* she echoed quietly.

"Yes," Etherus replied. "Eventually you won't be able to stop the flood. All you can hope to do is buy time."

"Time for what?" Colonel Drask growled. "It sounds like the only reasonable course of action is to surrender and hope that the Faros don't break our treaty."

"There is another option," Etherus replied. "Abaddon has cloned himself billions of times, giving each of them his memories and personality. He maintains a cohesive sense of self by synchronizing his clones through the Forge, and that is also how the original Abaddon keeps all of the others under control. He can kill any of his clones from there if they get out of line."

"The Forge... we heard about that at Freedom Station," Garek said, joining the conversation for the first time.

"Yes, from Oorgurak, the runaway slave that you rescued," Etherus said.

Again, Tyra found herself wondering how Etherus knew so much about everything that had happened. Perhaps the faithful were right, and he really could read everyone's thoughts. Still, that didn't necessarily make him a god. All kinds of technology could read a person's mind, and some aliens were natural telepaths.

"What is the Forge?" Admiral Wheeler asked.

"It is the source of all consciousness, the Tree of Life—or it was, until Abaddon stole it during the Great War. He used it to create all of the species beyond the Red Line and to give them life, but he failed to create true consciousness, and he had to settle for creating endless copies of the Faros.

"He copied their minds, wiped their memories, and put them in the bodies of new alien species; then he enslaved those aliens to the original Faros, whose minds they were created from. All he has done is to enslave the Faros to themselves, but not even that, because all of the beings Abaddon created with the Forge are nothing but life-like drones. They lack the subjective experience of consciousness and the crucial element of free will provided by souls. The same holds true for all of Abaddon's clones, so they are right to say that they are helpless to do otherwise than the evil that they do. Only the original Abaddon is free to change his path, and he does not wish to do so."

Tyra's eyes narrowed. As a scientist, she considered free will to be a fiction, but here Etherus was claiming that some missing piece of the puzzle allowed people to have such a thing.

"You allow the Faros to enslave everyone beyond the Red Line because they're doing it to themselves?" Addy asked.

Etherus nodded to her. "They wanted to live in a chaotic universe. That's why they started the Great War. I gave them what they wanted, and allowed them to steal the Forge so that they could create the chaos they wanted, but the Faros and their soulless slaves are the only ones who will ever suffer because of the chaos they created, and their suffering is ultimately self-inflicted."

"But now Abaddon is planning to add Laniakea to his empire," Wheeler said. "And according to what you're saying, all of the beings inside the Red Line are free, conscious beings."

"That is why I am speaking to you now. To give you a chance to prevent what is coming. You need to hold the wormhole with everything you've got, while a smaller force goes looking for The Forge.

"When you find it, you must destroy it. Abaddon has linked his clones to The Forge in such a way that if it is destroyed, all of his copies will be killed. That is to prevent any of them from defying him. He has also linked the minds of every other being on his side of the Red Line to The Forge, and he can kill any of them on a whim. That is ultimately how he maintains control over his empire, but if The Forge is destroyed, slaves and dissident forces everywhere will seize their opportunity to finally rise up against their masters, and the Farosien Empire will disintegrate."

"Wait, I thought the Faros' slaves are all mindless automatons?" Tyra asked. "Why would they defy him if they can't think for themselves?"

"They're not mindless," Etherus said. "The mind is a predictable computer, but that doesn't mean it isn't intelligent. Abaddon's creations are *soulless*. There is a difference."

"If it looks like a snake, and slithers like a snake, then it is a snake," Wheeler said.

Tyra frowned and shook her head. "Souls don't exist. You admitted that when you helped us to defeat our AI ruler, Omnius, all those years ago. You showed us that our human minds were linked to sleeping Etherians on the artificial planet, Origin, and you told us that we were just avatars for those Etherians to experience the free, chaotic universe that the Faros wanted. Although back then you didn't mention the Faros. Anyway... you said those sleeping Etherians *were* our souls. So was that all a lie?"

"No, it was all true, but I never said that *Etherians* don't have souls. After you decided to remain human, their souls passed on to you. That is what Abaddon could not do for any of his clones, or for any of the alien species that he created with the Forge. He could not give them souls."

"Then my daughter is still alive?" Garek asked.

Etherus's gaze swept to him, and Garek squinted

against the glare. "Yes, her soul lives on, and you will see her again."

Garek nodded slowly, and some of the tension left his face.

Tyra shook her head. "You're just justifying your apathy toward the Faros in a way that we'll never be able to prove. I think the truth is that you let Abaddon get out of hand. You gave him too much time to build his empire, and whatever forces the Etherians left behind aren't enough to defeat them now. That's why you haven't gone to war with the Faros, because you know that you'll lose. You abandoned this side of the universe, and us along with it."

Etherus regarded Tyra steadily. "You are upset because your husband is in a coma and your daughter is injured, and now you are lashing out at me, but it's not my fault that they came to harm, or that any of the people from *Astralis* died. You were the ones who decided to leave the Etherian Empire against my wishes, and by doing so you have put everyone else at risk. Now you want someone to blame for the repercussions, but I am not responsible—*you* are. With freedom comes responsibility, and you have misused yours, but it is not too late. Find the Forge and destroy it. It is the only way to prevent what is coming."

"Then help us!" Tyra said. "Tell us where the Forge is, and send whatever ships you have on this side of the universe to help us destroy it."

Etherus tilted his head to one side. "You refuse to trust me, but you want my help. You refuse to listen to me, but you want me to share what I know. You defy my rules, and then you expect me to wave away the consequences. You don't believe I am God, but you ascribe god-like powers to me with your demands and wait for me to prove that I have them. You are like spoiled children demanding that their parents solve all of their problems for them."

"If you did prove that you really are God, then we would obey you," Tyra said. "In fact, if you'd just done that from the start, we could have avoided this entire mess!"

"If I proved to you that I am God, you would not need faith to believe in me, and if it were a matter of proof and not faith, then you would have no choice but to do as I say. You would obey me because you have to, not because you want to. Who would knowingly defy the creator of the universe?" Etherus asked.

"That depends whether or not you promise to punish the ones who go their own way," Tyra pointed out.

Admiral Wheeler shook her head. "Let's cut to the chase. You want us to deal with the consequences of our actions now and solve our own problems. That means we need to find the Forge and destroy it, while simultaneously defending this wormhole from the Faros. I don't suppose you have any suggestions about where we should start looking for this Forge? It's a big universe out there."

"Wouldn't a simple query to the fleet's data banks reveal its location?" Addy asked.

"No," Etherus replied. "The fleet's sensors have unlimited range, but the Forge's location is not indexed."

"So we need to send scouts looking for it," Admiral Wheeler mused.

"What if we only find it after our defenses have failed?" Colonel Drask asked.

"Then you will have lost the war," Etherus replied.

"You'd let us fail?" Tyra asked.

"Do you trust me?" Etherus replied.

Tyra said nothing to that. She could have lied and said yes, but she was fairly certain Etherus would see through her.

"I don't know," she finally replied.

This time it was Etherus's turn to say nothing.

Colonel Drask squinted at him. "If the outcome is uncertain, then evacuate us all to Etheria."

Etherus shook his head. "There is no time to do so."

"You have to do something!" Tyra burst out. "We're talking about the enslavement of trillions of sentient beings, and not all of them are guilty of defying you. Only *Astralis* did that."

"That is true, but you are all guilty of wanting to live in a chaotic society where my control is not absolute and my interference is minimal. Being subjected to the poor choices that other people make is an inevitable result of such chaos."

Tyra gaped at Etherus. The blinding light of his gaze made her eyes ache, but she refused to look away. Etherus's stance felt all wrong to her.

"I need to go see my family," she said, turning to leave the bridge once more.

"There is one other thing you should know, Tyra..." Etherus said as she strode for the exit. "One of the agents you discovered, whose mind Abaddon was supposed to release—was not in fact released, and she has recently reverted back to her subjugated state."

She...? Tyra wondered. *Atara. No, it can't be her.* But Tyra's heart was already in her throat, and her steps had faltered. Her legs were shaking as she turned back to Etherus.

He looked distraught. "I am sorry, Tyra. Abaddon was angry about the way you treated him during your negotiations. He took his revenge by pretending to release your daughter."

"If that's true, then *you* should release her," Tyra said slowly. "A good god would never allow a five-year-old to languish as a prisoner in her own mind."

Etherus shook his head. "She is gone, Tyra, but you will see her again someday."

Tyra's horror and outrage grew unbearable. She wanted to scream at Etherus and punch him in the face. She wanted hurt him just as much as his inaction was hurting her.

"You can't claim to be good and let innocent *children* suffer!"

"It is what you wanted," he replied, his eyes dimming and his expression grim.

"Then I've changed my mind! Take me and family to Etheria and bring Atara back!"

He just shook his head. "It doesn't work that way. You can't be free of me when it pleases you and be my faithful follower when it doesn't. I've intervened as much as I can without removing your freedom. Now the rest is up to you."

With that, Etherus vanished and the light of his presence left the bridge.

Tyra was panting with rage, glaring at the spot where he had been standing a moment ago.

For long minutes, no one spoke.

Finally, Admiral Wheeler broke the silence, "We'd better start preparing. We have an invasion to repel, and scouts to send out looking for the Forge."

"So we're going to break the treaty?" Colonel Drask asked, sounding incredulous as he turned to Wheeler with dark eyebrows raised. "We're just going to open fire on the first Faro ship that dares to cross the wormhole?"

"I don't see that we have a choice. The wormhole is the only advantage we have. If we let the Faros cross it, and they realize they can't reach their real target..." Wheeler trailed off with a grimace. "Etherus is right; they'll turn on us next."

"Send us to look for the Forge," Garek said.

Admiral Wheeler turned to him. "Excuse me?"

"I mean, send us, *ma'am.* Myself, Addy, Brak... we were all disguised by Abaddon to look and sound like Faros so that we could search for the lost Etherian fleet. We can even speak their language. We'll blend right in with their people."

"And we still have the Faros' boarding shuttles on *Astralis*..." Wheeler mused. "Yes, that could work. You think you can fly one of their shuttles?"

Garek shrugged. "There's only one way to find out."

Tyra shook her head. She couldn't deal with this right now. She was too angry to think straight. She needed to go see her husband, to make sure that at least *he* was okay—and to see for herself if what Etherus had said about Atara was true. "I have to go," she said.

Wheeler called after her as she reached the bridge doors. "Don't let your daughter know that we're suspicious of her! If she's a Faro agent, we might need her to feed misinformation to the enemy."

Tyra bit her tongue to hold back an angry retort. She waved the doors of the bridge open and breezed through.

The Marine Sergeant standing inside the doors followed her out with his squad of bots. The Sergeant strode by her and took point, but he looked just as dazed as Tyra felt.

Etherus's revelations had come as a shock to them all, and his refusal to help Atara boiled her blood. *How can a good*

God stand by and allow innocent children to suffer? It was a question as old as time, and as far as Tyra was concerned, the preservation of people's freedoms, or—*because that's the kind of universe you wanted to live in*—weren't good enough answers.

I'll find a way to bring you back, Atara. With or without Etherus's help.

CHAPTER 11

The Lost Etherian Fleet

When Tyra reached the corridor outside her quarters, she found dozens of people wounded and nine people dead. Doctors were busy attending people's injuries as best they could, but they didn't have the facilities or the supplies to treat everyone properly—Lucien in particular. Soon after Tyra arrived, medics transferred him to the bed in his and Tyra's quarters.

Now Tyra stood at his bedside with their two daughters, watching Lucien sleep and listening to the rhythmic beeping of a portable heart monitor. She kept hoping to see his eyelids flutter open and a smile grace his lips, but he didn't even twitch. Atara had an odd expression on her face as she watched her father, but Tyra wasn't ready to draw any conclusions from her behavior yet.

"Dada!" Theola exclaimed suddenly and pointed at Lucien. She jumped in Tyra's arms, trying to reach him.

"Yes, that's Dada," Tyra said.

Doctor Reed, the physician attending Lucien, took out a portable scanner and passed it over his head. "The swelling is getting worse," he said. "If it continues, it will cut off blood flow to his brain and he will die."

"Can't you relieve the pressure, somehow?" Tyra

asked.

"If I had the right tools and an operating room, maybe."

"There isn't a medical center on board?"

"It's crowded with people. We'd have to clear them all out, and even then, the sterility of the environment has already been compromised. We could be exposing your husband to a lethal infection if we operate there. We'd do just as well by operating right here."

"So what are you waiting for?" Tyra demanded.

Doctor Reed hesitated. "I'd need to find the proper instruments, but..."

"But what?"

"I understand your husband has a healthy clone on board."

"He was arrested for insubordination."

"Perhaps those charges can be dropped if he is integrated with this Lucien."

Tyra frowned and glanced at her husband once more. It actually wasn't a bad idea.

"Even if we treat your husband now, there's no guarantee that the swelling hasn't already caused irreparable brain damage."

"Then how do you know that the data you extracted isn't compromised?"

"We copied his brain data immediately, before the swelling had a chance to set in, so there's no reason to expect that the data is incomplete."

Tyra hesitated to approve the procedure. For one thing, she'd been hoping her husband wouldn't be asked to integrate with his clone, because that other Lucien was romantically involved with his crew mate, Addy Gallia.

"What if we integrate them and then this Lucien wakes up and he's fine?" she asked.

The doctor shrugged. "Then we can have the judiciary rule who should be integrated with whom. Until then—" He broke off suddenly as Lucien's heart monitor stopped beeping and instead issued a solid tone. "He's crashing!"

"Do something!" Tyra demanded.

"Frek... I don't have the equipment to restart his heart!" Doctor Reed hurriedly peeled back the covers and planted his hands on Lucien's chest to start compressions.

Tyra looked on in horror as he conducted CPR. Several minutes passed, but Lucien's monitor didn't give so much as a single beep.

Finally, the doctor stepped back, gasping for air, exhausted. He shook his head. "I'm sorry. The decision has been taken out of our hands." He walked around and pulled the plug on Lucien's heart monitor to silence the annoying flat line tone. With that, he turned back to her. "You can wait until we arrive at New Earth to have him cloned and revived in a new body, or you can revive him now by integrating him with the clone we have. It's your choice."

Tyra stared at Lucien's lifeless face for a long moment.

"Is he dead?" Atara asked, and poked Lucien's cheek with one finger. When he didn't respond, she poked him again.

"Atara!"

"What?"

Tyra grimaced. *Is he dead?* No emotion. No sign of grief. That didn't sound like normal behavior from five-year-old who'd just lost her father. Tyra shook her head and turned back to Doctor Reed. "Let's integrate them," she said. "Assuming the prisoner gives his consent."

Doctor Reed nodded. "Perhaps you'd like to accompany me to see the prisoner? I suspect you'll be more convincing than I."

Tyra nodded. "Let's go—Brak would you stay here with Theola and Atara please? Keep them safe, and make sure they don't... tease each other," she added, glancing at Atara.

"I shall guard them with my life," Brak replied.

Tyra passed Theola to him, and he held her awkwardly in one arm. Theola gazed up at the Gor with big blue eyes.

"Doctor Reed?" Tyra prompted.

He nodded and started for the door to her room. She followed him out, all the while wondering about Admiral Wheeler's plan to send out the survivors from the *Intrepid* to find the Forge. Would Admiral Wheeler send Lucien, even after he had defied her orders? If she did, integrating *her* Lucien's memories with his surviving clone wasn't going to bring him back to her.

* * *

The Lost Etherian Fleet

"Colonel Drask, have the first group of ships jump to New Earth," Admiral Wheeler said.

"Aye, Admiral," he replied.

Wheeler listened as he got on the comms and gave the order. They'd divided the fleet up into ten groups, and now they were sending them to New Earth one at a time to disembark the refugees.

Meanwhile, New Earth was busy deciding what to do about everything Etherus had told them. Apparently he'd appeared on New Earth to speak to its Chief Councilors at the same time that he'd appeared on the bridge of the *Gideon.* He'd told New Earth all of the same things, and now they were deliberating over what to do about the coming Faro invasion.

As far as Wheeler was concerned, there was nothing to deliberate about. Soon the Faros would come streaming through the wormhole with everything they had, and if New Earth didn't also put everything they had into defending their side of the gap, the entire human race would soon be enslaved to the Faros. Yet that defense was a losing battle, nothing but a stalling tactic to give them time to find and destroy the Forge.

With that in mind, Wheeler looked up from her control station to address her crew. "Lieutenants Addy Gallia, Garek Helios, and Brakos—" All three turned to look at her, and Wheeler went on, "Report to Hangar Bay Seventeen. It's time for you to prepare for your mission to find the Forge. I'll find replacements to fill in for you here on the bridge."

All three of them stood up from their control stations. Wheeler noted Garek's dull eyes and despondent expression, and she wondered if she should even be sending him. He'd recently learned that his daughter, Director Nora Helios, had been killed during the fighting inside the Resurrection Center. Etherus had promised Garek would see her again, but Wheeler didn't see how that was possible with the Res Center and all of its data gone.

"What about Lucien?" Addy Gallia asked.

"A good question," Wheeler replied, tearing her gaze

away from Garek to address the other woman. She rubbed her chin as she considered the matter. Lucien had refused to follow orders, but it turned out that he'd been right to do so. If they hadn't negotiated with the Faros, New Earth wouldn't be in jeopardy right now. Besides, they only had four officers that they could send looking for the Forge. "I'm going to drop the charges against him," Wheeler decided.

Garek's gaze sharpened. "He refused to follow orders, and he would have sacrificed *Astralis*. You'd be dead right now if we'd left him in command."

"Perhaps," Wheeler replied. "But everyone else would be safe. That's what a good commander does—he minimizes casualties, and that's exactly what Lucien was doing. You, however, appear to have based your decisions solely on concern for your daughter."

Garek's lip twitched at the mention of her, but he said nothing.

"Report to the hangar bay and get ready. Pick one of the Faro shuttles for your mission, and consolidate whatever supplies you can from the others. Remember, you won't be able to take any non-Faro items with you. Meanwhile, I'll see that Lucien is released from the brig and sent to join you there."

"Yes, ma'am," Garek replied.

"Our fate is in your hands," Wheeler said, looking to each of them in turn. "Failure is not an option. Dismissed."

They all nodded and saluted her before turning to march off the bridge. Garek led the way, while Addy and Brak trailed behind him. Wheeler watched them go, wondering if they actually had any chance of success.

Failure might not be an option, but it's definitely a

strong possibility.

CHAPTER 12

The Lost Etherian Fleet

Lucien watched as Chief Councilor Tyra *Ortane* strode into his cell. A doctor followed her in, and they explained the situation with his dead clone. He listened politely to what they had to say, but he wasn't ready to consent to anything yet.

Lucien ran a hand along his hairless scalp, and leaned back against the wall behind his cot as he considered the offer. He began bouncing his knee with restless energy. Being cooped up in the *Gideon's* brig was making him stir-crazy.

Another knock sounded at Lucien's door before he could make a decision.

"Yes?" Tyra answered, half turning to face the solid metal door of the cell. A small window in the top of the door allowed them to see out, but Lucien couldn't get a good look at whoever was standing there.

"Admiral Wheeler is here to see the prisoner, Madam Councilor."

Lucien recognized the voice of the Marine Sergeant assigned to guard his cell. *The admiral came to see me personally?* he wondered. That could either be very good or very bad.

"Let her in..." Tyra replied. Her tone was wary, making

Lucien suspect this visit wasn't a good thing.

The door slid open and Wheeler strode in, followed by a pair of Marine bots.

Tyra and the doctor stepped aside, and Admiral Wheeler moved to stand just a few feet from Lucien's cot with hands clasped behind her back. Lucien smiled and patted an empty space on the cot beside him. "Make yourself comfortable, Admiral."

Her eyes narrowed at that. "No thank you, Commander."

"Commander? I thought I'd been stripped of my rank?"

Wheeler frowned. "Have you heard about our recent contact with Etherus?"

Lucien's brow furrowed. *Contact with Etherus?* "Doesn't contacting him violate your treaty with the Faros?" he asked.

"That treaty was bound to be violated, anyway. I'd like to make this brief, so keep your mouth shut and listen." Wheeler proceeded to explain everything that Etherus had told them.

Lucien couldn't believe it. The result of negotiating with the Faros had turned out to be a lot worse than he'd imagined. The visions that the extra-dimensional Polypuses had shared with him of Etheria being conquered by the Faros obviously weren't accurate. Apparently they couldn't see the future, after all.

"I was right," Lucien said when Admiral Wheeler finished speaking. "We never should have agreed to negotiate."

"Perhaps," the admiral replied. "Regardless, we can't change the choices we've made. All that's left is to make better ones from here. Etherus told us that if we destroy the Forge, all of the Abaddons will be killed, and all of his slaves and subjects will finally be free to defy him."

"If that's true, then the Forge must be very well-defended."

"Or well-hidden," Wheeler replied. "The first step is to find it. We won't be able to plan an attack until we know where it is. That's where you and your crew mates come in. Thanks to Abaddon, you've been disguised to look and sound like Faros. You can use those disguises to infiltrate the enemy and find the Forge. What do you say, Commander?"

"What did the others say?" Lucien replied.

"They're already preparing to leave."

Lucien turned and nodded to Councilor Tyra. "What about her request that I integrate with my clone?"

Wheeler regarded the councilor with eyebrows raised. "If he integrates, he won't be able to stay with you, Councilor. It would be better for you to keep your husband by your side while we wait for his clone to return."

Tyra's expression twisted with grief, and she shook her head. "He won't be able to stay with me. He's dead, killed in the riots. The doctor who attended him managed to extract his data, but we still need a body to put it in."

"I see," Wheeler replied. "I'm sorry to hear that. If that's the case, you might still be better off waiting for a new clone to be grown for him on New Earth."

Tyra frowned. "By then we may already be overrun, and there's no guarantee that we'll win. Lucien will stand a better chance of success if he has something to lose. *This* Lucien doesn't know he has a family. Mine does. Integrate them and he'll have more to live for and more reason to fight."

"Good point," Wheeler replied. She regarded him once more. "Well? What do you say?"

Lucien's head was spinning. "In exchange for my help finding the Forge, all of the charges against me will be dropped."

"Done," Wheeler said, nodding.

"And as for integrating..." Lucien couldn't explain it, but he felt strangely compelled to do so. Maybe it was because the thought of his clone being dead and languishing in limbo as static data made his skin crawl. Or maybe it was because Tyra's arguments had swayed him. He had to admit he *would* be more motivated to find the Forge if he had a family to think about... two little girls. The family he'd always wanted but never had. "I'll do it," Lucien decided. He nodded to the doctor Tyra had brought with her. "I'm ready when you are, Doc."

"I'll go get my equipment," the doctor replied, nodding back.

* * *

The Lost Etherian Fleet

Lucien woke up screaming: "Atara!" He sat up quickly, his eyes wide and his breathing shallow. He could feel his entire body buzzing with adrenaline, and overwhelming concern for his children. "What... what happened to Atara? Is she okay? What about Theola? Where—"

"Shh..." Tyra whispered and squeezed his hand. "She's okay. They're both okay. Take your time. Deep breaths."

Lucien looked around, shaking his head. This wasn't the corridor where he'd been knocked out. It wasn't even a med center. *And why is my head so cold?* He reached up to find all of his hair mysteriously missing.

Then more memories came rushing in to fill the gaps, and he understood. He was in the brig. He'd been arrested for defying orders from Admiral Wheeler.

He looked around quickly. Tyra and his doctor were the only ones present. "Where is Atara? And Theola?" Lucien asked, his gaze returning to his wife.

Tyra bit her lower lip and tears welled in her eyes.

"What's wrong?" he demanded, his heart suddenly pounding again.

Tyra released his hand so she could wipe her eyes. "Abaddon didn't release Atara. She's back to the way she was. Infected with his consciousness."

"What?" Lucien blinked rapidly as he tried to process that.

"Etherus told me she's still infected, and I think he's right. She's not acting normal, even though all the others former agents seem to be fine. Abaddon singled Atara out because of me, because of the way I spoke to him during the negotiations."

Conflicting thoughts raced through Lucien's head. He felt a flash of anger toward his wife, but it quickly faded at the sight of the tears slipping down her cheeks.

"I never should have provoked him..." she said.

Lucien reached for Tyra's hands and pulled her down into his lap. "Listen to me. Abaddon is the one who shouldn't have provoked *us*. I'm going to find the Forge, and when I do, we're going to kill him."

"Etherus said we'll see Atara again, but..."

"Then we will," Lucien said.

Tyra nodded slowly, uncertainly. "Admiral Wheeler suggested we use her to feed misinformation to the Faros."

"What?" Lucien shook his head. "She's a five-year-old for frek's sake! Not a weapon! Don't let that happen, Tyra."

"I won't," she replied, shaking her head.

Lucien grimaced and reached up to wipe fresh tears from her cheeks with his thumbs.

"You need to go before the Faros arrive and the battle starts," she said. "The others are waiting for you."

Lucien pulled her lips down to his and kissed her long and hard. When she withdrew, he replied, "I need to say goodbye to the girls first."

Tyra shook her head. "You can't. Atara thinks you're dead, so she won't expect to see you again, and if she does, she'll wonder where you went. She might find a way to warn Abaddon."

"What about Theola?" Lucien asked. It was one thing not being allowed to say goodbye to Atara—with Abaddon in control of her again, the real Atara might not even get to hear his goodbyes, but Theola deserved to hear them, and he *needed* to see her.

"We can't risk it," Tyra replied, shaking her head. "Theola might say something to make Atara suspicious."

Lucien exhaled shakily and scowled. "I didn't expect this to be so hard. Maybe I shouldn't have integrated."

Tyra shook her head. She stood up from his lap and pulled him to his feet. "I'm glad you did, because at least now *I* get to say goodbye. I love you, Lucien."

"I love you, too." He wrapped her in a fierce hug and

started to kiss her again, but this time a knock at the door interrupted them.

"Madam Councilor, Commander Ortane—we need to hurry."

Tyra pulled away with a grimace. "Go," she said. "And... may Etherus be with you."

He arched an eyebrow at that. Tyra was far from a believer, but she knew that he was. He nodded at that acknowledgment of his faith.

Admiral Wheeler had said that Etherus wasn't going to help them, but maybe that wasn't entirely true. Maybe He would still find some way to help.

"Keep an eye on Atara," he said, remembering the obsession she'd had with hurting him and Theola while she'd been under Abaddon's influence on *Astralis*. "And keep Brak close."

"I will," Tyra replied.

Before either of them could say anything else, the overhead lights flashed dark crimson and a klaxon blared, followed by a muffled announcement coming from the corridor beyond his cell: "General quarters, general quarters! All hands to battle stations! This is not a drill."

Lucien blinked. It's too late! They're here.

The door to Lucien's cell slid open, and the Marine sergeant stepped in, looking grim. "We're out of time, Commander. You need to come with me, *now*."

"We're under attack already?" Tyra asked, her blue eyes huge and blinking.

The sergeant's gaze shifted to her. "Not yet, Madam Councilor, but I'm told that our ships on the other side of the wormhole are coming through with scan data that shows a massive Faro fleet headed this way."

"How long before they arrive?" Tyra replied.

"I don't know, ma'am, but if we're already at general quarters, it can't be long. Commander—" The sergeant nodded to Lucien. "—your shuttle is leaving soonest possible. We need to hurry."

"Lead the way, Sergeant."

"Yes, sir."

The sergeant matched action to words, taking off at a run. Lucien raced after him. He flicked a glance over his shoulder and waved to Tyra as he crossed the threshold of his cell. She waved back just before they lost sight of each other.

Lucien grimaced as he looked away. *This is going to be close....*

CHAPTER 13

The Lost Etherian Fleet

Lucien arrived in Hangar Bay Seventeen and raced across the deck toward the Faro shuttle that the Marine Sergeant escorting him indicated. As he drew near, he saw Addy waving to him from the top of the boarding ramp. She was already wearing a sleeveless black Faro robe.

Lucien glanced at the Marine Sergeant and nodded to him before running up the ramp. Addy stepped aside to let him into the shuttle, and he waited in the airlock while she cycled the outer doors shut and raised the landing ramp.

He watched her with a frown, remembering that she'd done nothing to stop Garek's mutiny, but those memories felt distant now, and somehow less significant than his new memories from *Astralis.*

That was the life he felt most drawn to now—his life with Tyra and his two daughters. His memories of Addy felt more like memories of an ex-girlfriend, except that his memories of her were scattered between his memories of his family. Remembering his relationship with Addy was like remembering an extra-marital affair he'd never had.

Addy spared a glance at him as she moved to cycle the inner doors open. "Stop it," she said.

"Stop what?"

"Stop looking at me like that. There was no time to intervene before Garek stunned you," she said.

Lucien frowned. "I know." He decided not to tell her that he'd actually been thinking about his recent integration and what that meant for the two of them. Did she even know that he'd been integrated with the other Lucien? Probably not, but now wasn't the time to talk about it. He shook his head. "You could have done something after he shot me," Lucien replied.

"Yeah, *two* mutinies—that's exactly what we needed. Besides, if we'd sacrificed *Astralis,* there'd be no way to bring all of those people back now. At least this way they have a chance for survival."

The inner doors irised open and Lucien followed Addy into the shuttle. The inside looked less alien than he'd expected: gray metal walls and scuffed metal floors, exposed conduits in the ceiling, glow panels lining the bulkheads, deck, and ceiling. This could have passed for a shuttle from New Earth. Sealed metal crates were stacked to the ceiling on both sides of the compartment where they now stood—the cargo bay?

"There's no point arguing about it now," Lucien decided.

Addy nodded to him. "Then stop taking it so personally. It has nothing to do with *us*. I still care about you just as much as ever."

Lucien nodded slowly in turn, but still said nothing about his integration. "Where are Garek and Brak?"

"Up in the cockpit, trying to figure out the flight controls."

"We should probably join them and get an update on

the situation."

"Yeah..." Addy trailed off uncertainly, her eyes narrowed in bemusement.

"Lead the way," he prompted.

Addy walked to the end of the cargo bay. She keyed the doors open and took him through a small galley, then down a short corridor with six doors, and finally to the cockpit. There were only two seats, one for the pilot, and one for the co-pilot.

"Small ship," Lucien commented.

Garek turned. "Good, you're here." Like Addy he was already wearing one of the Faro's black robes, while Brak wore one of the shapeless black garments of a Faro slave—a shadow robe, Lucien remembered it was called. "Brak—let the *Gideon* know we're leaving."

"Yess," Brak replied, hissing softly. The shuttle hovered up, and the hangar bay sprawled out to all sides of them with a dozen more matte black Faro shuttles, as well as several of the gray, cylindrical ones from *Astralis* that had carried refugees aboard.

"Any sign of the Faros yet?" Lucien asked.

"Not yet," Garek replied. "But our sensors can't see through the wormhole, and the last of our fleet is already through. We're sending probes back for updates, but I'm told they could be here in less than two hours."

"Is that enough time for us to get away?"

"This shuttle's fast, but it's still going to take the better part of an hour to cross the wormhole. From the other side we can start calculating a jump somewhere else, but we'll need at least half an hour to get clear of the interdiction field around the Red Line."

"So it's going to be close."

"Very close," Garek replied.

Lucien blew out a breath and silence fell inside the cockpit. He watched as Garek banked the shuttle toward the fuzzy blue static shield covering the exit of the hangar bay.

"I'm sorry about Nora," he thought to say as Garek accelerated toward the shield. He'd been there to witness Director Nora Helios's death in the Resurrection Center. Now that he had both sets of his memories to draw on, he understood who both Nora and Garek were, and who they were to each other. Garek's daughter, Nora, was the reason he'd joined *Astralis's* mission. She was the only person in the universe that he really cared about, and now she was dead.

Garek gave no reply, but Lucien noticed his shoulders stiffen at the mention of his daughter. They passed through the opening of the hangar with a sizzle of static shields scraping theirs, and as soon as they were out, the cockpit canopy became crowded with stars.

"You sure you're up to flying us out of here?" Lucien asked. "I can take over from here."

"You didn't spend the last two hours familiarizing yourself with the controls," Garek replied. "I'm fine. You want to do something useful? Go change your clothes for something a Faro might wear."

Wheeler had restored Lucien's rank of Commander, so he was still the ranking officer on board. That meant he was in charge, but after the mutiny, Lucien wasn't sure Garek saw it the same way.

"I'm going to change," Lucien replied, making it sound like his idea. Now wasn't the time to fight over who was actually in command. "Send me a message via our ARCs if there are any new developments. Addy?" He turned and nodded to her. "Maybe you'd better show me to my quarters."

"Sure... follow me."

* * *

Aboard the Captured Faro Shuttle

"There's only *two* rooms?" Lucien asked, looking around the pilot's quarters. The room was cramped, with just one bed—a double, at best; a closet, and an en-suite bathroom. "What about the other doors in the corridor?"

"Gunwells, and storage," Addy replied.

Lucien grimaced. "Where are we all going to sleep?"

"You and me in here. Brak and Garek in the other room. It has two bunk beds."

Lucien frowned. His eyes skipped from Addy to the bed and back again. She obviously meant for them to share the bed. That would have been no big deal before he'd integrated, but now he had his wife to think about, and his relationship with Addy couldn't continue the way it had before.

"I can sleep on the floor," he said. "There must be extra bedding and pillows somewhere."

Addy sidled up to him with a furrowed brow. "Look, I'm sorry I didn't try to stop Garek...."

"It's not about that," Lucien replied.

She grabbed his hands, her gaze searching his. "Then what is it?" She released his hands to wrap her arms around his neck, but he pulled away and took a step back. He saw the hurt and confusion flash in her eyes.

"I'm married, Addy," he blurted out. "We can't..."

Realization dawned, but the hurt in her eyes remained. "You integrated with him?"

Lucien nodded.

"You didn't even ask me first!"

"I didn't have a chance. The other Lucien died, and Admiral Wheeler and Tyra—the Chief Councilor—both asked me to integrate. They argued that I'd be more motivated to accomplish our mission if I had a family to fight for... if I had something to lose. I agreed."

Addy's lips twisted sarcastically. "So I'm not a good enough reason to fight?"

Lucien opened his mouth to object, but the words wouldn't come. He didn't know what to say to that.

She turned away and pointed to the closet. "You'll find Faro robes and a translator band in there."

He nodded and went to the closet to get changed. He stripped out of the orange *Astralis*-issue jumpsuit they'd given him to wear in the brig, and waved the closet open to find three black Faro robes hanging inside. He took one of them and pulled it on. It adapted to fit his body, lengthening and broadening to accommodate his height and build.

"Where's the translator band?" he asked, turning to look for Addy. Her back was turned and she was already keying the door open to leave.

"Look for it. It's there." The door slid open and she walked out.

Lucien watched her go with a grimace. If she hadn't actually sided with Garek before, she would now. Establishing a proper chain of command was going to be harder than he'd thought.

CHAPTER 14

Dauntless

Crusader Ethan Ortane sat in the command control station of his star galleon, the *Dauntless,* listening to Serenity Talos, the High Praetor of the Paragons, explain the situation. *Astralis* had returned—or rather, it's people had. His son, Lucien, had to be with the refugees. Ethan's heart swelled at the thought of seeing him again. It had been almost nine years since Lucien had left, and they hadn't even heard from him since.

Ethan could feel his wife's own eagerness radiating off her in waves from the control station beside his. Unfortunately, there wouldn't be any time for a family reunion. The refugees had returned with a massive alien invasion fleet chasing him, and all Paragons everywhere were being recalled to help defend the wormhole that was apparently the only way across the Red Line.

"Shouldn't Etherus be leading the charge against these Faros?" Ethan asked.

The high praetor shook her head, sending her long, straight black hair skipping over her shoulders. Ethan saw the skin around her piercing rose-colored eyes tighten, and her lips formed a grim line. She was visiting a neighboring system, which was how they were able to conduct a real-time conversation.

"We've petitioned Etherus for help, and He's gone to speak with the Etherians on our behalf, to ask them for volunteers to man their fleets in our defense... but after *Astralis* sold them out, or *thought* they did, I doubt they'll be eager to help us."

Ethan scowled. "But *we're* not the ones who sold them out. We didn't even know what was happening! And besides, even if they all die, Etherus will just resurrect them back in Etheria, so they're not actually risking anything."

"You don't have to convince me," the high praetor replied. "Regardless, you have your orders. Our entire fleet will be joining the defense, including all the facets of New Earth. We'll break it up into its individual facets and use them to help hold our lines. That will more than double the strength of our fleet."

"There's trillions of civilians on board New Earth!" Ethan objected, as if the high praetor didn't already know that.

"The facets are heavily armed and shielded, and we're going to need the extra firepower."

Ethan shook his head. "The facets have all of our resurrection centers. If they're destroyed..."

"We're well aware of the risks, Crusader. The facets will sit safely behind the lines and use their long-range beam cannons to join the fight. Now if you'll excuse me, I have more fleets to contact, and time is short."

"What about our allies in Laniakea? This is their fight, too."

High Praetor Serenity Talos nodded. "They've been contacted. So far seven of them have agreed to send ships to help us, but not enough to make a difference. They're sending token forces of barely a few hundred vessels each."

"What? That's absurd!" Alara objected, joining the conversation for the first time. "Any one of them should be able to send several thousand ships without breaking a sweat—not several *hundred*."

The high praetor's gaze shifted to Alara. "They're afraid if they send more, their neighbors will take advantage of their weakness and attack—particularly since we're withdrawing all of our forces from their current peace-keeping missions."

Ethan grimaced. Laniakea was far from unified, with the strongest species all vying for dominance, and humanity in the middle, keeping a tenuous peace. "So we're on our own," he concluded.

"Yes. Get your fleet to the rendezvous, Crusader. There's no time to waste."

Ethan nodded. "Aye, ma'am."

And with that, the high praetor vanished from the main holo display.

Ethan turned to the Helm. "Confirm receipt of rendezvous coordinates and begin calculating our jump."

"Coordinates received," the officer at the helm replied. "Jump calculating."

"ETA?" Ethan asked.

"Eight days, three hours," the helm replied.

"Carry on. Comms, inform the rest of the fleet about our change of orders and send them the coordinates. Have them begin calculating their own jumps."

"Yes, sir," the comms officer replied.

Ethan turned to his wife and executive officer next.

"We'll see Lucien soon," he said in a quiet voice. "One week."

"Eight days," she replied with a sigh. "I'm going to kick his ass when we do see him."

Ethan nodded grimly. "Not if I kick it first." He shook his head. "They never should have left. Etherus warned them not to. Now they've put us all in jeopardy."

Alara frowned at him, her violet eyes skeptical. "Maybe you should leave the ass-kicking to me."

"What's that supposed to mean?" he replied.

"If you didn't have a family to think about, you'd have signed up for *Astralis's* mission yourself—and don't try to deny it. Lucien got his rebel spirit from someone, and it wasn't me."

Ethan snorted. "I suppose Trinity got her level-headedness from you, then."

Alara smiled and patted his shoulder. "And her good looks," she added with a wink.

"What? You don't think I'm good looking?"

Alara studied him with an appraising eye. "Rakish. Scruffy. You'd look okay if you took the time to shower and shave off that beard."

"Scruffy!" Ethan burst out and absently ran a hand through the over-grown stubble on his cheeks. "And what's wrong with my beard? You said it made me look *distinguished.*"

Alara shrugged and smiled. "Only because it hides the wrinkles."

"Wrinkles!" Ethan did a double-take. "I don't know why I take this abuse."

"Because you married me."

Ethan snorted and shook his head. Their banter was a

nice reprieve from the seriousness of the situation. They were about to fight a technologically superior enemy with *trillions* of ships. The Paragons' entire fleet only numbered in the tens of millions of capital ships, most of them star galleons. Add to that the few hundred ships their alien allies had managed to spare, and the odd one thousand Etherian vessels already guarding the wormhole, and they didn't even come close to matching the forces arrayed against them.

Even with the narrowness of the wormhole, it didn't take a mathematician to figure out that it would only be a matter of time before they were overwhelmed.

There'd better be more to this plan, Ethan thought. He frowned and looked up, out the *Dauntless's* holo displays to his and Alara's Fleet, the One Hundred and Tenth.

Silver specks beetled across the black, schooling together like fish. Their fleet was comprised of exactly one hundred star galleons, each with its own complement of two dozen fighters. Ethan had always thought of the 110th as a powerful armada, and they'd proved that time and again through the years, but now Ethan saw their fleet for what it really was: a pinch of sand, scattered in an infinite black sea.

And the Faros are the tidal wave coming to dash us against the rocks.

CHAPTER 15

The Lost Etherian Fleet

Twenty Minutes Until the Faro Armada Arrives...

"This is Chief Councilor Tyra Ortane to the commander of the Faro armada. We have just learned that your stated target, Etheria, remains unreachable." Tyra paused and then went on to explain everything that Etherus had told them. When she finished, she concluded, "Under the circumstances, we will allow five of your vessels to cross the Red Line so that you may independently verify our claims. We will ensure their safe passage through our territory, but if any additional ships are sent, it will be seen as a violation of our peace treaty and a declaration of war. We await your response."

Tyra ended the recording there, and sent the comms probe from her control station. Tyra was back on the bridge at the *Gideon's* comms station. Between her, Colonel Drask, and Admiral Wheeler, they were in complete command of the ship. The admiral had appointed new officers to the control stations vacated by Garek, Addy, and Brak, but they were still learning how to use them.

"The probe is away, headed for the wormhole," Tyra announced. That probe would have to carry her message through to the other side of the wormhole, since no comms signals could cross the Red Line.

"Good. Now we wait," Wheeler replied.

"What if they refuse to accept our terms?" Colonel Drask asked.

"They'll accept," Admiral Wheeler replied.

"And what happens when they find out that we're telling the truth?" Drask pressed.

"Then Etherus's prediction will likely be fulfilled and the Faros will turn on us," Admiral Wheeler replied. "They might think they can somehow draw Etherus and the Etherians out by threatening us."

Drask snorted. "Then they obviously didn't get the memo: Etherus isn't going to help us."

"He's already helped us by telling us how to defeat Abaddon," Admiral Wheeler said. "There's an old story about a man sitting on his roof during a flood. The water is rising all around him and then a hover car with rescue workers comes by to save him, but he turns them away, saying that he's waiting for God to save him. The man drowns. The moral of the story is—"

"That God doesn't exist?" Tyra suggested, half-turning from her station to face the admiral.

Wheeler frowned. "No—that God helps those who help themselves. All we need to do is buy Commander Ortane enough time to accomplish his mission, and that's what these latest negotiations are for."

Drask looked skeptical. "Even if they find the Forge, we still have to find a way to destroy it, and with all of our forces pinned down and trapped inside the Red Line, that might not be possible."

"One problem at a time, Colonel. We can't fret those details until we have more information."

Tyra grimaced. The colonel was right—even if Lucien managed to find the Forge, destroying it presented a whole new set of challenges. Etherus had given them an impossible task.

* * *

Aboard the Captured Faro Shuttle

Five Minutes Until The Faro Armada Arrives...

"How long until we can jump out?" Lucien asked quietly. The Faro shuttle's cockpit was dark and quiet, devoid of the usual hum of engines and life support. As soon as they'd crossed the wormhole, Garek had cloaked the shuttle and powered down everything except for passive sensors and the navigation computer. Ever since then, they'd been cruising with their momentum. It was slow going, but eventually they'd reach the edge of the Red Line's interdiction field.

By then, hopefully the Faros still wouldn't have arrived, and they'd be able to power up the shuttle's jump drive to get away. If not...

"Ten minutes to reach the edge of the field, give or take," Garek replied.

"And the Faros?" Lucien said. "How long before they get here?"

"Without active sensors, there's no way to tell how close they are, but if you ask me, they should already be here."

Lucien directed his attention to Addy. She'd taken Brak's place at the co-pilot's station. "What about the probe that followed us out? Is it still broadcasting the Chief Councilor's message?"

"Looping on repeat," Addy replied.

"So maybe the Faros are thinking about what to do next?" Lucien suggested.

A chime sounded somewhere in the cockpit.

"Looks like they're done thinking," Garek said. "We've got contact: five ships headed for the wormhole, just like the councilor ordered."

Lucien leaned over Garek's shoulder for a look at his displays. Sure enough, five blips had appeared on the middle holo display. "Those are Etherian ships," Lucien said, noting the familiar stream-lined shapes of their hulls. "Five out of the ten that we gave them. Looks like they accepted Tyr—the chief councilor's terms."

Garek nodded. "Looks like."

"Can they see us?" Lucien asked.

"They're not reacting to our presence," Garek replied.

"Why send Etherian ships?" Addy asked. "Why risk five of the ten most valuable vessels they have?"

"Maybe they think Etherian ships have a safe way to jump from one side of the universe to the other?" Lucien asked.

"Yeah, I wouldn't put it past Etherus to be holding out on us," Garek replied.

Addy shook her head. "Unless he outright lied about the other side being made of antimatter, I don't think the Etherians have some secret way of traveling from one side to the other. You can't take matter ships to the other side without them being annihilated."

"Actually, I wouldn't be too sure about that," Lucien said. "Space is a vacuum. The particle density of deep space is so minuscule that you'd never even notice the matter-antimatter annihilations going on around you. The Faros could potentially still attack Etheria if they can find a way to cross the great divide at the rim of the universe, or whatever barrier is at the center. What they definitely *can't* do is conquer or enslave the Etherian people. That would require close contact. But they could bombard Etherian planets from extreme range."

"Why bother?" Garek asked. "All they have to do is crash a few of their ships into the atmospheres of Etherian worlds. The annihilation of that much matter would release so much energy it would probably blast their atmospheres into the next solar system and crack the planets in half. Every ship in their fleet will become a planet-busting super weapon."

Lucien felt horror twist inside of him with Garek's conclusion. "Maybe we should warn the chief councilor to back out of the negotiations."

"Here we go again..." Garek said.

"They need to know that Etheria might still be at risk! Etherus told us how to beat the Faros, and with the wormhole restricting entry to Laniakea, our forces should be able to hold them off long enough for us to find the Forge."

Garek swiveled the pilot's chair to face him. "And then what? How are we supposed to destroy it?"

"Etherus didn't tell us to negotiate with the enemy for a reason. If the Faros could be dissuaded by simple diplomacy, don't you think he would have told us to do that instead?"

"Not if he's hiding something—like the fact that Etheria really *can* be reached, and they really *are* in danger."

"Maybe because if we knew that, then we wouldn't agree to defend them," Lucien suggested.

Addy turned around now, too. "If Etherus lied to us, then he deserves what's coming."

Garek snorted. "I guess time will tell, won't it?" He turned his chair back to the fore and nodded to the cockpit canopy. "We're coming up on the edge of the interdiction field. Risk of scattering is down to five percent... four... three..."

"Still no reaction from the enemy ships," Addy declared.

"And they haven't tried to hail us?" Lucien asked.

"No," she replied.

"Zero percent," Garek said. "We can jump away safely now."

Lucien eyed the five enemy ships still cruising toward the wormhole. "We can't risk powering our jump drive yet. Those ships will spot us."

"Etherian sensors can see clear across the universe, with no propagation delay—what are the odds that they haven't already seen us through our cloaking shield?" Garek asked.

"I don't know, but that doesn't mean we should go around broadcasting our location. We wait for them to cross the throat of the wormhole. Then we jump," Lucien said. The throat was an impenetrable barrier to quantum and electromagnetic signals, so they'd be safe from detection as soon as those five ships crossed the wormhole.

"Fine," Garek replied. "Better get comfortable. It could be a while."

Lucien sat on the deck behind Addy, watching stars through a viewport in the port side of the cockpit. Garek and Addy passed the time in silence.

Twenty minutes later, Garek spoke up: "They're through. Let's get out of here before someone else shows up."

Lucien stood up and went to look over Garek's shoulder. A star map glittered on his primary display. He selected stars at random and checked the recorded data, skipping from one to another like they were channels on the holonet.

"Any ideas about where should we jump to first?"

Addy leaned over from her seat to examine the map. Lucien was just about to suggest a star system when a bright flash of light illuminated the cockpit. He whirled around, searching for the source of the light—

And saw a ghostly apparition lurking behind them. Glowing tentacles waved lazily in an unseen breeze. Garek and Addy both turned to look at the creature—a *Polypus,* one of the squid-like extra-dimensional aliens who'd occasionally appeared to help them since leaving the Red Line. If it weren't for them, they'd never have found the Lost Fleet.

Among their many mysterious qualities, the Polypuses had revealed that they could move through physical barriers. They were seemingly unaffected by the physical world, ghosts in all but name, yet they'd demonstrated that they could also read people's thoughts and interact with the physical world when they chose.

"What's it doing here?" Addy whispered.

Lucien shook his head, watching as the creature drifted

toward them. He hurried to get out of the way before it could pass *through* him, and Garek leaned as far over in his chair as he could without falling out. The Polypus floated up to the star map and slowly extended one tentacle to point at a particular star system.

"I think it wants us to go there," Addy whispered, her blue eyes huge and unblinking.

Before any of them could say anything else, the apparition floated out through the cockpit canopy and into space. It dwindled to a pinprick, blending in with the stars, and then they lost sight of it entirely.

"What system was that?" Lucien whispered.

Garek tapped the star the Polypus had indicated, and a list of details appeared, along with a name: *The Fortuna System.* It was only fifteen light years away. Calculating a jump there would take less than a second.

"Powering the jump drive," Garek announced.

"Punch it," Lucien replied.

Brak walked in, covering a giant yawn, as if he'd just woken up. "Are we there yet?"

They all stared at the Gor.

"What? What do I miss?" Brak asked, his eyes darting between them.

Only a Gor could sleep at a time like this. Nothing seemed to rattle their nerves.

Garek snorted and shook his head. Lucien looked away just as Garek executed the jump. The stars beyond the viewport vanished in a bright flash of light, and as the glare faded, three bright specks of varying sizes appeared around a dazzling blue sun.

"Report," Lucien said.

CHAPTER 16

The Lost Etherian Fleet

"Abaddon," Tyra said, trying not to let her revulsion and hatred show. She wasn't surprised that he had decided to join the Faros' expedition personally. He had enough clones that he could afford to risk the lives of a few. "I see that you have accepted our terms."

"For now," Abaddon replied. "If you are lying and stalling for time, you will regret it."

"We are simply relaying what Etherus told us."

"And what makes you think he told you the truth?" Abaddon challenged.

Before Tyra could reply to that, he waved his hand to dismiss whatever she might have said.

"Send five of your own vessels, the same class and size as our own to accompany us. We will wait for them to join us behind your lines."

Tyra hesitated. "We may not be able to find five of the exact same ships."

Abaddon scowled. "No? I see plenty of the same ship classes in your fleet. I can choose them for you if you like."

"That won't be necessary. We'll find them."

"The *same* ships, Councilor. We'll be waiting."

With that, the alien king vanished from Tyra's holo

display, and she turned to face Admiral Wheeler. "Do we have five identical ships?"

The admiral nodded. "Yes."

"Good. Who are we going to send to command them?"

"I think both of us should go," Admiral Wheeler replied.

Tyra frowned and shook her head. "I'm needed here to continue the negotiations, and you're needed to coordinate our defense."

"New Earth is on its way. They'll be in charge as soon as they arrive."

"They won't be here for at least another week," Tyra objected.

Admiral Wheeler nodded. "Fighting won't break out before we return. And even if it does, we'll be able to jump back here in a matter of hours. Besides, Etherian comms are instant, so we can always coordinate negotiations and defense strategy from a distance before we arrive."

"Not if you're dead," Colonel Drask replied.

"We'll be evenly matched. Their five ships to ours. I like those odds. It's better than what we'll be facing here," Wheeler replied. "Besides, we can't trust anyone else with these negotiations. Who else can we send? We need a competent commander in case they decide to double-cross us, and we need an experienced diplomat to help us delay the war for as long as we can."

Or to manage the fall out if the Faros discover that Etherus was lying about Etheria being unreachable, Tyra thought. She gave in with a reluctant nod. "All right, but I'm taking my kids with me."

"I wouldn't have asked you to do otherwise," Admiral

Wheeler replied, rising from her control station. "Colonel Drask, you have the conn until I return."

"Aye, ma'am," he replied.

* * *

Aboard the Captured Faro Shuttle

"There are ships all over this system..." Addy said. "Some of them are registering friendly—which I'm assuming means they're Faros; others are neutral—native species of aliens, maybe?"

"None of them is headed toward us, so our disguise must be working," Garek said. "Where to, Commander?"

Lucien regarded Garek for a moment. "We need to make contact with the locals to see what we can learn about the Forge. Take us to whatever planet seems the busiest."

Garek nodded and turned back to his displays. "That would be... Meson I and Meson II."

"Meson?"

Garek shrugged. "Don't ask me. The Faros probably named those planets." He magnified them on the main forward display, and Lucien gaped at the scene: two worlds of almost equal size locked in an impossibly-close orbit around each other. They were so close that their atmospheres were actually touching, warped by their mutual gravity into a strange, wispy hourglass shape that glowed brightly in the system's sun.

"Are we watching two planets collide?" Addy whispered.

"It is amazing," Brak added.

Lucien shook his head. "What are the odds that we'd arrive just in time to witness a catastrophic collision between two planets? Besides, we'd be able to see them getting closer to each other, but both planets are still separated, defying gravity in some kind of impossible equilibrium."

"I'm getting some very strange gravimetric readings at lagrange one," Garek said.

"Lagrange one?" Brak asked. "What is this?"

"The point between the two planets where their gravity cancels out," Lucien replied.

"There's some kind of facility there," Garek added. He touched a button on his displays, and the image zoomed in on the hourglass-shaped band of atmosphere between the two planets.

A hazy, donut-shaped space station appeared floating in the center of the hourglass.

"That space station must be stabilizing the gravity fields," Lucien said.

"What's that?" Addy pointed to a darker, thicker column of air running through the hole in the center of the facility.

"I'm not sure..." Garek replied. He zoomed back out, and suddenly Lucien saw that column for what it was—it ran straight from the blue, water-covered planet to the blue freckle on the desert planet below.

"It's water..." Lucien said. "They're siphoning off water to the desert planet. Whoever built that facility and moved those planets into such a close orbit must have done it to make the desert planet more habitable."

"How do you move a *planet?*" Addy asked.

"Etherus did it with Origin," Lucien pointed out.

"And we still don't know how he did that," Addy replied.

"Interesting," Garek said, "but not relevant to our mission. Which planet should we go to first? My vote is for the desert planet. The water-stealers probably know more than whatever aquatic creatures evolved on the other planet."

Lucien considered that. "Let's try the space station first."

Garek's eyebrows shot up. "You're assuming they'll allow us on board."

Lucien shrugged. "If they don't, then we head for the surface."

"All right. Hang on." Garek powered their engines and worked the shuttle's controls.

"Everyone activate your holoskins," Lucien said. "If someone hails us, we'd better be looking like Faros or this mission will be over before it starts."

No one replied, but Lucien saw the air shimmer around both Garek and Addy. When it cleared, they had the smooth blue skin of Faros. Lucien nodded to Brak. "Hood up, buddy."

Brak bared his black teeth with displeasure, but he reached behind his head and pulled his shadow robe's shapeless hood over his head, concealing his features.

Lucien gazed out the forward viewport at the bright, oblong speck of their destination—the binary planets of Meson I and Meson II.

What kind of alien species lived on those worlds? he wondered. *And would they be slaves or free? If they were slaves, they might not be for much longer.*

"If we pull this off, we're going to pave the way to

freedom for a lot of slaves," Lucien said.

"I'm not sure that matters anymore," Addy said.

Lucien stared at her in shock. "What do you mean it doesn't *matter?*" How could freeing untold trillions of sentient beings not matter?

Addy went on to explain what Etherus had said about all of the aliens beyond the Red Line being nothing but soulless bots—copies of the Faros' own consciousness stripped of their memories and repeated endlessly. She explained that that was why Etherus hadn't intervened to set the Faros' slaves free.

Lucien didn't like that explanation. "So it would be okay to clone myself without my memories and enslave that clone to me?"

Addy shrugged. "Don't ask me. I'm just the messenger."

"If it's true, then the argument for freeing the Faros' slaves is the same as the one advocating freedom for artificial intelligence," Garek said. "Are they really alive, or just pretending to be?"

"What about animals or pets? They don't have souls?" Lucien pressed.

"Etherus seemed to be implying that only the life he didn't create is soulless," Garek said. "So basically, everything outside of the Red Line."

That still troubled Lucien. "Did he say what souls are?"

"Nope," Garek replied. "But he did say that souls are what makes us free—that without them we're slaves to determinism, but that sounds like an old cop-out to me. There's no way we can prove that free will does or doesn't exist, so if he ties the existence of souls to the existence of free will, both become equally unprovable."

"That's not exactly true," Lucien replied. "We have run experiments to test for the existence of immaterial souls, and we did find something."

"Something random," Garek replied. "That doesn't make us free."

"Something unpredictable, not necessarily random," Lucien argued.

Before they'd met Etherus, a human-built AI called Omnius had ruled humanity, and Omnius had found that if he could kill someone and resurrect them in a cloned body, then they would become entirely predictable. That led Omnius to look for and ultimately find the missing piece of the puzzle—the sleeping Etherians whose minds were linked to human bodies on Origin. But not all humans had been linked to Etherians, and nowadays none of them were.

More recent tests conducted on *Astralis* by the Academy of Science seemed to corroborate Omnius's results. Cloned minds were predictable, and the originals were not, but if the originals died leaving the clones to live on in their stead, then those clones became just as unpredictable as the originals. It was as if only one copy of a person could possess their soul, and that soul didn't move to a new body unless its current body died.

Those tests seemed to prove the existence of a soul, and it was the proof most often cited to support Etherus's law against creating simultaneous copies of people.

But given Lucien's own experience with living a double life through clones, he was beginning to wonder what difference a soul really made, and if it even mattered. In theory, only one of his bodies could have retained his soul, and it was probably the original Lucien, the one who'd found the lost fleet and whose body he currently inhabited. Yet his memories from *Astralis* felt equally real and significant—if not more significant—so how did not having a soul make a person less alive, or any less deserving of their fundamental rights?

Lucien shook his head to clear it, but he couldn't shake off the feeling that the lives of hypothetically soulless beings were just as important as the lives of soulful beings.

"They deserve to be free," Lucien decided.

Garek shook his head. "Even if we set them free from the Faros, they'll still be slaves to determinism. Unless Etherus was lying, in which case all bets are off."

Lucien wasn't ready to call Etherus a liar, but was it that simple? No soul equals no freedom, only the illusion of it? Lucien wished he could test the aliens beyond the Red Line for predictability, to see if their behavior really was subject to determinism.

"They are all slaves to the universe," Brak mused. "Perhaps the universe is the one we should be fighting...."

Lucien smiled at the unlikely image Brak's suggestion triggered in his mind, of stars and planets rallying into fleets for a cosmic war.

"Well, this is all very fascinating gents and *lady*, but it's not important," Garek said. "We can't afford to waste time setting aliens free, so hypothetically asking ourselves whether or not they actually *can* be free is pointless."

Lucien sighed. "It doesn't bother you that we might have some kind of immaterial ghosts guiding our behavior, and we don't even know where they come from or what they are?"

Garek arched an eyebrow at him. "Sounds like the Polypuses to me."

Lucien blinked. It actually did sound a lot like them. "I didn't think of that."

"I did," Garek replied.

"We can see them," Addy said. "If they were souls, then we'd see them floating free of people's bodies when they die."

"Unless they only appear when they want to..." Lucien said.

Addy shook her head. "Doesn't make sense to me, unless you're saying the existence of souls is some kind of grand extra-dimensional conspiracy."

A chime sounded, interrupting their debate. "What was that?" Lucien asked.

"We're being hailed by a Faro cruiser," Addy said. She looked up at him with a blue alien face and wide glowing green eyes.

"It's headed this way," Garek said.

CHAPTER 17

Aboard the Captured Faro Shuttle

"We'd better answer that hail before they get suspicious," Lucien said. "Brak, maybe you should leave the cockpit first. It could seem strange to the Faros that one of their slaves is allowed in such a sensitive area."

Brak hissed loudly—no doubt at being referred to as a slave. "I am to be in the galley," he said as he left.

"Addy?" Lucien prompted. "Answer it."

She nodded and a blue-skinned Faro appeared on one of her displays. This one wore a black robe like them, not the gray robes that Abaddon preferred, and its eyes glowed green like Addy's.

"This is Lord Korvas of the *Ravager.* We've been expecting you. Please proceed to the Nexus. Our fighters will escort you in. The political situation here has become increasingly volatile, and we wouldn't want you to fall prey to separatist terrorists."

Expecting us? Lucien wondered. He leaned over the co-pilot's station until he came into view of the holo recorder. He nodded to the Faro on the other end and tried not to let his confusion show. "Thank you for your consideration, Lord Korvas."

Lord Korvas's features screwed up in confusion and

contempt. "Why is this... *commoner* speaking for you, Lady Tekasi?"

Lady...? Lucien hesitated, taken aback.

Addy flicked a scowl at him and made a shooing gesture before turning back to her displays. "My apologies, Lord Korvas. He spoke out of turn and will be punished."

Korvas nodded uncertainly. "I will see you aboard the Nexus soon."

"I look forward to it," Addy replied, just before Lord Korvas ended the comms from his end.

"Lady Tekasi?" Garek asked, arching an eyebrow at Addy.

Lucien grimaced. "We should leave. We don't know what we're getting ourselves into here."

"I agree," Garek replied.

"They bought it," Addy objected. "They're obviously expecting someone, and for whatever reason, they don't know that I'm not the one they're waiting for. It's the perfect cover. Why should we give that up?"

"Because the counterfeit ID Katawa gave you won't match this *Lady Tekasi* that you're supposed to be," Garek replied.

Addy shook her head, smiling. "My ID says that I *am* Lady Tekasi."

"They don't know who's coming..." Lucien mumbled. "They must have checked your ID and they just assumed that whoever you are, you're the one they're waiting for. Maybe because of your rank—*Lady?*"

"How can we check our IDs?" Garek asked, looking puzzled.

"Via the comms," Addy explained.

"Katawa never mentioned that," Garek said.

"Probably because the IDs weren't actually necessary to find the lost fleet," Addy replied. "We didn't need to know how they work. Katawa just had to allay our suspicions long enough to get us to Mokar."

"So who are *we?*" Lucien asked.

"Garek is Lesot Berandol, and you are Rikel Dromas—my concubine."

"Your *concubine?*" Lucien echoed.

Addy nodded and flashed a wry smile at him. "I guess we'll have to share a bed after all."

Garek's gaze skipped from Addy to Lucien and back again. "If he's your concubine, then what am I?" Garek asked.

"Your ID says that you're my aide."

"Maybe we'd better read the data on our IDs before we get to this *Nexus* place," Lucien said.

"There isn't much to them. Look, here's yours," she said, keying the comms to pull up the info.

Lucien leaned over her shoulder and found a display with his face on it—Faro-blue, but still recognizable. He read the block of text beside it.

Name: Rikel Dromas
Rank/Title: None
Occupation: Concubine
ID: A1S-TRQ-P21-LZT
Birth Date: 1-24789
Home World: Tosia

Lucien grimaced. It wasn't much, but at least it gave him some kind of identity to work with. Addy brought up

Garek's info next. Lucien glossed over the ID code and birth date, which only Garek would need to know, focusing instead on his home world—Aarakett—and his name—Lesot Berandol.

Garek briefly scanned the info before looking back to his displays. "Here comes our escort," he said, pointing to a pair of silver specks silhouetted by bright red engine glows. The fighters grew rapidly larger as they approached, taking on aerodynamic wedge shapes that would make them perfect for maneuvering inside planetary atmospheres.

The fighters sped by them in a blur, but reappeared a few seconds later with the business end of their engines facing the shuttle.

Those banked to port and accelerated away. Garek pushed the throttle forward and banked after them until they were all headed directly for the hourglass-shaped band of atmosphere connecting Meson I and II.

"I'm guessing the Nexus is what they call that donut-shaped facility," Garek said.

Lucien nodded. "Seems like. Why do you think they're expecting us?"

"You mean why are they expecting *Lady Tekasi*," Garek replied.

"Right."

"Could be anything, but if my grasp of the Faro word for *Lord* and *Lady* is accurate, Addy holds a combined political and military title reserved for the rulers of star systems or groups of star systems."

"So what system do you rule?" Lucien asked.

Addy shrugged. "I have no idea. If we're lucky no one will ask, or someone will mention the name of the system in passing. We're going to have to be very careful what we say around the Faros to avoid getting caught."

"You mean *you* are going to have to be very careful," Garek said. "We're just commoners, remember? They probably won't even speak to us."

Addy grimaced. "Right. Good luck to me then."

* * *

Aboard the Etherian Ship, *Veritus*

"What is that?" Tyra asked, pointing to a fuzzy white speck at the absolute center of the universe.

Tyra and Admiral Wheeler sat in the Operations Room of the *Veritus,* the largest of the five ships they'd sent to join the Faros. Both groups of ships were busy calculating the first of three jumps to reach the coordinates that the Faros had chosen to investigate. According to the *Veritus's* nav computer, it would be twelve hours before they arrived at those coordinates.

"Good question," Admiral Wheeler replied. Her eyes fell from the large holo display in front of them to examine the controls in the armrests of her chair.

Tyra went on studying the map. She noted that Etheria sat in the grayed-out southern hemisphere of the torus, and so far they'd been unable to find any data about either Etheria itself, or the surrounding star systems and galaxies. All they knew were those coordinates, and that their nav computers refused to calculate a course to reach them.

Suddenly the map zoomed in on the fuzzy speck that Tyra had identified, and a dazzlingly bright sphere appeared, dominating the holo display. It was labeled: *The Gates of Etheria.*

"Aha," Wheeler said. "There we go."

"This is where we're headed?" Tyra asked, shaking her head.

"It looks like the white hole that Etherus mentioned," Wheeler said.

"White holes are purely theoretical," Tyra objected.

"Until now."

Tyra frowned. "Assuming that's what this is, then not even light can cross into it."

"Well there sure is a krakton of light pouring out of it. It has to be coming from somewhere."

Tyra shook her head. "White holes are the inverse of black holes. Black holes don't let light or matter out, and white holes don't let it in. I suppose that would explain why we've never seen the universe on the other side even though it's spatially close to us here in Laniakea. Light can't take the shortcut through the center of the universe because there's a white hole blocking the way."

"So Etherus was telling the truth?" Wheeler asked. "There's no way through?"

"You'd be better off trying to cross the Big Empty, or the Great Divide, as Etherus calls it," Tyra said. "In fact... if Etherian comms are instantaneous and really do have an unlimited range, then that's probably exactly how the Etherians left this side of the universe. They must have transmitted their consciousness all the way around to the other side. That's probably what they do when humans visit Etheria, too."

"So why haven't aliens from the other side tried to

contact us?" Wheeler asked.

"Maybe we don't have the right technology to listen? Our receivers are limited, and we're far from the Big Empty. Who knows, but whatever the case, the Faros are leading us into a dead-end."

"It doesn't matter," Wheeler said with a shrug. "This is just to buy time, remember?"

"That's what *we're* doing," Tyra said. "But what are *they* doing? Why travel to the white hole in the center of the universe if everyone knows there's no way to cross a white hole?"

Wheeler blew out an exasperated breath. "Maybe they want to snap a few pictures for posterity, or scrawl some space graffiti in Etherus's neighborhood—does it matter?"

"It might. Maybe there's something else at those coordinates that we haven't noticed yet."

Wheeler gestured to the map. "Look for yourself. There's nothing there. Not even a star system."

"Try zooming in some more," Tyra suggested.

"All right..." Wheeler trailed off as she did so. The blindingly bright sphere vanished, the outermost edges of its radiance were reduced to a bright, gauzy veil for the stars. *A nebula?* Tyra wondered.

In the middle of the display, right beside the coordinates the Faros had chosen, was a gleaming cube, the sides of which were luminous, transparent, and vaguely golden. Through the transparent walls of the cube, Tyra saw a complex maze of structures on countless different levels, with what looked like elaborate gardens growing inside. A label above the cube read: *The Holy City.*

"There," Tyra pointed to it. "That's where they're

going."

Wheeler shook her head. "But what *is* it? It's..." she broke of, shaking her head. "That can't be right."

"What?" Tyra asked, leaning over to check her displays.

"It's 2250 kilometers long on every side."

Tyra blinked in shock. The wedge-shaped facets of New Earth were each only two hundred kilometers on a side, and just twenty kilometers thick. This *Holy City* would be able to hold at least a few thousand of them inside its walls.

"It must be some kind of space station," Tyra suggested. "I wonder what makes it *holy*?"

"Maybe that's where Etherus lives," Wheeler suggested.

"So he lives on our side of the universe—not in Etheria with his people?" Tyra asked.

"He might have another holy city on the other side," Wheeler said.

"Maybe we should search the ship's databanks for more information," Tyra replied. "There's a reason the Faros are headed there. They must already know what it is. It might have some kind of strategic significance."

Tyra summoned a holographic interface from her chair to query the ship for information about The Holy City. It didn't take her long to find what she was looking for. Reams of text appeared, and she began scrolling through the data, scanning it for pertinent details. Thankfully Etherian interfaces were all self-translating, but there was still a lot of information to get through.

Dwelling place of Etherus... focal point of power... capable of generating extra-dimensional barriers in quantum space...

Tyra's blood ran cold. That sounded familiar. "I think that city might be what's generating the interdiction field around the Red Line...."

Wheeler leaned over to read the information off Tyra's displays. "Frck. You're right. If that's true, and the Faros find a way to deactivate the interdiction field, we'll be overrun in minutes. We need to kick them out now, while we still have the rest of the fleet here to support us."

"They're already behind our lines," Tyra said. "If they realize we're onto them, they'll jump away, and we'll have to chase them all the way to The Holy City."

"You stay here and search the databanks for more information. See if you can confirm our suspicions. Meanwhile, I'm going to get back up to the bridge and see if I can maneuver us close enough to the Faros that we can stop their ships from jumping away."

"They might not like us getting that close," Tyra pointed out.

"I'll try to allay their suspicions," Admiral Wheeler said as she stood up from her chair and ran for the exit.

CHAPTER 18

Aboard the Etherian Ship, *Veritus*

"If you come any closer we will open fire."

Admiral Wheeler glared at the blue-skinned Faro on the other end of the comms—one of the Abaddon clones. "You're still in range of our fleet. We have you outnumbered."

"Then perhaps we should even the odds," Abaddon replied.

"We let you in so that you could investigate the truth of our claims that you cannot reach Etheria."

"And that is exactly what we are doing," Abaddon said.

"By going to The Holy City? How does that help you find a way to Etheria?"

"When a gate is shut, you go to the gatekeeper for the key," Abaddon replied. "Etherus is the gatekeeper, and he is in The Holy City. He could save us the trip if he would reply to our hails, but he is not responding."

"A white hole isn't a gate that can be opened or shut," Wheeler said, remembering what Tyra had said about them.

"Then why did the Etherians call it the Gates of Etheria? You can see where my confusion arises."

Wheeler frowned. "Etherus won't allow you into his

city, and he might attack you himself if you try to force your way in."

Abaddon grinned. "He is a pacifist. What makes you think he has any means to attack us? Weapons would defile his home."

"We're not going to allow you to reach The Holy City," Wheeler replied.

"Why?" Abaddon asked. "Are you afraid we'll find a way to deactivate the interdiction field at the Red Line and go around the wormhole?"

Admiral Wheeler tried not to react to that. The Faros had obviously spent plenty of time reading through the Etherian databanks themselves. They knew what she knew and then some. There was only one course of action left.

"Abaddon, I'm warning you. Turn around now."

"No."

"Then you leave me no choice—gunnery! Weapons free!"

"Aye, Admiral!"

The screeching reports of laser fire came shivering through the deck, and Abaddon's smile grew broader than ever. His glowing blue eyes glittered. "Last one to The Holy City gets to watch it burn."

The comms connection ended there and Abaddon's face vanished from the holo dome.

"They've jumped away!" the ship's sensor operator announced. "And I'm detecting an unidentified vessel de-cloaking at the entrance of the wormhole. They're flying through to the other side."

"With updated orders for the rest of their fleet..." Wheeler mused. "They're coming." She scanned the holo dome around the bridge, looking for the glassy sphere of the wormhole. She found it between the nine and ten o'clock position. She imagined the glinting specks of enemy ships streaming through the wormhole, explosions flashing around them like firecrackers.

"Your orders, ma'am?" the officer at the helm asked.

Wheeler shook her head. "Comms, contact Chief Councilor Ortane, tell her she has command of the *Veritus*, and she is to pursue the Faros to the Holy City and stop them if she can. I have to get back to the *Gideon* to command the rest of the fleet. The Faros are coming."

"Aye, ma'am..." the sensor operator announced.

"You're leaving the Chief Councilor in command?" the helmsman asked. "Are you certain that's—"

Admiral Wheeler's gaze swept to him. "She was captain of the *Inquisitor* before she was the chief councilor, and give her the same respect you would me, is that understood, Lieutenant?"

"Yes, ma'am."

"Good. You have the conn until Captain Ortane arrives."

"Aye, Admiral."

Wheeler stood from her station an strode for the recessed entrance of the bridge. New Earth and its fleets were still a week away. That meant all they had to hold the wormhole was the refugee-crowded Etherian fleet, and all of its ships were staffed with tired, badly inexperienced, and ration-starved crews.

Admiral Wheeler had a bad feeling it was going to be impossible to hold back the flood of Faros until reinforcements arrived.

* * *

Aboard the Captured Faro Shuttle

"Here we go..." Garek said as the hourglass-shaped band of atmosphere connecting Meson I and II loomed large before them. The fighters escorting them in slowed down, and Garek hauled back on the throttle to match their speed.

The edges of the cockpit canopy began glowing orange, and the shuttle shuddered around them as they hit atmosphere. Gauzy white clouds swept by the viewports, and condensation beaded on them as friction with the air slowed their momentum to a crawl. Within minutes the Nexus itself emerged from the clouds, a gleaming silver torus with parallel bands of viewports stacked hundreds deep. A shimmering column of water raced through the hole in the center, falling toward the rocky desert planet below, while the water planet sprawled above, its surface a vast and rippled blue canvas peeking through scattered clouds.

"Which is Meson One and which is Meson Two?" Addy asked.

Garek pointed up to the water world—"Meson One"—then down to the desert planet—"Meson Two."

Lucien stared into the shimmering column of water. Glowing bands of light rimmed the inner-side of the Nexus, no doubt something to do with whatever was driving the water and holding the planets in such a close orbit. "That's got to be the longest waterfall in the universe," Lucien said.

Garek nodded slowly. "Incredible."

The Nexus swelled in their canopy until it was all they

could see, and the shuttle began shivering again as the atmosphere grew thicker. Garek was forced to throttle down some more, but this time it didn't help. Violent winds buffeted them from all sides, swirling like a vortex around the station, and soon their cockpit was streaming with rivulets of water.

"It's raining," Addy said.

"But are the rain drops falling, or are we just running into them?" Lucien asked.

"We're at the point where the gravity between the two planets cancels out, so I'd say running into them," Garek replied.

The Faro fighters escorting them headed straight for a small rectangular bar of light in the side of the station. From a distance it looked like a viewport, but as they drew near, it resolved into the shielded opening of a hangar bay, and the glowing rectangles of light around it proved to be big rectangular *blocks* of viewports.

Lucien counted thirty-two viewports stacked beside the hangar, making it at least that many stories high, and he estimated it was about two kilometers wide.

As they passed through the shielded opening, tiny specks appeared on the deck below, waving them down to three small circular landing pads along one side of the hangar. Only a handful of other ships were landed inside the hangar, all of them small fighter-class vessels, leaving the bigger berths in the center of the deck empty.

"I guess their garrison is out on patrol," Garek said.

"I guess so..." Lucien replied.

They landed between the two fighters that had escorted them in, and the canopy of the one in front of them popped open. The pilot hopped out, wearing a black flight suit and helmet. The pilot removed his or her helmet, revealing a green-skinned head with broad masculine features. This was a member of the Faros' green-skinned caste.

A slave? Lucien wondered, as Garek powered down the shuttle's engines. The constant hum of the ship's drive system diminished to a fading whine, leaving their ears ringing with silence.

Garek and Addy both stood up from their control stations.

"Time to meet our hosts," Garek said. He gestured for Addy to go first. "After you, Lady Tekasi."

"Thank you, Lesot. Rikel?" Addy asked.

He stared blinkingly back, waiting for her to continue. Then he realized that he was blocking her way. "Right," he said, and moved aside.

Addy led the way from the cockpit and he fell in beside Garek. On their way aft, they found Brak in the galley, finishing off a pile of raw, reconstituted meat from the fabricator.

"Time to go," Lucien said. Brak let out a thunderous belch and rose to follow them. "Hood up, buddy," Lucien reminded him, and Brak lowered the hood of his shadow robe, concealing his features.

From the galley they walked into the cargo bay, and through to the airlock. Addy cycled the inner doors open and they all piled in, waiting for her to cycle the outer ones. A moment later, the inner doors shut and the outer ones irised open, followed by the groaning sound of servomotors extending the landing ramp from the back of the shuttle.

Lucien spied the blue-skinned Faro they'd spoken with over the comms waiting for them on the deck below. Four guards in shiny black suits of armor stood behind him, their faces hidden behind their helmets, and four shadow-robed slaves stood behind them.

Lucien's mind flashed back to their original first encounter with Abaddon, where Brak had killed several of his shadow-robed slaves in an attempt to get to Abaddon.

Fortunately this Faro wasn't one of the Abaddon clones. He probably would have seen through their disguises in an instant.

The landing ramp touched the deck below, and Addy started down. "Lord Korvas," she said as she approached.

Lucien and Garek followed uneasily in her wake, with Brak bringing up the rear. None of them were armed. Lucien had suggested they arm themselves, but Addy had argued that it might look suspicious for them to bring weapons aboard a friendly station.

"Welcome to the Nexus," Lord Korvas replied as Addy reached the bottom of the ramp. His gaze flicked to Lucien and Garek, and then to Brak before returning to Addy.

"It's a pleasure to be here," Addy said.

Korvas nodded and inclined his body to her in a shallow bow. Addy mimicked that bow somewhat awkwardly, and an even more awkward pause followed.

"As you can see, we're shorthanded to deal with the separatists. They were quick to take advantage of the fleet's absence. They haven't attacked us yet, but I fear that it is only a matter of time if their demands are not met. Hopefully you can negotiate a peaceful resolution while we wait for our fleet to return from Etheria."

Addy nodded. "Yes. I'm confident we'll be able to do that."

"I'm surprised Abaddon was able to send a negotiator so soon, and that you arrived without a more... *substantial* vessel to convey you here." Korvas's glowing green eyes flicked up to their shuttle as he said that.

"The situation here is precarious, as you say, so I got here as soon as I could. As for my ship, available vessels are few with all of them being summoned to join the war with Etheria. I was lucky to arrange transport aboard a passing vessel. I requisitioned one of their shuttles for the final leg of the journey."

Lord Korvas nodded slowly, apparently having bought the lie. "Well, I'm relieved to have you with us. Come, let me show you to your quarters." The Faro turned and crossed the hangar, heading for a large set of doors in the side of the cavernous space, some fifty meters distant.

"What are the separatists' demands?" Addy asked, as she walked up beside their Faro host.

"That we stop transferring water from Meson One and return the planet to its original orbit. They also want us to pay for the water we've already taken in the form of supplies for their fleet. None of that is acceptable to us. The Nexus was expensive enough to build as it is. If we had to forfeit our operation, or pay for the water we're taking, we'd go bankrupt. Ideally, you'll find a way to stall the separatists until our fleet returns to deal with them."

"Leave it to me," Addy said. "I won't disappoint you."

"I am sure that you won't."

The hangar doors parted automatically as they reached them, revealing a long gray corridor lined with windows. As they walked down the corridor, Lucien saw that it was actually a bridge crossing over a vast garden—*no, a farm,* he realized, noting the orderly rows of colorful alien plants.

Brown, bug-like aliens skittered about, periodically rearing up on their back four legs to pluck ripe fruits and vegetables with their front four. They dropped those foods in hovering metal carts that preceded them down the aisles of crops.

As Korvas and Addy came to the end of the bridge, another set of doors parted for them, and they proceeded to wind their way through long, dull gray corridors lined with doors. They passed a few blue-skinned, black-robed Faros along the way, and Lucien wondered at their attire. He had yet to see a Faro wearing anything more colorful or stylish. Either the Faros had no concept of fashion, or their robes were a kind of uniform and they had yet to meet any Faro civilians.

After passing down several more corridors, they came to a broad set of glass doors. Above them a glowing sign read, *The Grotto*.

They walked through those doors into a high, circular room. The ceiling was at least ten stories. Walkways with glass railings girded each level, giving access to various doors. A giant crystal tree stood in the center of the room with a translucent, luminous trunk and branches. Broad crystalline leaves sparkled like amethysts and sapphires in the light of the tree's trunk and branches.

Lucien wondered if that tree was some kind of living crystal, or just an elaborate sculpture.

Lord Korvas led them to an elevator on the far end of the lobby, and they all crowded in—except for Korvas's guards. There was no room for them inside the elevator, so he left them waiting on the ground floor.

Korvas selected a floor from the control panel and the elevator whisked them up. When it opened and they all walked out, Lucien saw that they were now at the top of the chamber. A transparent dome capped the space above the crystal tree, with some kind of aquarium or water reservoir inside.

Lucien thought he saw something large and shadowy swimming in there, but it was hard to be sure.

Lord Korvas led them around the circumference of the level they were on until they reached a golden door. Holographic text identified it as the *Grand Suite.* Korvas worked the keypad beside the door until a flickering red fan of light snapped out from a black lens above the door. *Some kind of scanner?* Lucien wondered.

Korvas stepped aside and turned to Addy, clearly waiting for her to do something. *Step in front of the scanner maybe?*

Lucien held his breath, and Addy hesitated.

"If you please, Lady Tekasi," Lord Korvas said, and gestured to the flickering fan of crimson light.

"Of course," Addy replied and stepped in front of the scanner.

Lucien held back a grimace, wondering if the scanner would be able to tell that she wasn't really a Faro.

The fan of light passed up and down her body, scanning her from head to toe, and then a pleasant chime issued from the control pad, and the door swished open.

Lucien blinked and swayed on his feet, almost dizzy with relief. Or maybe hunger.

Lord Korvas nodded to Addy. "I trust you'll find the

accommodations here adequate, but don't hesitate to call me if you need anything."

Addy nodded. "Thank you, Korvas. Are we the only ones staying in The Grotto?"

A glimmer of suspicion appeared in Korvas's glowing green eyes. "Our distress call mentioned that we evacuated all of our non-essential personnel after we received the threat from the separatists...."

A cold prickle of sweat trickled down Lucien's back.

Addy nodded and smiled, as if she'd simply forgotten that detail. "Yes, it was wise of you to do so."

Korvas indicated the open door of the suite. "Make yourself comfortable. Tomorrow we travel to Meson One for the negotiations."

Addy nodded and walked through the doors. Lucien followed her with Garek and Brak, being careful to avoid Korvas's gaze. The Faro's glowing green eyes tracked Lucien disdainfully as he passed through the doors, as if he were some contemptible *thing*. Lucien supposed that was exactly how the Faros probably saw their slaves.

Once everyone was inside, Addy fumbled with the control panel to shut and lock the doors behind them. Fortunately, Korvas didn't stick around to see her furiously tapping random commands into the panel. Eventually she found the right one, and the doors slid shut.

Garek blew out a breath. "He suspects something."

"He left his guards in the lobby," Addy replied. "That has to count for something."

Garek snorted and began wandering around their suite. It was a sprawling, luxuriously appointed space with a jutting balcony with glass walls and floor running along the far side of the living and dining areas.

Through the glass Lucien saw the gushing waterfall in the center of the Nexus, and he went to stand there and gawk at the view. Meson I hovered directly above, a rippled blue marble streaked with white. Through the glass floor, Lucien saw the blue freckle on the desert planet below. It was partially covered by thick white clouds, and fat ripples marked the surface of the blue—what had to be towering waves caused by the falling water.

"Amazing..." Lucien whispered.

Addy and Garek joined him on the balcony.

"These separatists might be able to help us," Garek said as he admired the view.

Lucien glanced at him. "What do you mean?"

"If they realize that we're actually mutual enemies of the Faros, they might help us with our mission. If nothing else, maybe they can tell us where the Forge is."

"Assuming they *know* where it is," Lucien replied.

Garek shrugged. "At least it's a place to start. It's not like we can just ask Korvas. Real Faros would either already know where the Forge is, or they'd know better than to ask because it's a well-kept secret. Either way we'll make him suspicious."

"The separatists might want us to do something for them in exchange for their help," Lucien mused.

Addy glanced at him. "Are you suggesting we sabotage the negotiations in order to make the separatists happy?"

Lucien nodded. "But without letting Korvas know that's what we're doing."

"No pressure," Addy replied.

"Well, maybe a little," Lucien said.

CHAPTER 19

Aboard the Etherian Ship, *Veritus*

"Captain, we have an incoming message from the *Gideon,*" the *Veritus's* comms officer announced.

"Patch it through to the holo dome," Tyra said.

A familiar head and shoulders appeared on Tyra's primary display. "Admiral Wheeler here. I'm back aboard the *Gideon.* Are you ready to go, Captain? I could send someone else."

"I'm ready, ma'am."

"You should at least wait to have more ships join you."

Tyra shook her head. "My ships have already calculated the first jump, and they've already been emptied of refugees and crewed with our best officers. We can't afford to wait for reinforcements. By then the Faros will have jumped somewhere else, and we could lose their trail."

Wheeler frowned. "As soon as you execute that jump, you're going to be in the middle of a firefight. Your *children* are on board."

"You mean like the firefight you're about to be in here?" Tyra asked. She shook her head. "Stay or go, we'll be risking our lives, but we need to go, and we can't afford to deliberate any longer."

"Good luck then, Captain," Wheeler replied.

Tyra saluted. "We'll be in touch."

Admiral Wheeler returned her salute and ended the comms from her end.

Tyra gaze snapped to the gunnery control station. "Gunnery, report!"

"Ready for action, ma'am."

"Good. Engineering—set full power to shields."

"Aye... Councilor," the woman sitting there replied.

"*Captain,*" Tyra corrected.

"Yes, ma'am."

"Comms, have our ships to stand by to execute the first jump."

"All ships standing by," the comms officer replied.

"Execute jump!" Tyra ordered.

The holo dome over the bridge flashed white, and then a clean slate of stars appeared. Tyra called out, "Sensors, report!"

"Five Etherian ships at seven thousand klicks! It's the Faros."

"Gunnery, what's the range of our—"

A flurry of bright red laser beams slashed out of the void and drew a hissing roar from the *Veritus's* shields.

"Weapons free!" Tyra ordered. "Target the engines on their largest vessel—the *Concordance,*" Tyra added, reading the name off her contacts panel.

"Aye—weapons firing," gunnery replied.

Fat green lasers lanced out from invisible hardpoints—invisible due to the artificially unobstructed view afforded by the holo dome.

Tyra watched the laser light show going on around them. *Green for friendly, red for enemy?* Tyra wondered. It was a fair bet. Those colors had to be simulated, since lasers couldn't actually be seen in space.

"Enemy ships are launching fighters—and missiles!" the sensor operator reported.

"Where did they get *fighters* from?" Tyra asked. The Lost Etherian fleet didn't have any on board—probably expended long ago in some ages-old battle with the Faros.

"They must have stocked their ships with their own fighters," the sensor operator suggested.

"Great. Gunnery—where are our missiles?"

"We don't have any, Captain. All of our launch tubes read empty."

"Perfect." They had five ships to the Faros' five, all equally classed and equally powerful—except that the Faros had taken the time to re-stock their vessels with their own compliment of ordinance and support ships.

This was far from a fair fight.

"Engineering, activate quantum jamming."

"Aye, ma'am..." the engineering officer trailed off uncertainly. Trapping one's enemy was a good strategy if you had them out-gunned, but the reverse was true here.

"Comms, get me Admiral Wheeler. It looks like we're going to need those reinforcements, after all."

"Aye, Captain."

Wheeler appeared on the holo dome, a floating head and shoulders overlaying the streaking red and green lasers of the battle going on around them.

"Is there a problem, Captain?" the admiral said, her eyebrows raised in question.

"We need—"

Wheeler vanished in a haze of static, and the

crisscrossing laser beams returned.

"What happened?" Tyra demanded.

"We lost the connection—the enemy is jamming our comms."

Tyra ground her teeth and shook her head. "Looks like we're on our own. Helm, get us away from the enemy fleet and out of here as soon as our jump drives have finished cooling down."

"They've activated *their* jamming fields, Captain. We're trapped," the helmsman replied.

"Then get us out of range!"

"Yes, ma'am. Coming about..."

Tyra shook her head and grimaced. She summoned a tactical map and watched as her five ships turned to flee from an identical five enemy vessels. A horde of smaller, wedge-shaped red blips streamed from the Faros' capital ships, and an even smaller cloud of glittering red specks preceded them—incoming missiles.

"The enemy is giving chase," the helm reported.

"Engineering, all power to engines! Comms—relay that order to the rest of our ships. Speed is of the essence here."

Both officers acknowledged their orders. The range between Tyra's ships and the enemy ones increased briefly, but stabilized just a few seconds later. The Faros had boosted power to their engines, too.

We can't outrun ships with identical drive systems, Tyra mused. That left them outgunned and backed into a corner. Her heart began to race, and her eyes flicked to the recessed stairway leading away from the bridge. Her thoughts went to Theola and Atara. She might be able to escape with them aboard a shuttle if it came to it. Or maybe she could send Brak away with them. Then she remembered the clouds of enemy fighters headed their way. *They'll be chased down and shot to pieces.*

Tyra's gaze returned to the battle grid and she saw that the cloud of missiles racing toward them had closed to less than a minute of reaching them.

"Incoming ordinance! ETA fifty-two seconds!" the sensor operator announced.

"All power to weapons and shields!" Tyra ordered.

"Aye!" the chief engineer replied.

"Gunnery—concentrate fire on those missiles!"

"Point defenses firing..."

Tyra watched on the battle grid as a flurry of smaller weapons fire stuttered out from her ships, raking through the waved of incoming missiles. Explosions sprinkled the grid with muffled *booms,* but not fast enough.

A handful of missiles sailed on to reach each of their ships.

"Brace for impact!" sensors warned.

The deck shook and explosions boomed. A panel flashed in the periphery of Tyra's control station—*Damage Report.*

"Shields down to ninety percent," the engineering officer reported. "We've lost one of our jamming field projectors."

"They're trying to take down our jamming field?" Tyra wondered aloud. "They're trying to get away from *us?*"

"Maybe that means they're not trying to kill us," the ship's chief engineer suggested, a hopeful quiver in her voice.

"That, or they're afraid we might have reinforcements coming," Tyra replied.

"It took three hours to calculate this jump. They have to know that we won't have reinforcements until then, and there's no way we'll last that long," the helmsman replied.

"No, we won't," Tyra agreed as the first wave of Faro fighters reached them. She looked up from her tactical grid to the holo dome. A dozen glinting specks were swooping toward them, riding on bright red thruster trails. Green pulse lasers and kinetic cannons tracked out from the *Veritus*, catching one of those fighters in the crossfire. It exploded and molten debris shot out in fiery tentacles.

The other fighters began jinking evasively. They fired back with red pulse lasers and dozens of glinting silver missiles.

Point defenses tracked those missiles, catching two of them before the remainder sailed on to impact on the *Veritus's* hull.

More muffled booms shivered through the deck.

"We've lost another two jamming field projectors!" the chief engineer announced. "Our field is down to half strength."

Tyra grimaced and shook her head, watching on the battle grid as the next wave of enemy fighters approached the *Veritus* from behind. Matching waves raced up behind the other ships in her fleet, each of them targeting her ships' field projectors.

After three more waves and just ten minutes, all of Tyra's ships had lost their quantum jamming fields, leaving the Faros free to jump away.

"There they go," Tyra said, watching as the Faro fighters flew back to their carrier ships. Long-range lasers still streaked between the Faros' five capital ships and Tyra's five.

"One of our ships has just lost its shields!" the comms officer announced.

"Have them fall back," Tyra said.

"The Faros have stopped firing..." the gunnery officer said.

"The *Concordance* is hailing us!" the comms officer added.

Tyra tapped the flashing comms icon on her display, and Abaddon's smiling face appeared before. "Had enough yet?" he asked.

"You hailed us just to gloat?" Tyra replied. "I didn't realize you were so petty."

"Pettiness is the language of petty people. I had to be sure you'd understand me."

Tyra gritted her teeth, but affected a thin smile. "And what is it you expect us to understand?"

"That resistance is futile. Your forces at the wormhole will also be overwhelmed. It is only a matter of time. Therefore, you have just two options: join me, or die. I know you don't believe Etherus is god any more than I do. If he were, don't you think he would have destroyed me a long time ago?"

Tyra said nothing to that. It was hard to defend a belief system that wasn't hers, but that didn't mean she thought Abaddon would be any better in the role of supreme ruler. Etherus might not be the conquering hero she wanted him to be, but at least his apathy cut both ways: he didn't actively harm or threaten his subjects.

"We won't submit to an empire of evil," Tyra replied.

"Evil? I'm not evil. I just want answers, like you."

"What about all of your slaves?"

"If it were wrong to enslave them, Etherus would have stopped me. Unless you're admitting that he's not as *good* as he claims to be."

Tyra refrained from poly-parroting the explanation Etherus had given them for his inaction. "Try defending your actions without invoking Etherus as a scapegoat."

Abaddon smiled. "How's this: if I were evil, wouldn't I keep attacking you until your ships are all destroyed? And yet, here I am, retreating while your jugular is exposed."

"We're not your target," Tyra said. "And if you stick around, you risk being overwhelmed by our reinforcements."

"Yes... the ones you failed to call for before we jammed your comms. Even if Admiral Wheeler realizes that you need her help and does send you reinforcements, those ships won't arrive for several hours. That's more than enough time for us to destroy you and leave."

"Then why don't you?"

"Because maybe I'm not as evil as you think? Dwell on that, Tyra, and perhaps by the time we arrive at The Holy City, we can arrive there as friends seeking answers together. After all, that is why *Astralis* left, is it not?"

With that, the comms ended, and Tyra was left gaping at a blank screen.

"Your orders, Captain?" the helmsman asked uneasily.

All eyes were on her. How much had they overheard from her conversation with Abaddon? How much had they believed of his lies?

"The enemy just jumped away," the sensor operator announced. "Should I try to find their signatures?"

Tyra shook her head. "Take us straight to The Holy City. We'll catch up with them there. Hopefully Abaddon is wrong about the city's lack of defenses, and Etherus will have some kind of firepower to add to ours by the time we arrive."

"Aye, ma'am."

"ETA until our next jump?"

"Two hours," the helm replied.

"Good. Comms—contact Admiral Wheeler with an update. Ask her to send whatever ships she can spare to The Holy City."

"Aye, Captain."

Those reinforcements would be running three hours behind them, but it would be better to have them than not. She rose from her control station on stiff, cramping legs. "If anyone needs me, I'll be in my quarters."

She turned to look at the helmsman and queried her ARCs for the man's name. "Lieutenant Gorman Argos," she said, reading the ID tag that appeared above his head. He had short black hair, indigo eyes and dark skin.

"Yes, ma'am?" he asked.

"You have the conn."

"Aye, Captain."

"Everyone else, carry on."

Tyra strode for the recessed stairway leading down from the bridge, and hurried down those steps. The marine sergeant guarding the doors stood at attention and saluted her as she approached.

"At ease," she said, and waited for him to open the doors. They swished open and she breezed through into a long, gleaming white corridor.

It was time to go check on her children. After losing one battle with the enemy, she now winced at the thought of having them on board.

Before they arrived at The Holy City and joined another potentially lethal confrontation, Tyra resolved to send them safely away with Brak aboard the fastest shuttle the *Veritus* had.

There was no sense in getting them killed along with her.

CHAPTER 20

The Nexus

"You can take the bed," Lucien said. "I'll sleep in the living room."

Addy just looked at him, her expression fraught with unspoken emotions. *Bitterness? Jealousy? No... anger,* he decided.

But all she said was, "Okay."

Lucien left the bedroom and went to lie on the couch in the living room of their suite. He didn't have a blanket or a pillow, but the room and his Faro robes were warm enough. The couch was comfortable at least.

He tried turning off the lights with a verbal command, and was surprised to find that it worked. The suite plunged into darkness, and he lay there listening to an aching silence.

He felt bad putting up walls with Addy. She didn't deserve it, and if he was being honest with himself, a big part of the reason he was pushing her away was that he was afraid of what might happen if he didn't.

He was badly confused. He had memories with both Tyra and Addy, and both sets of memories corresponded to the same points in time, making him feel like a married man with a mistress, even though he'd never actually cheated on his wife. Regardless, he had all of the corresponding guilt, and that made it easy to think about actually cheating. *If you've already done it, what's the difference in doing it again?*

Except that he hadn't.

Lucien frowned and shook his head to clear it. He and Addy had bigger problems than the love triangle they found themselves in right now. They needed to focus on finding the Forge and destroying it. After that, Lucien would have plenty of time to unravel his conflicting feelings and memories to figure out who he actually loved the most.

Lucien rolled over and cleared his mind. Sleep eventually came, but it brought no relief. His dreams were haunted by Addy. She was crying, accusing him of betraying her, of never really loving her.

He awoke with a start and lay blinking bleary eyes at the ceiling. Ghostly after-images floated before his eyes and the fuzzy darkness seemed to become a living thing, reaching out to suffocate him.

Then the room snapped into focus, and the ghostly shapes fled. Lucien turned to look out the balcony at the darkened viewports. They were almost entirely polarized to keep out the starlight and the reflected sunlight beaming off Meson I and Meson II.

Lucien lay awake and staring out at the shimmering curtain of water streaming through the center of the Nexus. It was mesmerizing.

Gradually, he became aware of a muffled sound coming from the suite's two bedrooms. He sat up, his ears straining to identify it...

It was Addy. She *was* crying. He hadn't dreamed that part. Frowning, Lucien got up from the couch and followed the sound to Addy's room. He waved the door open, and the sound grew suddenly louder, no longer muffled by the door—then it stopped.

"Go away," Addy said.

"Addy..." He moved to her side of the bed and sat down beside her. "Are you okay?" he asked, placing a hand on her back.

"No. What do you care?"

"I care."

She sat up, her glowing green eyes—a Faros' eyes—flashing in the dark. Lucien started at the sight, but forced himself to relax. She'd forgotten to turn off her holoskin. So had he. That was probably wise considering they didn't know what kind of surveillance systems their suite had. "You chose *her* over me," Addy accused. "Did you even give it a second thought?"

Lucien grimaced. "I haven't chosen anyone."

"You chose to integrate your memories. That's the same thing."

"You're just assuming that means I chose her."

"You've been pretty clear so far. You won't even sleep in the same room with me."

Lucien took a breath and shook his head. "It's complicated."

"You said you agreed to integrate because it would give you more reason to fight. More to live for."

"Because of my daughters, not necessarily because of my wife," Lucien explained. "Between you and her, I don't know who I love more... I have more memories with Tyra, but I have happier ones with you. The problem is I made vows to Tyra, and marriage is supposed to be forever."

"Really?" Addy asked. "So why does everyone get

divorced, then? Forever is a long time for immortals. Fifty thousand years from now, are you still going to be in love with your wife? Or even me? You probably won't even remember our names anymore."

Lucien considered that with a deepening frown. "People can grow together or apart. It's a choice you make every day. Marriage really can last forever, but only if both people are actively trying to make that happen. Unfortunately, Tyra never tried very hard. She was more in love with her job than me. I guess I stuck around for the kids."

Addy sniffed and wiped her cheeks. "So what are you saying? That your marriage is over?"

"I'm saying that I'm not pushing you away because I don't love you. I'm pushing you away because I'm afraid that if I don't, I'm going to cheat on my wife with you." He shook his head. "I owe it to both of you to make a decision about my marriage first, and I can't do that until we get back to Laniakea."

"You mean *if* we get back," Addy replied.

"Etherus wouldn't have sent us on this mission if he thought we were going to fail."

"You think he knows the future?" Addy asked.

"I think he must. Isn't that part of being an all-mighty, omniscient God?"

"If he knows the future, then we do live in a deterministic universe, and no one is really free. Think about it: you can't know the future, unless the future is *destined* to be, but Etherus said we have souls, and that's what gives us free will.

"You can't have it both ways. We can't be free and have a god who knows the future. So if he doesn't know the future, then he doesn't know that we're going to win."

Lucien nodded slowly. "Good points. Maybe there's a middle ground somewhere. Maybe he can only predict a *likely* future, not some pre-determined one."

"Then that still means he doesn't know whether we're going to fail. Our success isn't a given."

"So let's make sure we don't fail," Lucien replied. He reached out to place a hand on one of Addy's shoulders, but she grabbed his neck and pulled his lips down to hers for a kiss. He didn't have time to react until it was over, and by then there was no point in pushing her away.

"What..." He shook his head. "I thought I explained where I stand?"

"You did, but you didn't give me a chance to explain where *I* stand. Maybe Tyra loved her job more than you, but I'm not her, and you won't have to settle for runner-up on my list of priorities."

Lucien nodded and rose from Addy's bed. "I'll keep that in mind. Try to get some sleep. You'll need your wits about you if you're going to convince the separatists to help us tomorrow."

"I will. Goodnight, Lucien."

"Goodnight, Addy," he replied as he walked out the door.

CHAPTER 21

Aboard the Etherian Ship, *Veritus*

—EIGHT HOURS LATER—

"Why do we have to go away?" Atara asked.

Tyra bought herself time for an answer by kissing Theola's cheek and parting the long locks of dark hair hanging in front of Theola's eyes. She'd be turning two in a couple of months, and she was long overdue for a haircut—just one of the many things that weren't a priority when their survival was the only thing on Tyra's mind.

"Mom..." Atara tugged on Tyra's councilor's robes. "Why do we have to—"

"Because mommy has to go fight bad guys, and you need to stay somewhere safe or I'll be distracted worrying about you."

"You're going to fight the blue people?" Atara asked.

Tyra fixed her five-year-old daughter with a measuring look. It was impossible to tell if she really was still possessed by Abaddon. She seemed to be playing the part of an innocent five-year-old well enough—except for her lack of concern over her father's death and subsequent absence.

"Yes, the blue people," Tyra confirmed. "Brak—"

"I guard them with my life," Brak said.

Tyra studied his stalwart expression and nodded. "I know you will." She kissed Theola one last time and then set her down on the deck of the shuttle. Theola made a scrunchy face and pouted, raising her arms to be picked up again. Tyra smiled wanly and shook her head. "No sweetie, Mommy has to go." To Brak she added, "Make sure they... behave."

He nodded slowly and glanced at Atara.

Atara caught that look and crossed her arms over her chest. "I always behave!"

"Of course you do, honey," Tyra replied, and tousled Atara's long black hair. She went down on her haunches to look her in the eye. Atara gazed right back, her jaw set and eyes fractionally narrowed.

"Take care of your sister, okay?"

The tightness left Atara's gaze and she nodded grimly, suddenly all grown up.

Tyra lingered on her haunches a moment longer, waiting for Atara's innocent facade to crack, but it never did.

"Good." She leaned in and kissed Atara on the cheek. "I love you, Atty."

Atara wrapped her arms around Tyra's neck and sniffled in her ear. "Don't go, Mommy. I'm scared."

Tyra's heart ached with those words, but they didn't quite ring true after Etherus had declared that she was still infected with Abaddon's mind. Tyra withdrew to an arm's length and gazed into her daughter's green eyes once more, searching desperately for some hint of the truth, one way or the other. All she saw was her little girl, a real five-year-old who was genuinely afraid.

"Be brave, honey. Brak will keep you safe. I promise."

Brak grabbed Atty's shoulder with a giant gray hand

and squeezed. "Yes," he confirmed.

Tyra stood up and backed away.

"No..." Atara whined, tears springing to her eyes. She lunged after Tyra, but Brak caught her in one arm and swept her off her feet. She kicked and screamed under his arm. "Don't go!" Atara screamed, and Theola began to cry.

Tyra shook her head, her eyes blurring with tears. "I'll see you both soon." She blew them a kiss, and with that, she turned and strode back through the shuttle.

"Mommy!" Atara called after her.

Tyra steeled herself and shook her head. She had a battle to fight, and her daughters would be safer with Brak than they would be with her.

She blew out a shaky breathe as she passed through the airlock of the shuttle and down the ramp. Her footsteps clanged echoingly on the metal ramp. Once she reached a safe distance, she turned and watched as the shuttle's engines ignited with a roar of dazzling blue fire. Heat pulsed out in waves, and dust scattered out from under the ship's grav lifts. The shuttle lifted a few meters off the deck and rotated on the spot to face the fuzzy blue shields over the opening of the hangar bay.

For a second, the shuttle lingered there, hovering; then it went screaming out of the hangar with a blast of heat from its engines. The hangar shields hissed and rippled in its wake, and Tyra watched that ship dwindle to a fuzzy speck, tinted blue by the semi-transparent shield.

Tyra gave a deep sigh. It didn't feel like she'd just said goodbye to an undercover Faro agent. But as far as she knew, Etherus had never been caught in a lie—*just lies of omission,* she amended.

Activating her comms, Tyra placed a call to the helmsman of the *Veritus,* the man she'd left with the conn. "Lieutenant Argos—"

"Ma'am?"

"Is our jump to The Holy City finished calculating yet?"

"Five more minutes, Captain."

"Good. I'll be right there."

* * *

The Nexus

Lucien awoke to the sound of the door chiming. He got up from the couch where he'd slept, rubbing bleary eyes, and went to answer it.

The door swished open to reveal Lord Korvas and his cadre of shadow-robed slaves.

"Good morning—" Lucien began.

"How dare you greet me, concubine! Where is your master?"

Scrambling for an appropriate response, Lucien hesitated in the doorway.

"I'm here," Addy said, walking up behind Lucien and rudely shoving him aside.

Lord Korvas gave a shallow bow, and Addy returned it.

"We must go," Korvas said. "The separatists are waiting for us on Meson One."

Lucien's stomach growled noisily in protest. Were Faros supposed to be immune to hunger?

"We have not had the chance to eat this morning," Addy said.

Korvas waved his hand to dismiss that concern. "Food will be provided for you on the flight down, and the negotiations cannot wait any longer."

Addy nodded and half turned back to the sleeping quarters in their suite. "Brakos, Lesot! It is time to leave."

Lord Korvas's glowing green eyes narrowed at that, but he said nothing until both Garek and Brak emerged from the room they'd shared. They hurried over and joined Addy by the door.

Korvas nodded to Brak. "You call your slave by its name?"

Addy nodded in turn to Korvas's four shadow-robed slaves. "You do not? How do you differentiate between your servants otherwise?"

Korvas's eyes narrowed still further. "I do not need to differentiate. Their individuality is not important. If it were, I would allow them to show their faces."

"I see," Addy replied, offering a disapproving frown of her own. "I find that treating my slaves as if their lives matter compels better service. You should try it."

"Perhaps I will..." Korvas replied, and his gaze flicked to his own slaves, as if considering the advice. "Please follow me." Korvas turned and led them back along the circular walkway to the elevator they'd ridden up the night before. From there they walked through the lobby, and followed Korvas down the Nexus's long, winding corridors.

Ten minutes later, they walked out into another cavernous hangar, a different one this time. Korvas led them to a medium-sized starship, and they proceeded up the landing ramp together, past a pair of faceless guards in shiny black armor. The guards turned and followed them up the ramp. Before they even reached the top of the ramp, it began rising with a pneumatic *hiss*, groaning under their combined weight. Dust swirled out from under the ship as grav lifts powered up, and a reverberating roar shuddered through the ramp.

Once they were all inside the airlock, Korvas keyed the outer doors shut and the inner ones open. He led them through a yawning cargo bay filled with metal crates and more armored guards sitting on bench seats to either side.

They reached a door at the far end of the cargo bay, and Korvas keyed it open. From there, they followed him down a long, straight passage lined with doors and branching corridors. Near the end of it a pair of ramps appeared—one leading up, the other down. The ramp leading up gave a glimpse into what might have been the cockpit or bridge, while the ramp going down showed a semicircular room filled with rows of seating.

Korvas descended the ramp to the lower room. Once inside, he turned to Addy and gestured to the empty rows of seats.

"Please make yourself comfortable, Lady Tekasi. I will have food sent down for you and your entourage."

"Thank you," Addy replied.

Korvas bowed once more and then left.

Lucien turned to watch him leave under the guise of examining his surroundings. The two black-armored guards who'd followed them up the ship's landing ramp had taken up positions just outside the doors. As Korvas walked through with his slaves, the doors swished shut with a muffled *boom,* and Lucien turned back to the fore. A broad set of viewports spanned the semi-circular front wall of the space.

"I don't like this," Garek whispered.

"At least we all have window seats," Lucien said.

Addy shot him a look, and waved a hand in his face as if to silence him. "We will be more than comfortable enough. It is a short flight to the surface."

Her superior tone held a note of warning. She was still in character, and for good reason: most starships had internal surveillance systems, and if Korvas held any suspicions about them, he would be watching.

Garek nodded slowly and went to sit along the front row of seats, near the center of the room. Addy followed and went to sit beside him. Lucien waited for her to sit before taking a his seat beside her, thinking that's what a submissive concubine would do.

Once he was seated, Lucien directed his attention to the view. He watched the transport hover up and slide out of the hangar. They passed through hangar shields with a faint shiver of exchanging energy, and then the star-field appeared, but those stars were almost as fuzzy and washed-out as they had appeared from inside the hangar. The atmosphere surrounding the Nexus made them appear as faint, twinkling pinpricks, vanishing into a thick white mist.

The view whirled around them as the transport turned, and then the rippled blue and white marble of Meson I appeared, looming large before them. The transport raced down into its atmosphere, and beads of moisture ran in rivulets along the viewports. Before long their acceleration and friction with the air made those water droplets evaporate instantly. The edges of the viewports glowed orange with heat as they plunged into Meson I's atmosphere, and the surface of the planet grew progressively clearer and larger.

The doors to the passenger cabin swished open and four shadow-robed slaves came in carrying covered silver platters. They stopped in front of Addy and wordlessly uncovered those platters, waiting for a command. Addy pointed to the most appetizing meal of the four, and the slave holding it handed it to her. They gave Garek second choice, and then Lucien third, leaving Brak with the meal that everyone else had already passed over—a plate full of mushy-looking greens and a pale, roasted leg of some or other animal.

The slaves filed out, and Lucien ate his meal in silence—some kind of hot sandwich. It wasn't bad, so long as he didn't wonder what kind of animal was on it. For all he knew of the Faros, they ate sentient aliens.

The transport hit fluffy white clouds and began shaking violently around them. They didn't feel anything thanks to the ship's inertial management system, but the appearance of movement without the accompanying sensation of it made Lucien's stomach churn.

Before long their speed dropped enough that the turbulence ceased, and the clouds parted, revealing the rippled blue surface of a planet-wide ocean below. The water shimmered in the sun, and Lucien spied a group of giant metallic spheres sitting half-submerged in the water. *Floating cities?* he wondered.

As they drew near, finer details emerged—viewports, decks, sensor dishes, comms receivers, and weapons emplacements—and the size of the spheres became apparent: each of them had to be at least several kilometers in diameter.

Near the waterline of the sphere a shielded rectangular hangar bay swelled ahead of them. The hangar grew rapidly larger as they approached, until it dwarfed even the giant hangar bays of the Nexus. With that, Lucien had to dramatically revise his estimate of the spheres' size to at least a hundred kilometers in diameter each.

As they cruised into the cavernous hangar bay Lucien saw hundreds of wedge-shaped fighters crowding the deck, with larger rectangular and cigar-shaped vessels sitting between them. They landed beside one of the larger ships.

"These guys look like they're spoiling for a fight," Garek commented.

Lucien had to agree. No wonder Korvas was so anxious about the negotiations. This crowded deck was a far cry from the Nexus's empty hangars. But there was something else that had caught his eye—the fighters from the Nexus and the fighters in this hangar were the exact same type. Whoever these separatists were, they had Farosien ships.

The doors swished open behind them, and Lucien turned to see Lord Korvas standing in the entryway.

"It is time," Korvas said. "Lady Tekasi?"

Addy rose from her seat, careful to mind the platter of half-eaten food she'd left at her feet. "We're ready," she said. Lucien joined her in standing, followed by Garek and Brak.

Addy led the way. When they reached Korvas, he turned and led them back down the corridor to the cargo bay. At the rear airlock they found two full squads of black-armored Faro soldiers waiting for them.

They all crowded into the airlock, and Korvas cycled the doors. Lucien peered between Addy and Korvas as the outer doors irised opened, trying to get a glimpse of the separatists waiting for them below.

"Lord Korvas," a familiar, buttery smooth voice greeted.

It can't be... Lucien thought.

The voice went on, "I'm glad to see that you're taking our threats seriously. I was beginning to think a demonstration of our intentions might be needed."

Wordlessly, the party started down the landing ramp, and Lucien saw the speaker, his suspicions confirmed. Addy sucked in a noisy breath.

It was Abaddon, but this one didn't wear the glowing golden crown that all of the others did, and his robes were brown rather than gray.

"Who is this?" Abaddon asked, his glowing blue gaze flicking from Korvas to Addy and back again.

"Our negotiator, Lady Tekasi," Korvas said as they stopped at the bottom of the ramp.

A horde of humanoid aliens from at least a dozen different species stood behind the Abaddon clone, all of them aiming gleaming black rifles at Korvas and Addy.

Abaddon's gaze snaked from Korvas to Addy, and then to Lucien and Garek. His eyes were suspiciously narrowed. "How did a negotiator get here so soon?"

"The empire is more efficient than you think," Korvas replied, lifting his chin.

Abaddon snorted and shook his head. His eyes slid back to Addy, and a sly smile spread on his lips. He glanced at Korvas, suddenly smug and gestured to a set of doors behind him. "Let's get on with it, then."

Korvas nodded and started forward, but Abaddon

stopped him at the bottom of the ramp with a sneer and an upraised palm. "Not you."

"As the duly appointed ruler of this system, it is my right to be privy to all negotiations."

"It's not up for debate," Abaddon replied. "Consider it... one of my new terms."

Korvas's eyes flicked between Addy and Abaddon, as if he suddenly suspected that they might be in cahoots.

Addy turned to him with a reassuring smile. "Do not worry, Lord Korvas, I will convey the details to you as soon as the preliminary negotiations are complete."

Korvas nodded sullenly, and Addy started forward. Lucien trailed behind with the others, and Abaddon watched each of them carefully as they passed by, but he made no move to stop any of them. That had to irk Korvas even more. He was not allowed to witness the negotiations, but even Lady Tekasi's shadow-robed slave apparently could.

The ranks of humanoid aliens parted, clearing a path to the doors Abaddon had indicated. Lucien was just wondering if they would be allowed to walk through unattended when a blue blur and a brief gust of wind whipped by them.

Lucien blinked and suddenly Abaddon was there, walking beside Addy toward the doors, having run by them faster than their eyes could even register. Lucien remembered that the Abaddons and their elite warriors, the Elementals, were all bio-mechanical beings, capable of seemingly supernatural feats.

Just before they reached the doors, they rumbled open, and Abaddon led them down a broad corridor. Lucien glanced over his shoulder and saw Korvas glowering at them from the foot of the landing ramp. He also noted that

Abaddon's horde of alien soldiers remained where they were, their aim not wavering from Korvas and his guards. Either they already had standing orders to remain with Korvas in the hangar, or Abaddon had somehow communicated his orders to them telepathically.

Lucien's gaze drifted back to the fore and he eyed the back of Abaddon's bald blue head, wondering how it was possible for him to be fighting himself as the leader of this separatist group. Supposedly the original Abaddon maintained control of his clones through the Forge, so how had this one escaped his notice? And if one of them could, then how many others had done so? It meant that finding and destroying the Forge might not actually kill them all as Etherus had indicated.

Abaddon stopped beside a small door near the end of the corridor. The door slid open and he gestured inside to what looked like a conference room. "Please, take your seats."

Addy nodded warily, and they followed her through the door. A long white table surrounded by black chairs sat under a gleaming, tentacled light fixture that was shaped like a...

Polypus.

Lucien blinked at the likeness of one of the extra-dimensional aliens. Addy and Garek both eyed it as they sat down near the head of the table. Lucien took a seat on the other side of Addy, while Brak remained standing by the doors.

Abaddon strode in, and the door swished shut behind him. He took a seat at the head of the table. Noticing their fixation on the light fixture, he nodded to it with a smile. "The seraphs are curious creatures, aren't they?"

Addy tore her gaze from the light fixture to look at him. "Yes... shall we begin with the negotiations?"

Abaddon arched an eyebrow at that, and his smooth blue scalp wrinkled briefly. A moment later he replied, speaking in Versal, not Faro: "First, why don't you start by telling me what three humans and a Gor are doing beyond the Red Line."

CHAPTER 22

The Lost Etherian Fleet

Admiral Wheeler watched Faro ships streaming through the wormhole while her fleet circled in front of them firing bright green lasers. The enemy ships fell one after another, cracking apart in fiery bursts of light, but they just kept coming.

Buzzing clouds of wedge-shaped Faro fighters streamed from the larger vessels as soon as they emerged from the wormhole. The destroyers in Wheeler's fleet flew headlong into those clouds, cannons blazing to keep them away from larger, more vulnerable battleships.

So far it was working, but with each new ship that emerged from the wormhole, the Faros' line advanced. As Wheeler watched, the Faros' lead ship explode, but two more took its place. They returned fire in tandem with missiles streaking from their bows and bright red laser beams stuttering out.

Their fire converged on a medium-sized destroyer—the *Allegiance,* and the faint blue glow of its shields suddenly vanished, replaced by gouts of escaping atmosphere as enemy lasers pierced its decks. Enemy missiles reached it next, flying *into* those holes. The *Allegiance's* hull bulged and it glowed brightly from every viewport and seam. Then a split second later, it flew apart and the light faded, leaving a dark cloud of debris drifting in its wake.

"Admiral, we've just lost the—"

"I know," Wheeler said curtly, cutting the sensor operator off. How many refugees had been crowded aboard that ship? How many more were going to die before this was over? She shook her head and gritted her teeth, watching as the enemy ships responsible for destroying the *Allegiance* both succumbed to answering fire from her fleet.

New Earth's reinforcements were a week away, but what about Etherus's ships? He supposedly had fleets tucked away somewhere, and he'd gone to speak with the Etherians about joining the fight. So where were they while her people were dying? And they weren't just dying the temporary deaths of people who knew they'd be resurrected in cloned bodies. These were real, permanent deaths. With the loss of the Resurrection Center on *Astralis,* none of the refugees or crews aboard her ships had backups of their minds or consciousness.

Wheeler scowled. "Comms, why didn't the *Allegiance* retreat as ordered?"

"They reported engine failure, ma'am. Enemy fighters must have scored a lucky hit."

"Let's try not to repeat that. From now on any ships whose shields drop below fifty percent are to rotate to the back of our lines."

"Right now, that's all of them," Colonel Drask put in before the comms officer could reply. "And we can't pull our destroyers and cruisers back without exposing our battleships to their fighters."

Wheeler checked the contacts panel from her control

station. Drask was right. The ships in their forward lines were all down below fifty percent shield strength, and as Drask had pointed out, they couldn't have those ships fall back, because the larger vessels hiding behind them weren't equipped to deal with enemy fighters and missiles.

She grimaced and shook her head. "So if we pull back our forward lines, their fighters will take out our battleships, but if we don't pull them back, they'll all be destroyed and then their fighters will take out our battleships, anyway."

"That's about the size of it, ma'am," Colonel Drask replied.

"They've lasted eight hours so far. Given current rates of shield drain, how long before all of their shields fail?"

"Not another eight hours, that's for sure," Colonel Drask said.

"The colonel is right, ma'am," the sensor officer said. "The enemy's numbers have been steadily growing and based on current trends... we've got about an hour before we lose most of the ships in our forward deployment. After that, it won't be long before we lose the rest of the fleet."

Wheeler nodded slowly. "Comms, try sending another distress call to Etheria and The Holy City. Message reads: Our defenses are failing. Reinforcements needed urgently. Please respond."

"Aye, ma'am. Contact established... message sent."

Wheeler waited, hoping that this time they'd receive a reply. Her gaze fell to the battle grid and she tracked the enemy fighters and capital ships still streaming from the wormhole.

As the minutes passed, the Faros lead ships fanned out to three abreast, all of them firing at once on another destroyer, the *Stalwart.* It's shields flickered, then failed, and fiery jets of atmosphere burst from its hull in a dozen different places. Crimson lasers continued to lash the ship even after its engines went dark. Then the destroyer's weapons stopped firing and the light went out of its viewports.

Wheeler's gaze slid to the battle report on one of her auxiliary displays. *Stalwart (Derelict)* appeared at the top of the list of friendly casualties, followed by *Allegiance (Destroyed),* and then the names of a hundred more ships, each of them also either derelict or destroyed.

"Comms, any reply yet?" Wheeler prompted.

"Not a peep from either The Holy City or Etheria, ma'am, but I am getting scattered reports from our ships' captains of riots breaking out aboard their ships. The refugees are demanding that we surrender."

"How do they even know that we're under attack?" Wheeler demanded. Without simulated visuals it would be impossible to directly observe the battle going on around them. Lasers were invisible in space, and even a kilometer-long battleship exploding would be hard to spot at the ranges from which this battle was being fought.

"Someone must have leaked the info," the comms officer suggested.

"Again," Wheeler replied, scowling.

"We need to find out who's leaking information to the refugees," Colonel Drask said from the gunnery station.

Wheeler nodded slowly. Even if the refugees aboard one ship found out about the battle, the news shouldn't have been able to spread from ship to ship and cause riots throughout the fleet. *How do they even know that surrender is an option?*

Someone had to have told them about the negotiations with the Faros, but those negotiations had been handled aboard *her* ship, the *Gideon.* Wheeler's eyes darted around the bridge, landing on each of her officers in turn. These were the only people who could possibly have leaked all of that information.

A deafening *boom* shook the bridge and smoke gushed from the recessed stairway leading down to the bridge doors.

Six Marine sergeants came clomping up the stairwell, fully armored, their pulse rifles up and tracking. Colonel Drask shot to his feet, his sidearm in hand before anyone else could react.

"Drop the weapon, sir!" one of the Marines ordered. "Nobody move!" another said.

Drask flashed a scowl and reluctantly dropped his weapon. "You'll all be executed for this," he gritted out.

Five of the six Marines stood off at a distance, their rifles trained on the other members of the crew, while the sixth went to retrieve Drask's weapon. He removed the weapon's power pack and slotted it into his belt; then nodded to the colonel and said, "Better that than that we all die at the hands of the Faros."

Drask gave no reply, and the sergeant moved on to remove the power packs from everyone else's sidearms.

"Who's your leader?" Wheeler demanded, her eyes still skipping around the bridge, landing on each of her officers in turn. These Marines had to be working with one of them.

The Marine sergeant disarming her crew gave no reply, but as soon as he removed the power pack from the last sidearm, he walked back over to Colonel Drask, and saluted smartly. "The bridge is secure, sir."

"At ease, Sergeant," Drask replied.

Wheeler watched the sergeant hand him one of the power packs, and Drask bent down to retrieve his weapon. He promptly re-loaded it and turned it on her.

"You!" she said. "*You* were the leak. You're behind all of the riots!"

Drask frowned. "I'm sorry it had to come to this. I hoped you would see reason on your own, but we're losing ships too quickly now. I can't allow you to sacrifice any more of our people in this last stand of yours. We're going to surrender to the Faros before anyone else has to die."

Wheeler sneered at her former first officer. "You don't have any authority to negotiate on our behalf, and the captains of the fleet will want to hear their orders from me. What are you going to tell them to make *them* stand down?"

"I don't have to tell them anything," Drask replied. "Surely you recall that the entire Etherian Fleet is slaved to the *Gideon*. We don't need the other captains to be complicit in this surrender for us to power down their weapons and shields. We can lock them out of their control stations from here, and by the time they find out how to bypass those protocols, the Faros will have enough ships through the wormhole that no one will even consider fighting back." Drask gave her a grim frown. "Now, please step away from your station, Admiral."

Wheeler's mind raced for a way to thwart this plot. If she triggered the *Gideon's* self-destruct and destroyed the ship, they'd have no way to control the rest of the fleet....

She turned to her station and hurriedly summoned the engineering panel. Her finger grazed the self-destruct button just as Drask physically hauled her out of her chair. A dialog popped up, asking for a confirmation code that she didn't have, anyway, and then Colonel Drask jabbed his sidearm into her ribs, and she winced.

"Nice try," he said.

He pulled the trigger, and a searing wave of pain shivered through Wheeler's body, causing her to lose all control of her muscles. She collapsed to the deck with her back arching painfully, all of the muscles spasming at once. A spreading wave of numbness came, and she watched with heavy eyelids and rapidly dimming eyes as Drask sat down at the command control station to accomplish his treachery.

Darkness swirled. Wheeler railed against it, trying desperately not to blink, but her eyelids sank shut of their own accord and stuck to each other like glue, trapping her in the infinite expanse of her own mind.

CHAPTER 23

Aboard the Etherian Ship, *Veritus*

"This is it!" Tyra said. "Gunnery?"

"Standing by, Captain."

"Engineering?"

"All systems green. Shields up and charged at one hundred percent."

"Good. Helm, execute jump."

"Aye, jump executing..."

The holo dome over the bridge flashed white, washing out the stars. Then the stars were back, along with something else—dead ahead was a glowing, translucent golden cube. A floating label above it identified it as *The Holy City*. Thin red lasers periodically leapt out around it, impacting on the translucent golden walls of the cube, causing them to ripple like water.

"Sensors, report!" Tyra said.

"Five vessels dead ahead. They're firing on the city."

"Helm, all ahead full!"

"Aye, Captain."

"Gunnery, open fire as soon as we're in range."

"Yes, ma'am."

"Sensors, can you get any readings from the city? How are their shields holding up?"

"Their shields at one hundred percent and holding steady, ma'am."

Tyra breathed out a sigh and nodded. "Good. This might turn out to be a fair fight, after all." They'd lost the last battle because the Faros had loaded their ships with fighters and missiles, and Tyra's ships had neither. But now with the Faros' fire focused on The Holy City, they'd have to choose between dropping its shields so they could get inside, or fighting back against Tyra's ships.

"We're in range! Weapons firing," the gunnery officer announced.

Tyra watched green lasers snap out from her ships and converge on the nearest Faro vessel. Its shields dropped steadily, but after just a few seconds, the Faros stopped firing on the city and came about to return fire. Their fighters banked away from the city forming in waves and flooding out to greet Tyra's ships.

"Helm, maintain our current acceleration. Fly us straight through the enemy formation and then circle back around the city for another pass."

"Aye, Captain."

"We're being hailed by the *Concordance,*" the comms officer announced.

Tyra nodded. "Patch them through to the holo dome." She wanted the whole crew listening this time.

Abaddon's head and shoulders appeared dead ahead, seeming to float among the stars. "You obviously didn't get the memo," he said. "Your fleet surrendered. Why are you still attacking us?"

Tyra snorted and shook her head, smiling at the obvious lie. "Admiral Wheeler would never surrender to you."

"Perhaps not, but she's not in command anymore. Colonel Drask is, and he's a far more... *enlightened* commander."

Tyra's smile faded and her gaze snapped to the comms station. "Contact the *Gideon* and ask for a tactical update."

"Aye, ma'am."

Abaddon smiled smugly. "I'll wait."

"If you're stalling..."

"I'm not."

"We'll see," Tyra said and then shut down the connection from her station.

A moment later, the comms officer replied: "It's true, ma'am. Admiral Wheeler has been forcibly removed from the bridge, and Colonel Drask is now in command. He has formally surrendered. The battle is over."

Tyra slumped in her chair, unable to believe it. There'd obviously been some kind of mutiny, but it was hard to believe that all of the captains would go along with it. Regardless, she was out of options. She couldn't fight a war on her own with just five ships.

"Weapons hold!" she said.

"Aye, weapons hold," the gunnery officer replied.

"Comms, hail the *Concordance* and put them back on the holo dome."

"Aye, Captain."

Abaddon's smiling face appeared once more. "I see you've come to your senses."

"Colonel Drask didn't leave me much of a choice. Let me guess, he's one of your agents?"

Abaddon's eyebrows floated up, and he shook his

head. "No, but he should be. Perhaps I'll recruit him and start a human branch in my fleet. Would you like to join it? We could use your help dropping the city's shields."

"Frek you."

"Aren't you curious what you'll find there? Don't you want to know what Etherus is?"

"I'm sure you'll be happy to tell us once you find out."

"*I* already know, but you're right, once I'm in control of the city I will open its gates so that everyone can come and see the truth for themselves."

"Good for you," Tyra replied. "And good luck with those shields." She glanced down at the battle grid and saw that The Holy City's shields were still registering at a hundred percent. "It looks like you won't be getting in anytime soon."

Abaddon waved a dismissive hand. "I only have five ships. When there's a trillion more here, those shields will fall in the blink of an eye."

Tyra smiled tightly. "I guess you'll just have to wait until then. Aren't Faro ships slower than Etherian vessels? It took us half a day to get here. Your fleet will take... what, three to five days to get here? Pity. The suspense must be killing you."

"On the contrary, I've waited billions of years for this. I can wait a few more days. Do let me know if you reconsider my offer."

With that, Abaddon vanished from the holo dome, leaving Tyra scowling into empty space.

"What are your orders, Captain?" Lieutenant Argos asked from the helm.

"Hold steady just outside of weapons and jamming range, and calculate a jump to a nearby system, but don't execute it yet. We're going to wait here for now."

"Wait for what, ma'am?"

For a miracle, she thought, but didn't say. Instead, she said, "You have your orders, Lieutenant."

"Aye, Captain."

"Comms, get my children back here. We're not at war anymore, so there's no danger to them."

"Yes, ma'am."

* * *

Meson One

"If you know we're not Faros, why didn't you expose us in front of Korvas?" Lucien asked.

Abaddon's gaze flicked to Lucien briefly before nodding to Addy. "Because Lord Korvas will be forced to abide by your decisions here until he realizes that you're not the negotiator he was waiting for, and by then it will be too late to stop us from getting what we want."

"And what do you want, exactly?" Lucien asked.

Abaddon tapped his chin, seeming to consider the question. "What do I want?" he asked, as if he were only thinking about it now for the first time. "It's hard to say. I want so many things... revenge would be nice, but unfortunately you can't help me with that."

"Revenge against Etherus?" Addy asked.

Abaddon's blue eyes glittered. "Perhaps."

"Korvas mentioned your demands. He said you want them to pay for the water they've taken and to return Meson One to its original orbit."

"Yes," Abaddon replied, nodding. "I'll take payment in the form of supplies for my fleet. Food, weapons—whatever they have aboard the Nexus."

"*That's* what this is about?" Addy asked. "Food?"

"An army marches on its stomach, as they say," Abaddon replied.

"Let's say we can convince Korvas to give you whatever supplies he has," Addy said. "But the Nexus and Meson One remain where they are, and the water keeps flowing. Does that sound like a reasonable compromise to you?"

"No," Abaddon replied. "I could take the supplies from the Nexus myself, and then return Meson One to its orbit and destroy the Nexus for good measure."

"So why haven't you?" Addy asked.

"I have my reasons."

"Then accept the compromise," Addy replied.

"Assuming you can get Korvas to agree..."

"We'll emphasize your point about simply taking the supplies and whatever else you want by force," Addy said. "I'm sure Korvas won't want to risk that."

"No, he won't," Abaddon agreed. "Let's say I agree. What do you get out of it? What are you all doing posing as Faros?"

"Well, in exchange for our help with these negotiations, we do want something for ourselves," Addy said.

Abaddon snorted and flashed a sly smile. "Negotiators negotiating on the side. How very Faro of you. Well, what is it that you want?" Abaddon asked.

"We need to know the location of the Forge," Lucien

said.

Abaddon's smile faded to a bemused frown. "That is common knowledge."

"It is?" Addy asked.

"Of course," Abaddon replied. "Every Faro knows where the Forge is. How else would they make the pilgrimage?"

"The pilgrimage?" Garek echoed, joining the conversation. "What's that?"

"When Faros come of age, they are required to visit the Forge, to study its secrets and learn the truth behind our exile."

"Well, if its location is not a secret, then you shouldn't mind revealing it," Addy said.

"I don't, but I am curious: what do you want with the Forge?"

"We want to destroy it," Lucien said. Addy shot him a sharp look, but he ignored it. "Can you help us?"

Abaddon barked a laugh. "I could, but why would I want to? If I destroy the Forge, then I'll die!"

Lucien nodded. "Etherus mentioned that, but you must have found a way to break free of the Forge, or else the original Abaddon would have used it to eliminate you already."

This Abaddon shook his head. "I've managed to insulate myself from an active purge, but my mind and body are still tied to the Forge. You can think of me like a computer virus that can't be deleted by ordinary means, but if the computer carrying it is destroyed... no more virus."

Addy frowned. "Then you won't help us?"

Abaddon shook his head. "No."

Garek stood up from the table. "If the location is common knowledge, we can just go ask someone else."

"Of course. Finding the Forge is easy, but good luck getting past its defenses. You'll need a fleet to do that."

"We have plenty of fleets, thanks," Garek replied.

"Ones that aren't already engaged with ours?" Abaddon asked.

Addy blew out a breath and planted her palms on the table. "Either you just like to gloat, or you're considering helping us. So which is it?"

Abaddon's gaze slid out from under hers and found Lucien once more. "There is one way that I'll agree to help."

"And that is?" Addy pressed.

"Allow me to transfer my mind to him," Abaddon replied. "If I'm allowed to do that before the Forge is destroyed, then I'll be safe."

Lucien felt the blood drain from his face. "And what happens to me?"

Addy placed a hand on his shoulder. "We'll make a copy of your mind." To Abaddon she said, "You have the means to do that?"

"No. All of our resurrections are conducted through the Forge, and there's a long waiting list. That's just another way that Abaddon maintains control over his people."

"You're a leader of a dissident group," Addy replied. "You're telling me you found a way to prevent Abaddon from actively killing you with the Forge, but not a way to copy your mind to a new body?"

"There are kill switches to prevent unscheduled transfers. They prevent us from *moving* the data in our minds from one body to another, but they don't stop us from copying the data to create a new simultaneous copy. The copies aren't tracked or tied to the Forge because they aren't dangerous; they have no authority in the Empire, and no rights. I'm afraid there's no way to save us both—unless you brought some kind of resurrection device with you?"

Lucien looked to Addy, but she shook her head.

"We weren't allowed to bring any human technology that might expose us," she explained.

"Can someone else stand-in for Lucien?" Garek asked.

"No. Etherus deliberately engineered Lucien's brain structure to make it identical to my own. Transferring my mind to anyone else would be like becoming a slightly different person, and I like myself just the way I am."

Lucien remembered that his daughter Atara was supposedly still infected with some part of Abaddon's mind, but her mind was also in there somewhere.

"So keep us both," he said. "We'll find a way to separate our minds later."

"There's no room for that. I'd have to make a partial transfer, leaving my memories behind in order to preserve yours."

Lucien's heart sank. That explained Atara. She didn't have Abaddon's memories, just his personality.

"There must be another way," Addy said.

"I'm afraid there isn't," Abaddon replied. "You *could* go looking for another rebel fleet, but I assure you mine is the only one strong enough to have any chance of destroying the Forge." He held Lucien's gaze, waiting for a reply, but Lucien's was too horrified to offer one.

He had a family, two girls, a wife... Addy. Abaddon nodded and looked away, as if he'd read Lucien's thoughts.

Speaking to Addy, he said, "Tell Korvas about our agreement. I expect supplies to begin arriving within the hour."

Addy nodded and slowly rose to her feet. Garek stood with her and both of them went over to the doors.

"Lucien?" Addy asked.

He'd remained seated where he was. "I'll do it," he said.

Abaddon's gaze shifted to him, looking mildly impressed. "One life to save trillions. You are a good mathematician."

"I have one condition," Lucien said.

"And that is?"

"Two actually."

"Very well."

"Allow me to stay alive until it's clear that the Forge *will* be destroyed. I don't want to die if I don't have to."

Abaddon inclined his head. "I can agree to that. And what is your second condition?"

"That when this is all over you find my daughter, Atara, and you release her."

"And she is... a captive of some kind?" Abaddon asked.

"One of your clones transferred himself to her without his memories," Lucien explained.

Abaddon's eyes widened and he nodded. "I see. Very well. I accept your terms. I will free her. You have my word."

For whatever that's worth, Lucien thought, rising to his feet now, too, and joining the others by the door.

"As soon as Korvas finishes transferring supplies to my fleet, I will find a way to send you rendezvous coordinates. Fly there in your shuttle. I will be waiting with my fleet, and we will leave for the Forge together."

Addy nodded, and Abaddon joined them by the door. He opened it and they followed him back down the corridor to the hangar.

Lucien's legs felt wooden, his entire body numb with dread at what he'd agreed to do.

He wasn't afraid of dying, but he was afraid of leaving his girls without a father, his wife without a husband, and Addy without a... Lucien stopped himself there.

Addy appeared beside him and slipped her hand into his. Her palm felt cold. He glanced at her and found tears shimmering in her glowing green Faro eyes—eyes that somehow looked more human now with tears shining in them.

"We'll find some other way," she whispered.

He shook his head. "There is no other way."

"What about the copy the medics made when they integrated you? They must have kept that data somewhere."

"It was data from the *other* Lucien, not both of us," he replied. "Which means the one you knew will still die." Lucien shook his head. "Besides, what are the odds that my data hasn't been overwritten with someone else's by now?"

A tear slid down Addy's cheek and she flung it away angrily. "You don't have to do this. You have a family to think about."

"And you," Lucien replied. Addy smiled wanly at that acknowledgment, and he went on, "That's exactly who I'm thinking about. If this works, at least I'll know that you and my family will be safe—not to mention everyone else."

Addy sniffled and scowled. "There has to be another way."

"There isn't."

"You'd better pull yourself together," Garek whispered gruffly. He pointed to the doors of the hangar looming ahead of them. "Korvas will get suspicious if he sees *Lady Tekasi* crying."

Addy nodded and wiped her eyes and cheeks with the heels of her hands, but Lucien could still see a sheen of moisture in her eyes.

"How do I look now?" she asked.

Garek grunted. "It'll have to do," he said as the hangar doors began rumbling open.

CHAPTER 24

Aboard the Etherian Ship, *Veritus*

—ONE WEEK LATER—

Tyra was on the bridge of the *Veritus,* pacing circles around the edge of the holo dome. Periodic flashes of light illuminated the deck, causing her to look up as straggling Faro fleets jumped in to join the trillions of ships already besieging The Holy City. They were running out of places to crowd in around the glowing cube. Dark, matte black specks were silhouetted against its golden sides in a dense cloud. Every couple of seconds, crimson lasers leapt out from those ships to converge on the center of their formation. Trillions of lasers all firing at once lit up the Faros' fleet like an angry red sun, blinking on and off, on and off.

Tyra stopped pacing long enough to catch her sensor operator's eye. "Lieutenant Asher—"

"Yes, ma'am?" the woman looked up, her blue eyes turning red with the glare of another salvo flashing out from the Faro fleet.

"How are the city's shields holding up?"

"Still at one hundred percent, ma'am."

"Incredible," Tyra breathed, shaking her head. "Let me know if there's any change."

"Aye, ma'am..."

Those were standing orders, but she had to keep checking, because she couldn't believe that the city's shields were actually holding steady under the combined assault of such a vast multitude.

Tyra went back to pacing the bridge.

Her five ships were standing off at a safe range of four million klicks, their quantum jamming fields engaged to make sure nothing snuck up on them, but the Faros were intent on their target, as oblivious to Tyra as an elephant to a flea.

The last she'd heard from the *Gideon* back at the wormhole, humanity's combined forces there were doing exactly the same thing. New Earth had arrived at the wormhole a day ago, and their reinforcing fleets were beginning to trickle in, but it no longer mattered. They were too late. The Faros were already through the wormhole. In fact, it no longer even seemed to matter whether or not the Faros could gain access to The Holy City. Who cared if they disabled the interdiction field now that they'd already crossed the Red Line?

One good thing had come from the arrival of their reinforcements, however: Colonel Drask had turned himself in, and Admiral Wheeler was back in command of the lost fleet. Apparently Drask had no personal interest in command, and he really had betrayed the admiral with all of the best intentions. *For whatever that's worth...* Tyra thought.

"Captain, we have an incoming transmission from... it's from Abaddon, but the signal appears to be coming from The Holy City," Lieutenant Teranik said from the comms.

"Play it for us, Lieutenant," Tyra said, and stopped pacing once more.

Abaddon's silky voice rippled out from hidden speakers, reverberating under the holo dome, and seeming to come from everywhere at once.

"Etherus, this is your last warning. If you don't surrender and drop your shields, we will hunt down and kill every human and alien inside the Red Line. You decide."

All the officers on the bridge looked up from their stations, and Tyra felt a sharp thrill of apprehension coursing through her veins. Her ships were first in line for the hunting. *I never should have brought my children back on board...* Tyra let out a breath and forced herself to focus, to think.

"That message was addressed to Etherus, not to us," Tyra said. "Teranik, you said it seemed to be coming from The Holy City?"

"Yes, ma'am," the comms officer replied.

Tyra nodded. "So this is Etherus repeating a message that was sent to him, for our benefit. He wants us to know that Abaddon is turning on us, just like he said he would."

"That may be, but it doesn't really help us, ma'am," Lieutenant Argos said from the helm. As her unofficial first officer, it was his job to challenge her ideas.

"That depends," Tyra replied.

"On what, ma'am?"

"On whether you think this is just Etherus saying *I told you so,* before we're all too dead to hear it, or if he actually thinks we still stand a chance of defeating the Faros. In the latter case, this is a warning for us to *run* while we still can.

"Execute our pre-calculated jump and start plotting a course back to the wormhole. It's time for us to join the rest of the fleet."

"Yes, ma'am," Argos replied. "Jump executing..."

The holo dome flashed white, and the pulsing crimson glow of the battle going on around The Holy City was replaced by crisp, steady white starlight.

Tyra strode over to her control station and sat down. It wouldn't be long before the Faros gave chase. With trillions of ships about to come looking for them, they couldn't hope to hide, but they could at least stand and fight with the rest of humanity's forces at the wormhole. Hopefully they could hold out until Lucien found the Forge—or until Etherus's reinforcements finally came.

The Etherians had supposedly left whole fleets of warships behind when they'd migrated to the other side of the universe, but they had yet to join the fight against the Faros, a fact which made Tyra doubt they ever would. They were safe on their side of the universe. They didn't need to fight. And maybe they would have volunteered to defend Etherus and The Holy City, but apparently he didn't need their help. His city was invincible.

If only the same could be said for New Earth, Tyra thought. Maybe Etherus will surrender to save us?

A skeptical thought countered that one: And after that the Faros will just leave us alone?

Tyra shook her head. That was one of the reasons Etherus had bounced Abaddon's message back to them: so they'd know what they were dealing with. If Abaddon were so keen to live and let live, he wouldn't be threatening to kill everyone if he didn't get what he wanted.

No, by sending them that message, Etherus was delivering a quiet warning: *you don't surrender to evil and expect mercy.*

"Exactly," a familiar voice said.

Tyra jumped and turned to see a luminous being standing at the top of the stairway leading off the bridge.

"Etherus?" she asked, wondering if it was really him. Why appear now, after more than a week of silence?

* * *

Aboard the Separatist Fleet

"It's been a week already! How much longer are we going to sit around here, doing nothing?" Garek asked, while pacing the living room floor. "Haven't you noticed that we're practically prisoners? We can't explore the ship freely. There are guards posted outside our door, and we've never once been allowed up to the bridge, so how do we know that *this* Abaddon is on our side, and that he's actually taking us where he says he is?" Garek stopped pacing long enough to fix them all with a scowl.

Lucien watched Garek from the couch in their living quarters aboard the *Redemption,* the largest of the Separatists' sixty-seven sphere ships. Lucien held Garek's gaze, noting the hardness around his eyes, and the tension in his scarred face—his real face. There was no point wearing their holo skins in private.

Addy was the first to reply to Garek's rant. "Abaddon told us we can't leave our quarters because he doesn't want his crew to find out who we are, or where we're going, in case there's a spy on board."

"How convenient," Garek replied. "Maybe when we arrive at the nearest Faro penal colony, you'll all realize that we've been duped."

"That's a pretty elaborate ruse," Lucien objected. "You're suggesting this Abaddon pretended to be a separatist leader just so that he could capture us? That would mean Korvas was in on it, too."

Garek shrugged eloquently.

"Why not simply kill us, then? Why bother capturing us?" Addy asked.

"I do not like the blue one. He smells wrong," Brak put in from where he sat in an armchair beside a broad viewport full of stars.

Lucien looked to him. "Wrong how?"

"Faros give off a sickly sweet odor. This one does not. He has no scent."

"The Abaddons are all bio-mechanical," Addy said. "I'm not surprised they don't have a scent."

"No," Brak said, shaking his skull-shaped head. The hood of his shadow robe was folded back behind him, revealing his face. "The other Abaddons we met all smelled sweet."

"But this one doesn't?" Addy pressed.

"Maybe he's wearing a deodorant," Lucien said with a small smile.

"Ha ha. You won't be laughing when the Faros kill us all in our sleep!" Garek said.

"So now they're trying to kill us? What happened to the penal colony?" Addy asked.

A knock came at the door, interrupting their conversation. They all turned to the sound and switched on their holo skins.

Lucien glanced at Brak. "Your hood," he whispered.

Brak hissed, but pulled the hood over his head,

concealing his features.

"Yes?" Lucien asked, now speaking in Faro rather than Versal.

"Your presence is requested on the bridge," someone said in a clacking voice that sounded like a bag full of marbles. Lucien recognized that voice as belonging to one of the orange, six-legged crab creatures Abaddon had left to guard their quarters.

"We'll be right there," Lucien replied. Rising from the couch, he nodded to Garek. "You ready to find out what's really going on?"

"Are you?" Garek challenged. "Even if I'm wrong, he's still going to kill *you,* remember?"

Lucien winced. "It'll be worth it."

"I hope you're right," Garek replied as they all walked up to the door.

Lucien keyed the door open to see one of the crab creatures standing there, peering up at them with four black eyes. An auto-cannon sat in a harness on its back, the barrel tracking restlessly back and forth.

The second guard skittered into view, its cannon also tracking. "Follow us," it said.

CHAPTER 25

The Lost Etherian Fleet

"Etherus, this is your last warning. If you don't surrender and drop your shields, we will hunt down and kill every human and alien inside the Red Line. You decide."

Admiral Wheeler glared up at the holo dome, waiting for some explanation from Etherus, but apparently that was the extent of the message. "That came from The Holy City?"

"Yes, ma'am," her comms officer replied.

"What are we supposed to do with that? Run?"

No one answered. Her new first officer, Major Calla Ward turned from the gunnery control station and shook her head. "If he doesn't surrender, then I think that's all we *can* do, ma'am."

"Then maybe he should surrender," Wheeler replied. But even as she said that, she knew peace with the Faros wouldn't last. They'd keep threatening humanity in an attempt to manipulate Etherus until they either got everything they wanted or lost contact with him. A brief flash of light suffused the bridge. Wheeler blinked and looked up, scanning the holo dome for some new arrival.

"Sensors, report! Was that one of our fleets jumping in, or one of theirs?"

"Neither," a familiar, resonant voice replied. Wheeler

shot up out of her chair and whirled around to see Etherus standing behind her, at the top of the stairs leading down to the ruined doors of the bridge.

"You," she said, her chest rising and falling quickly. "You have a lot of explaining to do. What happened to your reinforcements? They were supposed to help us hold the wormhole!"

Etherus shook his head. "I'm afraid you misunderstood. It was your job to hold the wormhole."

"Well, we failed. So now what? You've come to reprimand us for our failure?"

"No, I've come to rally your forces."

Wheeler narrowed her eyes. "For what?"

"The team you sent to find the Forge is about to reach it."

"How do you know? And why didn't they tell us?"

"Because they couldn't. No comms signals can get through the interdiction field, but I have my ways. You're going to have to trust me. They are about to arrive, and they have a fleet with them. The Forge will be destroyed, but only if you can keep the Faros pinned down here, inside the Red Line."

"How are we supposed to do that?" Wheeler demanded. "They outnumber us a million to one!"

"Fly through the wormhole, and hold it from the other side," Etherus replied. "You'll have the same advantage you had before Colonel Drask betrayed you, and this time all of your reinforcements are here. You don't have to win. You just need to buy time for the others."

Wheeler considered that. "So you're not going to surrender."

"Why surrender when you can win? Besides, my surrender would not save you. The Faros would threaten you again before long."

"All right, so why are you telling *me?* Tell the High Praetor, or the chief councilors of New Earth. They're in charge, not me."

"I *am* telling them," Etherus replied, and he looked pointedly to Wheeler's comms officer. "Lieutenant Sebal?" Etherus asked. "Don't you have something to share with the admiral?"

The comms officer was staring at Etherus, distracted by his sudden appearance, but he started when he realized Etherus was speaking to him, and his gaze slid away, back to his station.

"We're being hailed by *Halcyon...*" Lieutenant Sebal said slowly.

Halcyon was the capital facet of New Earth, its seat of government as well as the location of the High Praetor's citadel. "They're ordering us to fly through the wormhole and clear a path for the rest of the fleet."

Wheeler glanced at her comms officer and then back at Etherus.

"It's not over yet," he said, and with that, he faded from sight, vanishing into thin air just as he had appeared.

Wheeler whirled around to face Lieutenant Sebal. "Have our fleet make a line!" she ordered. "The fastest ships go through first."

"Aye, Admiral!"

"And get the *Halcyon* to dispatch a wing of fighters for us. I'd rather not go into battle without a fighter screen again."

"Yes, ma'am."

* * *

Aboard the Etherian Ship, *Veritus*

Tyra listened quietly to Etherus's speech. He'd instructed New Earth and its fleet to hold the wormhole again, but this time from the other side. Lucien was en route to the Forge, on his way to destroy it with whatever sympathetic forces he'd encountered beyond the Red Line.

"You knew this would happen," Tyra said.

Etherus cocked his head, and a small smile graced his lips. "Knew what would happen, Tyra?"

"You knew Colonel Drask would betray us. You wanted the Faros to cross the Red Line, so you could trap them inside and cut them off from defending the Forge."

Etherus inclined his head to that. "Yes."

Tyra frowned. "Why wait for a mutiny? Why not just tell us what to do?"

"The Faros had to believe your resistance and subsequent surrender was real, or else they would have seen the trap."

Tyra wasn't sure she agreed with that, but she decided not to argue about it. It was a waste of time to argue over what they could have done differently. "I guess you want us to join the rest of the fleet at the wormhole."

"No." Etherus shook his head, and suddenly he looked grim. "I want you to know that there's hope."

"What?" Tyra blinked, confused by the sudden change in his tone. "Why so fatalistic?"

"Because they're here," Etherus said, and with that, his presence faded from the bridge.

An alert chimed somewhere on the bridge, and Tyra spun around to see the holo dome flashing all around them with ships jumping in.

"Helm, get us out of here!"

Lieutenant Argos turned from his control station, his dark features drawn with grave lines and his indigo eyes wide with terror. "I can't. Their jamming fields are overlapping us on all sides. We're surrounded."

* * *

Aboard the Separatist Fleet

Lucien stepped through a pair of massive doors onto the bridge of the sphere ship. More crab-like guards swiveled to face them as they walked through. Dead ahead lay a vast, curving holoscreen, littered with windows and panels of data floating over a backdrop of stars. Abaddon sat in the center of the bridge, at what was apparently the only control station. His hands danced in the air in front of the screen, as if he were conducting a symphony. As he did so, the data rearranged itself, with some windows minimizing, and others appearing to take their place.

They approached his control station together, and Abaddon swiveled his chair to face them. "Good, you are here. We're just about to execute our final jump to reach the Forge."

Garek nodded to the curving holoscreen. "And what are we supposed to do? Stand here and watch?"

"If you like. I thought you might appreciate an update," Abaddon replied.

At that, the doors of the bridge slid shut, sealing them inside. Lucien turned and saw that the crab-like guards had stayed inside the doors. *Making sure I don't renege on my end of the deal?*

Looking away, Lucien nodded to Abaddon. "I'm ready."

"Good," Abaddon replied. "Executing jump..."

The stars on the holoscreen flashed white, and when they returned, Lucien saw a luminous, translucent golden cube in the center of the display. "Is that the Forge?" he asked, pointing to it.

"Yes," Abaddon replied. He waved his hands at the holoscreen, and suddenly the stars and the Forge were crowded out by thousands of pairs of red brackets, each one denoting the location of an enemy ship.

"That's a large fleet..." Addy said.

"Those are just the ships in range of us," Abaddon replied. He waved his hands again, and suddenly it was hard to see through all of the red. "That's *all* of them."

"There must be tens of thousands of them!" Garek said. "You only have sixty-seven ships. There's no way we can win this."

"Sixty-seven very large ships, plus supporting vessels," Abaddon corrected.

The bracket pairs diminished in number, once again focusing only on the ones in range of their guns. A second later, hundreds of bright blue lasers shot out to all sides, vectoring in on three of the enemy ships.

Those ships answered, firing back with an equal

number of *red* lasers. Lucien blinked against the glare and watched tiny clouds of silver specks swarm out toward the enemy fleet—*friendly fighter squadrons,* he realized—followed by larger supporting vessels.

The battle is on, Lucien thought. "We should call for reinforcements from our people," he said, turning to Abaddon. "How far are we from the Red Line?"

"Close enough, but comms can't penetrate the Red Line," Abaddon replied.

"Right." Lucien grimaced, remembering that restriction.

"We might have ships waiting outside the Red Line to hear us," Garek said. "We have to at least *try* contacting them."

"Even if you do make contact, they'll never arrive in time to help us. It took us a week to get here, and my vessels can calculate quantum jumps a lot faster than most of yours."

"The Lost Fleet is fast enough to make it here," Addy said.

"The lost...?"

"A fleet of a thousand Etherian ships we found out here in Farosien space."

"Aha," Abaddon replied.

"They can calculate a billion light years per day," Addy said.

"Then they'll still arrive in a week," Abaddon replied. "They are no faster than my ships. By then this battle will already be decided one way or the other."

Lucien fidgeted, his hands clenching and un-clenching with restless energy as he watched the battle unfold. Their fighters met the enemy's fighters and lit up the void with needle-thin lasers and streaking missiles. Thumb-sized explosions flowered, peppering the darkness with fire.

"There has to be something we can do," Garek said.

"There is," Abaddon replied. "You can let me concentrate."

CHAPTER 26

Aboard the Etherian Ship, *Veritus*

"What do you think you are doing?" Tyra demanded. "We surrendered."

"Drop your shields and power down your engines," Abaddon replied. His glowing blue gaze was sharp and filled with deadly intent.

"What for?" Tyra asked, still playing dumb.

"We're coming aboard. You and your crew are now prisoners of war," he replied, his teeth flashing white in a predatory sneer.

"If you don't honor our surrender, my people will fight to the death."

Abaddon shrugged. "That will save me the trouble of executing them."

Tyra bristled. "Is that what we can look forward to if we stand down and allow ourselves to be captured? Execution?"

"That depends on your god. He can either save you, or he can save himself and his precious city. Now lower your shields, or we'll lower them for you."

Tyra considered letting Abaddon make good on that threat, but it was too risky. Her ships were badly outnumbered, and too many people would die in the fighting.

"What guarantees do we have that you won't simply kill us, anyway?"

"None, but you have my guarantee that you will die much sooner if you don't surrender now. I'll make an example of your ship and destroy it."

Tyra took a deep breath. "Very well. We'll lower our shields."

Abaddon smiled. "I'm glad to hear that. I'll see you soon."

With that, his face disappeared from the holo dome, and Tyra dropped her gaze to address her crew. All of them were already looking to her, their eyes wide and expressions uncertain.

"Engineering—drop our shields. Helm, kill the engines."

"Aye, ma'am..." Lieutenant Argos reluctantly replied from the helm. Shades of his reluctance were mirrored on each of the other crew member's faces.

Tyra met each of their gazes in turn. "Etherus told us there's hope, that all we have to do is buy time. So let's do that, and let's hold onto that hope. I don't think these Faros know yet that the Forge is in danger. No signals can get through the interdiction field, so unless new ships come through the wormhole carrying news of the assault with them, the Faros' entire fleet will remain oblivious to the threat. The longer it takes for news to reach them, the longer our fleet will have to get through the wormhole and defend it from the other side."

Heads bobbed, and a few officers murmured their agreement, but Lieutenant Teranik wasn't so easily convinced. She spoke up from the comms station: "What if

Abaddon starts executing us to prove his intentions to Etherus? None of us have resurrection data anymore. We won't be coming back if we die."

"Discussing options here is pointless. We don't actually have a choice," Lieutenant Argos said quietly from the helm. "You heard him. We either allow ourselves to be captured and hope Abaddon takes his time executing us, or he'll destroy the *Veritus* now, and we'll all die anyway. We have to trust that Etherus has a plan. Maybe he can resurrect us from our souls?"

Tyra grimaced. That was a long shot, and she still wasn't convinced that they even had souls. "We should all be there to greet the Faros when they come aboard." Nodding to the ship's sensor operator, she went on, "Figure out which hangar they're headed for and get ready to meet them there."

"Aye, ma'am."

"Lieutenant Argos you have the conn. I'm going to see my children. Let me know which hangar to meet you all in."

"Aye," Argos replied from the helm.

Tyra turned and strode for the stairs leading down from the bridge. She now regretted her decision to recall Brak with her children. They would have been far better off staying in hiding with him aboard that shuttle.

Regret is a hole in the head, she thought. Hindsight wasn't going to do her any good now. Maybe she could hide them away somewhere on board the ship so that the Faros wouldn't find them.

Tyra nodded to herself as she breezed through the doors of the bridge. At this point that was their best chance, but if Atara really was still infected with Abaddon's consciousness, then she might give away their hiding place.

She'd have to split her children up and take Atara with her to meet the Faros, but then Atara would know that Theola and Brak were missing, and she'd give *them* away.

Tyra's heart felt heavy as she left the bridge. Surely Etherus wouldn't allow her children to be executed by the Faros. He *had to* have some larger plan in all of this, some way to prevent the loss of innocent life.

Despite her lifelong skepticism toward humanity's benevolent ruler, Tyra now found herself hoping and praying that he really was the deity he claimed to be, because only a real god could save them now.

* * *

The Lost Etherian Fleet

Admiral Wheeler's ship was one of the first in her fleet to go through the wormhole, since she couldn't command the fleet without at least being in comms contact. Fortunately, the other side of the wormhole remained clear until the first hundred of her ships were through. *Unfortunately,* the first Faro fleet that arrived on approach to the wormhole had more than twice as many ships as her own.

The Faros barreled on toward her, unconcerned by Admiral Wheeler's presence, but as more of her ships piled through the wormhole, adding to her numbers and tipping the balance of power in her favor, her comms panel lit up with an incoming message.

"We're being hailed, Admiral," Roth Sebal announced from the comms.

"I see it. Put it up on the holo dome." Wheeler replied.

One of the Abaddon clones appeared. "I was told that you had surrendered," he said.

"Strange..." Wheeler replied, shaking her head. "That doesn't sound like something *I* would do."

"You are blocking our way. Either you move your vessels, or they will be destroyed."

"May I suggest a third course of action?" Wheeler asked.

"And that would be?"

"Go frek yourself."

Abaddon's eyes flashed, and Wheeler abruptly ended the connection from her end. A self-satisfied smirk graced her lips, and she nodded to her new first officer and gunnery chief, Major Calla Ward. "Ready weapons," she said.

"Aye," Ward replied. "Standing by to reach firing range."

It took fully half an hour for the two fleets to reach weapons range, by which point Wheeler had almost all of her ships through the wormhole.

Now the Faros were badly outnumbered. She watched their ships explode one after another on the battle grid as lasers and missiles streaked between the two fleets. Her ships' shields were far stronger, and this time she had a fighter screen, so she was able to rotate the smaller vessels behind her lines when their shields weakened.

At some point the Faros' strategy changed from fighting a war of attrition to making a suicide run through her formation to get to the wormhole.

"What are they doing?" Wheeler wondered aloud, shaking her head. Even if they got through to the other side, they'd just be destroyed by New Earth's facets and fleet. They had to know that, so why were they making a mad dash for the wormhole?

The Faro ships raced ahead at full throttle, heedless of the fact that they were outnumbered and flying ever deeper into her formation. She watched her battleships and dreadnoughts cut down six ships simultaneously while another ten raced by, just seconds from reaching the wormhole.

Then, suddenly, Wheeler realized what they were after: they must have learned about the threat to the Forge, and now they wanted to cross the wormhole so that they could get a message through to the rest of their fleet and call for reinforcements.

"Concentrate fire on the lead ships!" Wheeler said. "We don't want any of them getting through."

Even if they did, it would still take the Faros' fleet half a day to get back from the Holy City, and by then all of New Earth's forces would be through. It would be too late to stop them from bottling the Faros inside the Red Line.

Admiral Wheeler gave a predatory smile, watching as the lead ships in the enemy fleet were cut down before they could enter the wormhole.

"Nice try," she murmured.

"Admiral, we're being hailed by the *Derringer,*" Lieutenant Sebal said from the comms.

"One of ours...?" Wheeler asked, already scanning her displays to locate the ship.

"Yes, ma'am."

"Patch them through to the holo dome."

"Aye."

A split second later, a harried looking man appeared,

wearing a black with white trim Captain's uniform. "Yes?"

"Admiral, we have an urgent message from the *Halcyon.* The facets of New Earth can't cross the wormhole. The throat is too narrow."

Wheeler felt her eyes widen with that revelation. There were half a million facets, and each of them was home to hundreds of millions of people. If they couldn't get them to safety, this entire plan was bust. Surely Etherus didn't mean for them to leave all of their civilians at Abaddon's mercy in order to keep the Faros from sending their fleets to defend the Forge...

"Have they tried contacting Etherus?"

"They're working on it, but there's been no reply, and there is some concern that the Faros will eavesdrop on our comms. If they do..."

"They might find out what we're up to and come running to stop us," Wheeler supplied.

The captain of the *Derringer* nodded.

Wheeler shook her head. "It doesn't matter if they find out. They're half a day from the wormhole and the Red Line, and besides, if Etherus drops the interdiction field for us, we can jump our entire fleet across in a matter of seconds, facets and all."

"Surely Etherus already knows that," the captain of the *Derringer* replied.

"Surely..." Wheeler agreed. *So why hasn't he dropped the interdiction field? Or appeared again to tell us he's about to do so?* A moment later, she answered her own question. "If he drops the interdiction field now, the Faros inside the Red Line will find out that the Forge is under attack, and they'll all come running. He's trying to buy us some extra time."

The captain of the *Derringer* nodded. "That's what the High Praetor suggested."

"Timing is everything. We have to trust that Etherus will drop the interdiction field when the timing is right."

"Yes, ma'am."

A flash of light drew Wheeler's gaze back to the battle grid, and she saw another Faro fleet appear to reinforce the last one. This time Wheeler's fleet was outnumbered. She looked back up to the holo dome with a grimace and said, "Form up, Captain. We've got company."

"Aye, Admiral," he replied.

CHAPTER 27

Aboard the Etherian Ship, *Veritus*

Tyra stood with her entire ship's crew in the *Veritus's* starboard amidships hangar bay, watching as a procession of just three Faros approached. One of them wore gray robes and a glowing golden crown, marking him as one of the Abaddons, while the other two sported bald blue heads and black robes. *Elementals,* Tyra decided with an accompanying frown. They'd boarded her ship with just *three* Faros to take more than a hundred humans prisoner. This was yet another symptom of the Faros' arrogance.

As per Tyra's orders, none of her crew were armed, which was a good thing, since someone might have taken the fact that they outnumbered the Faros so badly as an invitation to resist. Even bare-handed as they were, that was a risk, Tyra realized, as she glanced around at the belligerent expressions on the faces of the officers and Marines standing behind her.

"Is this all of you?" Abaddon asked, stopping in front of Tyra. His glowing blue eyes tracked through the crowd, as if performing a head count.

Tyra forced herself to breathe normally and keep her expression neutral. Despite her concern that Atara might still be infected with Abaddon's consciousness, she'd instructed Brak to hide with her children in one of the *Veritus's* storage rooms. So no, technically this wasn't *all* of them.

Abaddon's gaze landed on Tyra, and he cocked his head curiously. "Your entire crew is here?" he asked again.

Tyra nodded. "Yes."

Abaddon smiled. "Then why am I detecting three life signs below decks?"

"What? What are you talking about?" Tyra struggled not to stammer as her heart jumped in her chest with a painful stab of adrenaline.

Abaddon's gaze appeared to drift out of focus. "Two children and a... non-human," he decided, nodding to himself. "Your children and their guardian, I presume?"

Tyra said nothing to that, but the assembled crew shuffled their feat uneasily at the mention of her children. Tyra's mind raced to come up with a way out.

Abaddon turned and nodded to the Elemental standing to his right. "Go fetch them. If the non-human gives you trouble, kill him."

The Elemental nodded and started toward the nearest set of doors leading out of the hangar. As he went, the Faro drew a transparent blade from a scabbard on his back. A split second later it began humming and shimmering with an energy field. Tyra imagined Brak being cut in half by that blade as he tried to defend her children, and she winced.

"Wait!" she said.

"Halt," Abaddon called out. He smiled and raised hairless eyebrows. "Yes?"

"I'll call them up here," Tyra said. "No one has to die."

"Very well, but I'm afraid you are wrong. Someone definitely needs to die."

Tyra scowled. "If you're trying to convince us that

Etherus is the enemy and you're the misunderstood villain, you should probably stop threatening to kill people."

Abaddon's eyes appeared to dance with amusement. "Who is worse: the one who does something evil, or the one who could stop it from happening, but chooses not to?"

Tyra set her jaw and shook her head. "Etherus will stop you."

"Yes, I used to think that, too, but after committing the first few trillion murders, and taking quadrillions of slaves, one begins to doubt such things."

"You're doing it to yourselves," Tyra said, hoping Etherus's arguments for his inaction would put a dent in Abaddon's smug exterior. "You don't have souls. All of the beings you've enslaved are just empty copies of the original Faros' minds."

"I see you've been schooled in the latest dogma," Abaddon replied, smiling. "Let's say that's all true. Even if souls do exist, what difference do they make? Clone yourself and your mind a dozen times, then ask each of your clones if they think they're alive and free to make their own choices, and they'll all say that they are. Then kill the clones that you gave life to, and when you're done, won't you have committed twelve counts of murder? Or is it somehow acceptable for you to kill them because you were only killing yourself?"

Tyra frowned and shook her head, unnerved by that argument.

"Won't all twelve clones beg for their lives if they are given the chance?" Abaddon pressed. "Won't they scream and cry if you torture them?"

"They're like computers. Programs scripted to behave

a certain way..." Tyra replied, but even as she said that, she doubted the truth of what she was saying.

"You are a scientist," Abaddon said, nodding to her. "You believe in observable evidence. What is the observable difference between a being with a soul and one without? I know there have been experiments."

"People's clones behaved more predictably, in more deterministic ways than the original people. That unpredictability is attributed to souls," Tyra said.

"Exactly," Abaddon replied. "But if souls do exist, aren't they subject to their own higher-order version of deterministic forces? How is that any different? What is it that supposedly makes the soulful alive and the soulless dead?"

Tyra fumbled for a response, but she couldn't hope to answer those arguments without knowing exactly what souls were and how they gave people a free will.

"Food for thought, isn't it? Now enough stalling," Abaddon said, waving his hand imperiously. "Get your children up here. We have a shuttle to catch." He gestured to the ship they'd come in on, a medium-sized, matte black vessel.

Tyra grimaced and got on the comms to contact Brak. She told him to come to the hangar bay and warned him not to resist capture.

When she was done, Abaddon nodded and gestured to his Elementals. "Get the others on board."

Wordlessly the two black-robed Faros moved through the crowd, ushering everyone toward the transport. A few officers shuffled forward a few steps, but they were all obviously dragging their feet.

Tyra wondered how just two Faros were going to

compel compliance from her crew, but then they began gesturing to the stragglers, and invisible forces seemed to take hold of them, shoving them forward and drawing exclamations of shock from their lips.

When Tyra failed to follow the Elementals' directions, something invisible punched her between her shoulder blades, shoving her toward the Faros' ship. She stumbled and almost fell, but managed to avoid crying out in pain. She refused to give them the satisfaction.

They must have some kind of grav guns in their palms, she realized as she and her crew began a very literal *forced march* toward the Faros' shuttle. She thought of her children receiving similarly rough treatment, and felt a burst of rage building inside of her, goading her to action. She calmed herself thinking that Brak would probably pick Theola up, and Atara was technically one of the Faros, so she probably wouldn't mind walking on her own.

Tyra followed her crew up the shuttle's landing ramp into a cavernous space with bench seats along the sides. The Elementals moved between them effortlessly, pushing some people down onto the benches, and leaving others to stand. Tyra was one of the ones left standing. By the time everyone was inside, there was barely room to breathe, let alone to sit. The Elementals went to guard the top of the landing ramp and wait, their glowing eyes—yellow and orange—scanning the group with cold contempt.

The minutes trickled slowly by with the crew murmuring amongst themselves, passing nervous questions back and forth: What's going to happen now? Will Etherus save us? Who are they going to execute first?

The tension and fear in the room was palpable,

radiating from person to person in hot, noxious waves. Or maybe that was just their sweat.

Tyra refused to join the speculation. Her gaze remained fixed on the exit and the landing ramp, waiting for her children to arrive with Brak. Abaddon hadn't come in yet, so he was obviously waiting for them, too....

The thought of leaving him alone with her daughters, even with Brak to watch over them, was more than Tyra could take. Tyra pushed through the crowd, stepping on toes and elbowing her officers in the ribs to get back to the landing ramp.

"Ouch!" Lieutenant Argos said, his eyes flashing as she stepped on his foot. Then he appeared to notice that it was her, and his expression softened. "Captain? Is something wrong?"

She shook her head, her heart pounding and palms sweating. "I need to be there when my children arrive. I can't leave them alone out there with that... *thing.*"

Argos nodded and stepped aside. "Make way for the captain!" he called out.

Everyone turned and Tyra offered a grim smile, hoping they couldn't see how badly she was losing it. After a moment's hesitation, her crew began stepping on each other's toes to get out of her way, and Tyra pressed forward until she reached the top of the ramp. There one of the Elementals planted a palm on her chest and shoved her back a step, but Tyra barely noticed. Her gaze was fixed on the spot where Abaddon stood with her two daughters and Brak in the hangar below. She sucked in a hurried breath, and grimaced.

She should have known to expect something like this, but *seeing* the evidence with her own eyes was far more visceral than any verbal warning.

Brak stood a few steps away from Abaddon, shielding Theola hiding behind his legs. Atara stood in front of them, a mere arm's length from the Faro king, her back straight and a *reverent* expression on her face.

She'd had dropped the act. The five-year-old human child was gone, leaving nothing but a dutiful Faro soldier in her place.

CHAPTER 28

Aboard the Separatist Fleet

Lucien watched the battle play out from the bridge of the separatist sphere ship. There was no way for him to gauge who was winning, but ships in the Faros' defense fleet were exploding left and right, and so far the separatists had only lost one of their sixty-seven sphere ships.

"Who's winning?" Addy asked from where she was sitting on the deck, near the back of the bridge with Garek and Brak. Her voice held a note of apprehension, but her expression had lost most of its urgency. It had been almost three hours since they'd arrived at the Forge, and the battle had still barely begun. When Abaddon didn't immediately reply, Addy glanced behind her, to the exit and the crab-creatures guarding it. Turning back to the fore, she went on, "I hate to interrupt your concentration with mundane concerns, but we could use a break."

Lucien nodded at that. His stomach was aching with hunger, and his mouth was dry. This battle looked like it could be raging for days, and as much as he wanted to stick around to track every laser beam and missile, they weren't actually doing anything useful on the bridge.

"Abaddon?" Lucien prompted.

The alien's gaze was fixed on the holoscreen in front of

him. His glowing blue eyes were unblinking, his hands swiping furiously through the air to manipulate the display.

"Guards—take these four to the mess hall," he finally said.

One of the crab creatures replied in its bag-of-marbles voice: "Yes, master."

The bridge doors rumbled open and both creatures scuttled aside. Lucien walked up to them and the others joined him from the back of the bridge. One of the guards led the way, while the other waited until they were all through the doors before scuttling after them.

As soon as the doors rumbled shut behind them, Garek spoke up: "He never answered the question—about who's winning."

"Do you think it's because we're losing?" Addy asked.

Lucien frowned and shook his head. "I'm not sure we need to worry about that. Separatist or not, Abaddon isn't capable of sacrificing himself for a higher purpose. He'll retreat long before it comes to that."

"Leaving us back where we started, with all of humanity in danger," Garek pointed out.

"True," Lucien said. "But my point was, if we were losing, I think Abaddon would already be withdrawing from the fight. The fact that we're still fighting means there's at least a chance we'll win."

Garek nodded, and Addy let out a tremulous sigh. She glanced at him and bit her lip. "I don't know what to hope for. If we win, you die, if we lose... everyone else dies."

"Maybe not. The Faros wouldn't wipe out an entire species just because they can. They'd probably make slaves out of most of us."

"Doesn't sound any better to me," Garek replied.

"Slavery isss death," Brak agreed, hissing loudly. "Better to die free than to live a ssslave."

Lucien frowned, unable to agree. Better that humanity live to find some other way to defeat the Faros.

They followed the guard scuttling in front of them into an elevator. The one behind them squeezed in, stepping on Lucien's foot with a surprisingly heavy leg. He winced, and withdrew to the corner of the elevator as it dropped through the ship. Lights from passing decks strobed rapidly through the windows in the doors of the elevator. They must have passed at least a hundred floors before the elevator slowed to a stop and the doors parted once more.

They walked out into a giant room, filled with food stands and various kinds of adaptable seating scattered in-between. Every kind of alien imaginable crowded the space, from lumbering four-legged beasts of burden to two-legged humanoids, flying avian species, and hopping amphibians—even some kind of floating balloon-like creatures.

"Wow..." Addy breathed, her eyes skipping around the room.

Lucien nodded slowly. It reminded him of the mess hall on Freedom Station, where they'd met the Marauders, all runaway Faro slaves. Back then, in a mess hall not unlike this one, Oorgurak, the green-skinned Faro had first explained to them about the significance of The Holy City, the Forge, and the other side of the universe—although apparently not even he had known that the other side of the universe was made of *antimatter*.

Garek glanced down at the nearest of the crab-like guards who'd brought them here. "How do we know what's safe for us to eat?"

"If you do not know, how am I supposed to know?" the creature replied, membranes nictating over its upper two eyes, and then over its bottom two.

"Never mind. We'll risk it," Garek muttered, and started toward the nearest food stand. Lucien followed him there, with Addy walking along beside him. The aromas and odors wafting through the mess hall were overwhelming and confusing—some appetizing, others nauseating.

Lucien walked around the food stand Garek had chosen, sniffing at the colorful, steaming platters of food behind the serving counter. It was impossible to know what to order from sight and smell alone, but Lucien was determined not to make a mistake with what might be his last meal.

"What would you recommend for us?" Lucien asked the tan-colored reptilian behind this particular stand. Three bright pink eyes turned to them. The creature cocked its head, as if considering the question. Abruptly, a long pink tongue darted out of the creature's mouth, licking Lucien's lips.

Lucien jumped back a step, wiping his mouth on his sleeve with a wrinkled nose. He was about to give the lizard creature a piece of his mind when he noticed it was smacking its lips, sampling the flavor of something—*of me,* Lucien thought.

The creature spoke in a gravelly voice: "G'hartan root and roast dekku."

Lucien nodded slowly. "One order of that, please..."

Addy walked up beside him. "Make that two orders," she said.

The tan-colored reptile nodded and fetched two empty

platters in its upper two arms. Using its lower two, it scooped out pink chunks of what must be the *g'hartan root* before turning aside to retrieve two skewers of blackened meat from a sizzling grill. He passed both platters over the counter and then asked, "For drinking?"

"Water," Lucien said, not willing to take a risk on exotic food *and* beverages.

Addy nodded. "For me, too, please."

The lizard passed two metal cups of water over the counter and then Lucien and Addy went to take their seats on a nearby bench under a red-flowering green-leafed tree.

They weren't given any utensils, but Lucien was too hungry to care. He ate with his hands, stuffing the g'hartan root into his mouth in greedy handfuls, and biting off chunks of dekku from his skewer. The food was surprisingly delicious.

"Not bad for a last meal," Lucien said, washing it down with a swig of water.

Addy glared at him. "How can you be so blasé about your own death?"

Lucien snorted and shook his head. "I'm not, but if I don't make light of it, I'm afraid I'll lose my nerve."

Addy abruptly stood. "I need to use the restroom." And with that, she left.

"Me, too..." Lucien replied, but she was already striding away. He cast about for a place to deposit his leftover food, but before he could identify a waste-receptacle or locate a kitchen patrol bot (assuming these Separatists even had such a thing), a giant bird swooped down and landed in front of him. Standing on the deck, it was at least four feet tall, and its wingspan must have been twelve feet or more. It had short black fur all over its body, as opposed to feathers. The furry black bird spent a moment cocking its head at them. It had a sharp-looking beak, but also a mouth full of needle-sharp teeth sitting below that.

Glittering green eyes blinked at Lucien, and two long, spindly arms unfolded from its wings, reaching tentatively for Lucien's plate. "May I?" it asked in a fluty voice.

Lucien blinked, surprised that it could speak Faro. His brow furrowed with bemusement as he tracked its gaze to the leftovers on his and Addy's platters. "If you want, sure, but why don't you—"

The bird creature snatched his platter and began shoveling food into the mouth below its beak.

Lucien watched the alien eat, wondering why it didn't just get its own food. They hadn't been charged for anything they'd ordered, but maybe this creature's job was to help with clean-up? *And the way it does that is to eat the leftovers.*

Lucien looked away and spent a moment scanning the far walls of the mess hall for doors or markings to suggest where the restrooms were. He spied some glowing signs with suggestive symbols on them and headed that way. Once he arrived at those doors, he could see that he'd guessed right. As further confirmation, he ran into Addy on her way out of the door labeled *Female Humanoids.* She walked right by him as if she hadn't seen him. Lucien stopped and turned to watch her go, wondering if he should go after her.

They shouldn't split up on a ship this big with so many different aliens milling about—who knew what kind of trouble they could accidentally get themselves into?

But Lucien's bladder gave a painful stab, reminding him of more urgent matters. He winced and turned to enter the restroom marked *Male Humanoids.* The door swished open as he stepped up to it—

And a noxious cloud of fumes gushed out. He turned aside and sucked in a desperate breath before entering the restroom. Hurrying through the open door, he found a likely-looking row of dish-shaped urinals and emptied his bladder as fast as he could. Unfortunately, he ran out of air before he was done. A series of violent explosions issued from one of the stalls behind him just as he was forced to suck in another breath. His stomach heaved with the smell and his head spun.

As soon as he was finished, Lucien left the room at a run, not bothering to stop and wash his hands.

There's worse fates than death, he realized, as he stumbled out into the mess hall, gasping for air. Smiling ruefully to himself, he scanned the hall's tables, benches, chairs, and padded floor mats for Addy and the others.

While he searched for them, cold fear trickled in, stealing the smile from his lips.

Death was so final, so desperately hopeless and empty. Whenever he tried to picture it, he imagined the empty blackness lurking behind his eyelids just before he fell asleep at night—except that this sleep would be dreamless, and there'd be no waking from it.

Lucien shivered and shook himself, forcing his thoughts in a new direction. *At least my family will be safe,* he thought, picturing Theola's gap-toothed baby smile, and Atara's bright green eyes. *That's all that matters.*

There'd been a time in human history when the only form of immortality anyone could hope for had been for their genes to live on through their children, and maybe also, if they believed in such a thing, the hope that some immaterial part of them would live on after death.

Lucien's mind flashed back to the Polypuses, and he nodded slowly to himself. Maybe Garek was right. Maybe the Polypuses were souls, and maybe some part of him would live on as one of them. There were thinner hopes that a person could cling to.

Unable to spot his crew mates from the restrooms, Lucien began walking around the mess hall, searching for them, but the room was too big and too busy with milling crowds of aliens. Everywhere he looked, exotic aliens blurred together in a kaleidoscope of color and sound.

Then a strident voice came booming through the hall, drawing Lucien's gaze up to the distant ceiling. He noticed dozens of black-furred avians circling up there, waiting to finish off peoples left-overs. The noise in the mess hall quieted somewhat as others stopped what they were doing to listen.

After a few seconds, Lucien recognized the voice. It was Abaddon. Then he heard his name, followed by Addy's, Garek's, and Brak's. They were being summoned back to the bridge to deal with some 'urgent' new development.

Lucien's heart raced and his mind spun through possibilities: maybe they were losing; maybe Abaddon wanted them to see that for themselves before he gave the order to retreat.

To his chagrin, Lucien felt a spark of hope that that might be the case. He was looking for an excuse not to sacrifice himself.

The corners of Lucien's mouth turned down and he shook his head, pushing those feelings aside. He refused to hope for that outcome. Better that he should die so that everyone else could live. That was the only outcome worth hoping for at this point.

CHAPTER 29

The Lost Etherian Fleet

"Shields at nine percent!" the chief engineer announced. "I need to divert power from weapons or they're going to fail."

"Not yet. We need those guns!" Admiral Wheeler replied, watching on the grid as more than a hundred Faro capital ships and thousands of accompanying fighters barreled on, guns blazing in a solid wall of slashing red lasers.

She'd already lost two thirds of her original fleet, refugees and all. Since then thousands of star galleons had come through to support her on this side of the wormhole, but every one of the Etherian ships in Wheeler's fleet was worth at least a hundred galleons. Unfortunately, New Earth's forces weren't adding much to the fight, and to make matters worse, the Faros' straggling fleets just kept jumping in. Now they had upwards of twenty thousand ships headed for the wormhole.

"Admiral..." Her XO, Major Ward, caught her eye from the gunnery control station.

"Something on your mind, Major?"

"We're going to lose our entire fleet trying to make sure nothing gets through the wormhole. I say, if they want to get through, then let them. At least we'll have fewer ships to deal with on this end. We've got more than enough firepower on the other side to take care of whatever vessels slip through."

Wheeler chewed her bottom lip, considering the matter. Major Ward was right, of course, but if they let the Faros through, then they were going to call for reinforcements from all the trillions of ships they had waiting *inside* the Red Line. If that happened, they'd better hope that Etherus dropped the interdiction field so that the facets of New Earth could jump across the Red Line. If he didn't, they'd be stranded inside with countless enemy fleets incoming, and very nearly the entire human race on board.

"Admiral...?" Major Ward prompted.

Wheeler turned to her comms officer. "Give the order to retreat. Have all ships boost power to their engines and shields. It's time to lick our wounds."

"Aye, Admiral," Lieutenant Sebal replied from the comms.

"Here's hoping Etherus is watching..." Wheeler said, glancing up at the holo dome and the stars shining overhead as she said that.

Within minutes, the first Faro ships slipped through the wormhole. They formed up in a long line, going through single-file to squeeze through the throat. Wheeler imagined them colliding with inbound galleons along the way, but there was nothing she could do to warn them.

Time crawled by as Wheeler watched her forces retreat, streaming away from the enemy in clumps and trickling green lines. Now that her ships had withdrawn from the wormhole, the Faros were focusing less on obliterating them, and more on recharging their own shields. They'd need to last long enough on the other side to send a message to their forces at The Holy City.

Half an hour passed like that, with both fleets trading blows only sparingly. Wheeler's ship, the *Gideon,* now had her shields back up over fifty percent, and the Faros were still lining up to file through the wormhole.

And the interdiction field remained in place. A trickle of doubt wormed into Wheeler's gut. By now the Faros should have been able to alert the rest of their fleet. There was no point for Etherus to keep the interdiction field up any longer. At least, not until the Faros' reinforcements returned from The Holy City. By now Etherus should have seen what was happening and dropped the interdiction field so that the facets of New Earth and all their remaining galleons could join Wheeler's fleet outside the Red Line.

Her gaze strayed to one side of the battle grid, where a fuzzy grayed-out area extended off the side. That was the beginning of the interdiction field—the area that their comms and sensors couldn't penetrate. As far as they could tell, that field extended for at least a thousand light years in all directions, which was more than enough to prevent anyone from ever trying to cross it with conventional drive systems. If New Earth wanted to fly across the Red Line without using their jump drives, it would take them thousands of years. *And this battle is going to be decided in a matter of days. Etherus, where the—* She caught herself before cursing. *—are you...*

In that precise moment the grayed-out section of the grid snapped into focus, and Wheeler blinked in shock. Had Etherus somehow read her mind? She turned to look behind her, but he wasn't physically present anywhere on the bridge.

"Admiral, I'm detecting—"

"I know," Wheeler replied.

And a few seconds later, the grid came alive with flashes and flickers of light as new arrivals jumped in. It took several minutes before the light faded from the grid, and by then, Wheeler saw that New Earth and its entire fleet had arrived: over half a million of the giant triangular facets of New Earth, surrounded by literally millions of the cylindrically-shaped star galleons.

Not daring to blink, for fear that the fleet would prove to be an elaborate hallucination and vanish the moment she shut her eyes, Wheeler's gaze drifted down to the friendly ship count on her contacts panel:

106,435,678

And from there, to the enemy ship count:

27,329

Wheeler grinned. "Helm, set course for the nearest enemy ship! All ahead full."

"Aye, ma'am."

"Major Ward—ready weapons! It's time to press our advantage."

"Yes, ma'am," the major replied.

Let's see you frekkers break our lines again, Wheeler thought. Go ahead, I dare you.

* * *

Captive Aboard the Faro Flagship

Tyra sat on the deck of an empty hangar aboard the Faros' flagship. Theola squirmed and cried in her arms. "Shhhh, it's okay. Calm down," she cooed in Theola's ear, but she wouldn't be calmed. Her diaper needed changing and she hadn't eaten in hours.

Tyra's own stomach growled but she refused to focus on herself right now. She looked around, meeting the tired and resigned expressions on the faces of the crew from her five ships—some six hundred people in all—not counting Atara, who was no longer pretending to be Tyra's daughter, and thus not being held with the other prisoners.

Brak stood beside Tyra, a motionless gray wall of muscle, naked, but in a sexless way thanks to the Gors' lack of external genitalia. Tyra wondered if these Faros knew that Gors could cloak themselves. If they didn't, Brak's ability might present them with a chance to escape.

A sudden hush fell through the hangar, broken only by a rustle of clothing and a shuffling of feet. Tyra stood up for a better look and saw that the doors on the far end of the hangar were opening and a procession of three blue-skinned Faros were striding through. They looked like the same three that had taken Tyra and her crew hostage.

As they approached, officers stood up and challenged them with angry shouts, but the Faros simply gestured to them with glowing palms, and they went flying. The would-be dissidents crashed into the people next to them and fell in heaps to either side of the Faros, clearing a path. Tyra watched the blue-skinned aliens proceed wordlessly through the hangar, heedless of the seething wall of humanity closing in around them. No one dared to attack them— *yet*. The crews' restraint was remarkable, but Tyra feared it wouldn't last long. She tracked the three Faros through the hangar, wondering who or what they were looking for. Then Abaddon's glowing blue gaze caught hers and he abruptly swerved in her direction. Her heart leapt into her throat and began pulsing at a rapid rate. They were looking for *her*.

"We need food and water," Tyra said as soon as soon as Abaddon stopped in front of her. "And unless you want krak all over your deck, we'll need access to the ship's facilities, too."

Abaddon's eyes flashed, but then he smiled and nodded to the hazy blue shield covering the broad entrance of the hangar. "All of those problems can be solved with the flick of a switch."

Tyra caught his meaning and glared at him. "If you were going to kill us all at once, why bring us aboard? Besides, Etherus is more likely to respond to your threats if you give him a chance to save lives. If you jump straight to killing all of your hostages, he might think that negotiating with you is a waste of time. I would."

Abaddon scowled and made a cutting gesture with his hand. "Enough talk! You think you can fool me? You've been in league with Etherus from the start. You lured us here! For all I know, *Astralis* left the Red Line eight years ago with that very goal: to lure us to The Holy City so that you could attack the Forge."

Tyra opened her mouth to deny it, but Abaddon's hand flashed out and closed around her throat, cutting off any reply she might have made. Tyra's lungs burned for air, and Theola struggled in her arms, her tiny hands prying at Abaddon's fingers around her throat.

Tyra's vision clouded with dark spots, and a ringing began in her ears, but she battled to stay conscious. Brak loomed beside them. "Enough!" he boomed, and ripped Abaddon's arm away from Tyra's throat.

Tyra sucked in a hasty breath and clutched her aching throat with the hand that wasn't holding Theola.

Brak gave the Faro leader a mighty shove, forcing Abaddon back a few steps. He put himself between Tyra and the Faros, and then roared at them with deafening force, every muscle in his body flexing at once.

Tyra regained enough of her voice to warn him in a croaking voice: "Brak, don't."

But it was too late. A shimmering, transparent blade appeared and flashed through Brak's back. Tyra watched in horror as the blade slowly twisted inside of Brak, making a ragged, glowing circle. He roared in agony. His skin blackened and smoked with the nauseating smell of burnt flesh, and then his back burst into flames. The blade withdrew, and Brak stumbled away, his black teeth bared in a grimace. He was patting out the flames leaping from a matching hole in his stomach, and Tyra hurried to do the same on his back, burning her hands in the process.

As soon as the fire died, Brak hissed in fury and spread his feet in a wide stance, his hands balled into fists. Gors were hard to kill. His yellow eyes were fixed on Abaddon, and narrowed to deadly slits.

He was about to get himself killed. "Brak, no!" she said, and grabbed his arm to pull him back as hard as she could.

He didn't budge, but he *did* hesitate.

Abaddon smiled. "Yes, listen to your master, *slave.*"

Brak's muscles flexed once more, and his entire body shivered with rage. This time Tyra put herself between *him* and Abaddon. "What do you want from us?" she demanded.

"I'll ask the questions," Abaddon replied. "What do

you know of the attack on the Forge?"

"Nothing," Tyra replied. "I don't even know what the Forge is."

"Liar!" Abaddon's blade flashed out, the air around it blurring. The tip appeared just beneath Tyra's chin.

She froze, eyeing the weapon carefully. The heat radiating from the blade seared her exposed skin and she had to bite her tongue to keep from crying out. Thankfully Theola could sense the danger, and she shrank away from the blade rather than try to touch it.

Tyra's gaze bored into Abaddon's. All six hundred prisoners in the hangar were silent but for the occasional rustle of cloth and shuffling of feet.

"You are lying," Abaddon said again, more quietly now. "One more time. The truth." His eyes flicked down to Theola, and an evil gleam appeared.

Tyra's whole body stiffened with rage.

"Touch her, and I kill you," Brak spat over Tyra's shoulder.

"Good luck," Abaddon replied, his gaze not wavering from Tyra's face. "We're wasting time. Tell me what you know."

Tyra sucked in a breath. "I know as much as you. We sent out four people aboard a captured Faro shuttle to find the Forge so that we could destroy it."

Abaddon's eyes narrowed and his head tilted slightly to one side. "That much is true... but you're holding something back."

How could he possibly know that? Abaddon's blade drifted down, and Theola's eyes widened dramatically. Then she screamed as the heat radiating from the blade began to burn her face.

"Stop it!" Tyra screamed. She lowered Theola to the deck, but Abaddon's blade tracked her down. "That's all I know!"

"Who are the ones you sent?" Abaddon pressed, glancing up from Theola as she crawled behind Tyra's legs to get away from the scalding heat of the blade.

Tyra's mouth gaped open. She hesitated, scrambling for a way to avoid answering that question.

But Abaddon wasn't in a mood to wait. "Very well." He took a step forward, his eyes on Theola and his blade poised for a deadly thrust.

"Wait!" Tyra said, backing away quickly and pushing Theola back. "My husband is leading the team we sent. Lucien Ortane."

Abaddon stopped short. "Really? That is... very interesting... go on."

"We sent four people. All of them disguised as Faros and capable of speaking Faro. You gave them those disguises when you used them to find the Lost Etherian Fleet for you."

"Yes, I remember. Is that all?" he asked, and took a final threatening step toward her and Theola.

Tyra took another step back, pushing Theola back as she did so. "Yes! That's all I know! I swear."

"Very well," Abaddon replied, and the shimmering energy field around his blade vanished. He sheathed the transparent sword behind his back, and nodded slowly, as if coming to a decision about something. "Consider yourselves fortunate!" Abaddon said, turning to address the crowd. Tyra took the opportunity while his attention was elsewhere to pick up Theola and put some additional distance between herself and the Faros.

Abaddon went on, "You need no longer rely upon Etherus's mercies for your continued survival. Instead, you will be at the mercy of one of your own kind—Lucien Ortane. If the forces attacking the Forge agree to retreat, then you will all be spared, and a cease fire will be declared with humanity. If not, then you will all be killed."

Shouts of protest burst from the prisoners, and they surged toward Abaddon, but he and his Elementals hovered up out of the crowd, flying impossibly above their heads and out of reach. Tyra recalled that autopsies had revealed they had all kinds of technology inside of them to allow these kinds of seemingly supernatural feats.

Abaddon smiled down on her. "Thank you for your cooperation. I do hope for your sake that your husband proves to be as reasonable as you are."

Tyra shook her head. "He won't give in. Not to save six hundred people, and not when he knows that there are trillions of other lives at stake."

"Are you certain of that?" Abaddon cocked his head, his glowing blue gaze suddenly dancing with amusement. "Not even when he learns that he'll be sacrificing his wife and two daughters to win this war?"

Tyra glared up at him, speechless.

Abaddon nodded and flashed a smug smile. "Yes, I can see that I am right. He will think twice about killing his own family."

With that, Abaddon and his two black-robed Elementals all flew back the way they'd come.

Incensed by the Faros' threats, the crowd surged after them, reaching the exit just as the Faros hovered down for a landing.

This time they didn't bother pushing the prisoners back; they just opened fire. Hot white balls of plasma shot out of their bare palms, slamming into people and exploding with bright flashes of light and pulsating waves of heat that Tyra could feel all the way on the other side of the hangar. People screamed and scattered, giving the Faros the time they needed to depart.

The doors rumbled open and shut behind them, leaving the prisoners alone with the cries of the wounded and the aching silence of the dead.

Tyra blinked, her eyes scanning the chaos for Brak. She found him lying on the deck just a few feet away from her, his hands clutching the hole in his stomach, and his eyes wincing with pain.

She went over to him and dropped to her haunches by his side. "Brak..." she said slowly, shaking her head. "Thank you."

He nodded once. "It is nothing."

Tyra grimaced and looked back to the exit of the hangar. She couldn't see it through the forest of people in the way, but she could hear some of them banging on the doors, demanding to be let out, to have medics treat their injuries, food sent down...

Tyra's eyes drifted out of focus, her own hunger, and even Theola's muffled cries faded into the background, somehow insignificant in the face of Abaddon's threats. He was going to use Lucien's love for his family to force him to back down—but would it even work? Who had he found to join their mission to destroy the Forge, and would they even listen if Lucien asked them to retreat?

Furthermore, how was Abaddon going to contact Lucien to make his threat? Even if the Forge were close enough to allow communication, the interdiction field around the Red Line would prevent comms signals from getting out or back in. Abaddon would have to send a ship through the wormhole to get his message to Lucien, and another one to get Lucien's reply. With all of those barriers to communication, it could take a long time before their fates were decided.

Tyra grimaced. Suddenly their hunger and discomfort no longer seemed so insignificant. It could be days or even weeks before a comms message reached Lucien and his reply returned, and if food and water didn't arrive, it wouldn't matter what he decided: they'd all be dead, anyway.

CHAPTER 30

Aboard the Separatist Fleet

Lucien met back up with the others on their way out of the mess hall. The crab-like guards who'd brought them there from the bridge were waiting for them at the exit.

"Follow us," one of them said, and they turned to lead the way. On the way back up to the bridge, Garek and Addy speculated about the *urgent* reason that they'd all been summoned.

"Maybe we're about to destroy the Forge," Garek suggested.

Brak caught Lucien's eye and hissed. "You are sure you wish to die so that this blue-skin can live?"

Lucien grimaced and shook his head. "There's no other way."

Brak hissed again, clearly unhappy with the arrangement, but he nodded. He understood. Gors were more pragmatic and group-minded than most humans.

The elevator stopped, and they followed one of the crab creatures back to the bridge, while the other one trailed behind. As they approached the entrance of the bridge, the doors rumbled open, as if Abaddon could see them coming down the corridor.

The guards stepped aside, and Lucien walked through

first. "What's the emergency?" he asked.

Abaddon turned from the giant, curving holoscreen in front of his control station. His glowing blue eyes were sharp, and his lips were set in a grim line. "We have been hailed by the Forge. They're asking for you by name."

"Me?" Lucien asked, his brow furrowing with that bit of news. "How do they know I'm here? What do they want?

"Abaddon claims to have your family hostage at The Holy City. He's threatening to kill them and hundreds of other hostages if you don't stop attacking the Forge."

Lucien's blood turned to ice. "How..." he shook his head.

"They're bluffing," Garek said.

"Then how do they know that Lucien is here?" Abaddon asked. "They must have found out from someone."

Garek shrugged. "A spy probably leaked the information."

Lucien felt his own suspicions rise with Garek's skepticism. "How did the Forge get a message from whoever is holding my family hostage? If they're inside the Red Line and the interdiction field doesn't allow comms signals in or out..."

"They must have sent a messenger ship through the wormhole," Addy said. She walked up beside Lucien, her gaze seeking his. "Look, you don't have to do this. It's too much. No one can be expected to give up their own life *and* their family's lives for the greater good. No one would blame you for backing down."

"*Can* we back down?" Lucien asked, turning to Abaddon. "If I say we should retreat, will you?"

Abaddon held his gaze. "Yes. The choice remains

yours. If you decide not to press the attack, I will retreat. You will live, and your family will live—if the ones holding them hostage can be trusted to keep their word."

"But you've lost ships, crew members, resources... you're saying you'll just swallow those losses, no hard feelings?" Lucien pressed.

Abaddon inclined his head. "My enemy has also taken losses. That is sufficient payment for mine."

"How did they get a message all the way out here?" Garek asked. "Aren't we a long way from the Red Line?"

The separatist leader explained: "The Abaddons have a private network of quantum relays with pre-calculated routes that facilitate travel and communications at near instantaneous speeds. It's called the *quantanet*. It is not truly instant like Etherian comms technology, but it is close enough."

"How do you know that Etherian comms technology is instant?" Addy asked. "Not even *we* knew that their comms are instant until we found the lost fleet, and we have far more interaction with the Etherians than anyone outside the Red Line."

Abaddon replied, "There are rumors about them. Their fleet was lost beyond the Red Line for more than ten thousand years before you found it. That is more than enough time for such rumors to spread, wouldn't you agree?"

"I think the more immediate question is what are you going to do?" Garek asked, turning to Lucien.

Lucien shook his head slowly, and his eyes drifted to the holoscreen. Explosions sprinkled fire through the void; streaking red and blue lasers flashed back and forth; missiles spiraled and danced, bursting open in glittering clouds of debris as they reached their targets. Separatist sphere ships hovered all around the luminous gold cube that was the Forge, firing in steady streams. As big as those spherical warships were, they were dwarfed beside the Forge. Clouds of smaller ships swarmed around the sphere ships and the Forge—fighters and Faro capital ships, reduced to mere glinting specks at this range.

"What if we lose?" Lucien said, slowly tearing his eyes away from the holoscreen. "What if I end up sacrificing my family and my own life, and we lose this battle?"

Abaddon offered a sympathetic smile. "The enemy wouldn't be trying to force a surrender if they weren't worried that we can win."

"And what do *you* think?"

"We *will* win," Abaddon replied. "We are already winning. It is only a matter of time."

Lucien nodded slowly. His eyes slid back to the holoscreen, drifting out of focus as the conflicting thoughts racing through his head took all of his attention. He knew what he had to do, but he couldn't get the words out. They got stuck in his throat. His legs began to shake and his palms grew cold.

After a while, the separatist leader said, "If your goal is to save your family, we should not keep the enemy waiting for a reply. Abaddon is not a patient being—I would know."

"Don't answer," Lucien replied softly.

"Are you certain?"

Lucien's eyes fell shut, and he winced. He sucked in a shuddering breath and blew it out slowly. "Yes," he said, and with that one word, all the fight left him. He sank to his knees, a numb and broken shell of a man.

"Very well," Abaddon replied. He turned back to the holoscreen and the battle raging there, his hands once again sweeping through various displays and control systems as he gave orders to his fleet.

Addy sat down on the deck beside Lucien and rubbed his back, not saying anything. There wasn't anything she could say. They were going to win, and countless lives would be saved, but not the ones that mattered most to Lucien. Guilt stabbed Lucien repeatedly like a red-hot knife. This was more than anyone should have to bear.

"I have one request," Lucien said. His vision was blurry and hot. He wiped his eyes angrily on his forearm, only to discover that they were wet with tears.

"And that is?" Abaddon asked, sounding far away, no doubt distracted with the pressing concerns of managing his fleet.

"Transfer your mind to mine now. There is no reason to wait anymore."

Abaddon nodded. "I will do so as soon as I can, but it may be a while yet."

"Lucien..." Addy said, slowly shaking her head. "We could still lose, and if we do, there's no reason for you to—"

Lucien cut her off with a sharp look. "There are some fates worse than death," he said. "If I live, I'll be living with the knowledge that I sentenced my wife and children to die. Would you be able to live like that?"

Addy hesitated. Her mouth parted for a reply, but then shut, as if she'd just thought better of what she'd been about to say.

"I didn't think so," Lucien replied.

Addy muttered something under her breath, and

looked away, but before she did so, he caught a glimpse of tears shimmering in her eyes.

"It's okay..." he said, reaching for her hands, but she jerked them away.

"No, it's not!" she yelled, her eyes flashing. He was taken aback to see that she was angry, and not sad. "You're crazy, Lucien, you know that? I get that this is for the greater good, but no one should be able to make the choice that you just did! Are you even human?" Addy's fierce tone and the hurt look on her face confused him, but her words left him cold and unable to respond.

Her upper lip curled in a sneer, and she got up and walked away, moving all the way to the opposite end of the bridge to be as far from him as possible.

"Don't listen to her."

Lucien started at the sound, but recognized Garek's voice. He turned to face the scarred veteran, and saw grudging respect in the other man's eyes. "Very few people can ignore personal bias and emotional attachment in the face of duty. I couldn't. I *didn't.*"

Lucien remembered Garek's mutiny aboard the *Gideon* to save his daughter, Nora Helios, on *Astralis.* He also recalled the story of how Garek had fallen from grace in the Paragons: he'd brutally tortured and executed hundreds of aliens in revenge for them torturing and maiming his daughter.

"I consider it an honor to have met you," Garek went on.

"As do I," Brak added, striding into view. He stopped beside Garek and said, "The female human is only mad because you do not consider *her* reason enough to live in the event that we lose this battle."

Lucien blinked. Of course. He glanced behind him and saw Addy sitting against the far wall with her legs drawn up to her chest. Her green eyes glared coldly at him over her knee caps.

He thought of going over there to reassure her, but decided against it. It would be easier for her this way, thinking that he didn't care. In time she'd understand that it had nothing to do with her. The decision he was being forced to make now was simply too painful to live with.

Lucien looked out at the battle raging around the Forge, and wondered where Etherus was in all of this. He hadn't even lifted a finger to help them. Where were his reinforcements? Where was the proof of his divine power or of his supposed love for humanity? If he could help them and yet chose not to, then didn't that make him partially responsible for all of the lives lost in this war?

Lucien frowned, a cold knot of resentment forming in his heart. Something wasn't adding up. It shouldn't have fallen to *him* to save everyone. That was Etherus's job.

"You may all return to your quarters," Abaddon said, interrupting Lucien's thoughts. "It will be several days yet before this battle is won."

Lucien blinked in shock, and panic gripped him with the realization that Abaddon wasn't going to put him out of his misery yet. "What about my request? I thought you said—"

"I cannot transfer my mind to your body yet," Abaddon replied. "I will lapse into a coma after the transfer, and losing a few hours of consciousness in the middle of this battle could mean the difference between victory and defeat."

Lucien gaped at Abaddon. He would have to languish

with his guilt for several *days*. "But..." he trailed off, shaking his head.

"Come on," Garek said, hauling Lucien up by one arm. Brak helped on the other side, and the two of them half-carried him to the doors of the bridge. Addy was nowhere in sight, but Lucien heard an extra set of footsteps echoing softly behind theirs.

The doors rumbled open as they approached, and the crab creatures escorted them back to their quarters.

Lucien moved mechanically, his feet shuffling as Garek and Brak guided him.

Before long they arrived at their quarters, and Lucien had no recollection of how they'd even gotten there. He stumbled through the door and over to the couch to lie down. He shut his eyes, longing for sleep to come and take away the hollow ache now radiating from every part of his body. He felt like he was dying.

Time drifted by. Muffled voices babbled around him. Footsteps. Doors opening and closing...

At last sleep came, but it was no relief. His family's faces haunted his dreams, their eyes accusing, and in pain.

CHAPTER 31

The Lost Etherian Fleet

—FIVE DAYS LATER—

"A ship just crossed back through the wormhole. Should we give chase, Admiral?" Major Ward asked from the *Gideon's* gunnery station.

Admiral Wheeler pounded the arm rest of her chair. "Frek it!"

"Your orders, ma'am?"

"Hold your position," she replied. "It's too late to stop them now."

"Aye..."

Silence fell on the bridge. They all knew what this meant.

Five days ago the Faros had sent a ship through the wormhole with a chilling message, but it hadn't been directed at any of the human forces at the wormhole. Wheeler's comms officer had managed to decrypt and translate that message by using one of the translator bands found aboard the captured Faro shuttles. The message had been directed to Abaddon at the Forge, but it was actually intended for the forces attacking the Forge—specifically for Lucien Ortane. Abaddon was threatening to kill Lucien's family if he didn't back down.

Despite the concern that Lucien would give in to that pressure, the fact that Abaddon had even issued such a threat gave everyone hope. The Faros wouldn't be trying to get the forces at the Forge to withdraw if they weren't scared that the Forge might be destroyed. Within just a few days, the reply had come back to the Red Line: Lucien had not responded to the threat, and that had inspired even more hope.

Ever since then that message had been playing on repeat and the Faros had been struggling to get a ship through the wormhole to relay the news of Lucien's defiance, presumably so that his family could be executed. Wheeler's fleet was under orders to intercept and destroy any Faro ships heading back through the wormhole. But now, finally, the Faros had succeeded.

Wheeler shook her head and put the matter from her mind. There was nothing they could do to help Tyra or her daughters now.

May Etherus have mercy on their souls.

* * *

Captive Aboard the Faro Flagship

The stench of human waste was a physical thing, drifting through the hangar. Theola was spent from crying. She had a rash and what looked like a possible infection from the poor sanitary conditions in the hangar. Tyra had long-since removed her diaper and left her to run around bare-bottom, but there was only so much that the occasional sprinkle of water and air-drying could do for a baby's hygiene.

Making matters worse, Theola was desperately hungry for milk. This was a bad time to be a picky eater, but there's no reasoning with an eighteen-month old. Despite repeated requests, the Faros hadn't supplied anything even remotely analogous to baby formula.

Tyra's own stomach grumbled at the thought of food. There was never enough of it, and she regularly wasted hers by trying to get Theola to eat. Tyra's gaze drifted around the hangar, her eyes unfocused, her mind blank. The other prisoners moaned and muttered constantly. The sounds blurred into a regular rhythm and cadence: the dissonant refrain of human suffering.

"If they do not decide our fate soon, nature will decide it for them," Brak whispered.

Tyra nodded slowly, but said nothing to that. Her gaze drifted down to where Theola sat on the deck beside her. She had a vacant expression—her lips parted slightly, features slack, and dull staring eyes.

Something hot and ugly rose inside of Tyra at the sight of her daughter's suffering. It bubbled up from a dark, primal place and tore from her lips in an thunderous scream.

Heads turned, eyes widening at the sound of her outburst, but Tyra didn't care. She screamed again. And again. Theola began to cry, and other nearby prisoners cringed and looked away, a mixture of pity and unease crawling behind their eyes.

Abaddon would pay for this, Tyra vowed. He couldn't keep them locked up any longer, in these conditions, awaiting an uncertain end. *Better that we* choose *our fate,* she thought. She scooped Theola up and stood on shaking legs, her eyes wild as she looked around the hangar. All the exits, grilles, and access panels inside the hangar had already been checked for a possible avenucs of escape, but Tyra refused to accept defeat for even a second longer.

"You all want to die in here?" she demanded, scowling at each of them in turn.

Objections rose from several prisoners. A few of them climbed to their feet.

"It's been five days!" Tyra went on. "We haven't heard from our captors or even *seen* them in five *days*." Whenever they came to deliver food it was always with shadow-robed slaves and six faceless soldiers in matte black armor. Abaddon and the blue-skinned Faros had yet to make another appearance since they'd all arrived in the hangar. "I say, enough is enough!" Tyra roared. "If we're going to die, then let's die on our feet! Let's die fighting!"

Shouts of indignant fury rose up to replace the dismal sounds of human suffering. Heads bobbed and more officers climbed to their feet. Brak stood up beside her, too, but swayed unsteadily, still weak from the injury Abaddon had inflicted. Gors had remarkable healing abilities, but even they had their limits.

"The next time they come to deliver our meals, we ambush them! Let them try to stop us! If we die, we die free, the masters of our own fate. There's six hundred of us and only six guards. That's a hundred to one. I like those odds, don't you?"

Shouts of agreement tore out of the crowd and Tyra pumped her fist in the air. "Death to the Faros!"

The others prisoners echoed that sentiment and began to chant: "Death to the Faros! Death to the Faros!"

When their cries died down, Tyra said, "All former captains and bridge officers please join me to discuss our strategy. Everyone else, stand by for orders."

The majority of people sat back down, but a few scattered individuals wove their way through the crowd, heading toward Tyra. Before long, there were twenty officers standing around her in a circle. Tyra gestured for them all to sit, and then she began speaking in a hushed voice, outlining her plan of attack.

Every eight hours the Faros came to deliver their meals and a few basic supplies. At that time, several dozen shadow-robed Faro slaves would come in, pushing hover gurneys through the hangar, passing out meals and re-filling jugs of water. While they distributed supplies, six faceless, black-armored Faro soldiers would stand outside the hangar with the doors *open* and their rifles aimed, as if inviting an attack.

That attack had already been tried and failed. Within just a day of imprisonment, a small group of officers had tried rushing those guards, and they'd all been gunned down in seconds.

But this time would be different. This time they would surge out en masse, all acting as one, and drawing on their superior numbers to overwhelm the guards. And they had a secret weapon: they had Brak. His cloaking ability would allow him to slip out of the hangar unseen and attack the Faros from behind, distracting them at the precise moment that everyone else rushed them from the front.

"Are you all clear about your roles?" Tyra asked.

Officers murmured *yes, ma'am,* and *aye, captain,* but with dark eyes and grim expression. This would be a blood bath, and they all knew it, but they also had a good chance of success—at least in overpowering those first few guards. After that, six of their Marines would don the enemy soldiers' armor and attempt a more organized resistance.

"All right, go spread the word and get your crews in on this plan. When those doors open again, we need to be ready and waiting."

"Yes, ma'am," one of the ship's captains said. Tyra recognized him by his dark skin and silver eyes. It was Captain Orisson. She nodded back to him, and with that, the group of officers fanned out, whispering her plan to nearby prisoners and asking them to pass the message along.

Within just a few minutes everyone knew the plan, or at least some distorted version of it, but hopefully the gist remained. The plan wasn't complicated: swarm the guards; take their weapons; remove their armor; don't let any of them escape.

Tyra made her way to the hangar bay doors with Brak. The crowd parted for them as they went, and they reached the doors in short order. Tyra moved to stand to one side of the exit and wait. Theola squirmed and fussed in her arms. Tyra kissed the top of her head and whispered calming words. Then she felt something warm and wet trickling through her fingers and running down her leg, soaking into her already filthy uniform. Tyra paid no attention to it. She'd already been peed on so many times that her uniform had dried into a hard shell, creaking and cracking around her whenever she moved.

A familiar rumbling noise ground out, interrupting Tyra's thoughts, and a sudden, ringing silence fell among the prisoners. The doors were opening.

Tyra blinked, shocked that the Faros had come to deliver food again so soon. Had it been eight hours since their last meal already? Then came a collective rustle of cloth as hundreds of people simultaneously leapt to their feet, followed by a loud shuffling of feet as they all crowded closer to the doors.

Panic gripped Tyra, and her heart seized in her chest. It was time to act, and suddenly she realized she couldn't. She couldn't charge into battle with a baby, and she couldn't set Theola and run into battle by herself either. What if she died? Who would look after Theola?

"Stay back," Brak whispered. The air shimmered around him, and then he disappeared, having cloaked himself.

Tyra flattened herself against the wall and gazed back into the brave, desperate faces of the officers arrayed before her. A few of them nodded to her, and Tyra nodded back, still warring with herself. She couldn't do this. She *couldn't*.

The rumbling stopped, and Tyra heard a familiar voice call out: "Well! It looks as though you have finally found your back bones. Good. I was hoping you might."

There was no mistaking that voice. It was Abaddon. Precious seconds passed while Brak crept into position. The crowd fidgeted nervously. They must have been waiting for Brak to create a distraction, but surely by now he was already poised to do so. What were they waiting for?

"Well? What are you waiting for? Ah, I see... you weren't expecting *me,* were you?" Abaddon said.

Tyra couldn't see the Faros from where she stood beside the doors, but she could imagine Abaddon's smug smile, and the stolid expressions of the two Elementals standing to either side of him.

Captain Orisson stepped out of the crowd. His dark

skin gleamed with a fresh sheen of sweat, but his silver eyes blazed with a desperate, animal courage.

"Kill them!" Orisson roared, his arm snapping straight as an arrow to point at their tormentors.

Before anyone could so much as twitch, a blinding ball of plasma streaked out and exploded on Orisson's chest with a deafening *boom*. He flew backward, knocking over half a dozen people as he went. The crowd turned to watch as he skidded to a stop in their midst, and for a moment Tyra thought that would be the end of it.

But then they turned back to the fore, and Abaddon spoke again: "Who wants to die next?"

The prisoners roared with one voice, and surged forward like water rushing from a broken dam. They ran at top speed toward their enemy, their hands outstretched like claws. More radiant balls of plasma streaked out, three at a time, but the Faros' rate of fire wasn't fast enough to stop this many people. People fell as they were hit, but they were trampled and forgotten as the ones behind them rushed on.

Theola thrust out her hands toward the surging mass of humanity, her hands curled into tiny claws of her own, and something snapped inside of Tyra, her questions for Theola's safety all suddenly answered.

No one was going to walk away from this, and she didn't want to be the last one standing, left to suffer whatever retribution Abaddon had in store. Better to die a swift and merciful death than to be left at his mercy.

Tyra threw her head back and let out a shrill cry, and then she ran into the fray.

CHAPTER 32

The Lost Etherian Fleet

"*Halcyon's* shields are failing!" Major Ward announced.

Admiral Wheeler grimaced, watching as hundreds of Faro battleships surrounded the capital facet of New Earth. Crimson lasers speared the giant wedge-shaped facet from all sides. Tiny gouts of escaping atmosphere and debris appeared as those lasers punched through the facet's shields.

"They need to evacuate," Wheeler said, shaking her head. The muffled roar of an explosion rumbled through the bridge and shook the deck of the *Gideon.*

"They can't," Major Ward objected from the gunnery station. "They're surrounded. If they evacuate, their shuttles and transports will be cut to pieces. They're better off hiding below decks on *Halcyon.*"

"For how long?" Wheeler demanded. Silence answered that question, and she nodded slowly, coming to a decision. "Rally our fleet. We're going to clear a path for them to evacuate."

"But our orders are to hold the line at the wormhole and prevent more ships from coming through," Major Ward replied.

"New Earth's crusaders can hold the line without us

for now," Wheeler said. "The High Praetor and all of the chief councilors are on *Halcyon*. If they all die, there'll be chaos."

Major Ward gave a shallow nod. "Yes, ma'am."

"Helm, come about on a course for *Halcyon*. Full throttle."

"Aye, Admiral."

Wheeler's gaze fell from the holo dome to the displays at her control station. She checked the number of ships remaining in her fleet, wondering if she even had enough firepower to protect *Halcyon*. On her contacts panel, the grouping titled *Lost Etherian Fleet* now numbered just ninety-five ships. Wheeler's heart sank. That count had been a hundred and twenty-four just a few hours ago.

She was becoming so desensitized to their losses that she'd lost twenty-nine more ships without even noticing. Her fleet had started out with more than a thousand vessels, and now it was reduced to just under a hundred. The worst part was, all of those ships had been filled with refugees from *Astralis*. And the people from *Astralis* were actually better off than most. *Halcyon* wasn't the first of the other facets to fall. New Earth had arrived with more than half a million facets, and by current counts—Wheeler checked the contacts panel again—there were less than three hundred thousand left. Almost half of New Earth was missing—along with half of its people.

A soundless scream built up inside of Wheeler's chest at the thought of so many people dead. Where was Etherus? Where were the Etherians? Humanity had been left to fight this battle alone, and they were losing. All they could do now was hope that Lucien and his team succeeded in destroying the Forge.

Wheeler watched her fleet streaking across the grid to reach *Halcyon.* The distance between them ticked down steadily.

"Ready weapons!" Wheeler ordered.

"Standing by to reach firing range," Major Ward replied.

The nearest Faro ships slowly turned from their assault on *Halcyon* and lit their engines. Etherian ships had superior weapons range, so it was in the Faros' best interests to narrow the gap as quickly as possible.

"Range!" Major Ward announced.

"Open fire!" Wheeler replied.

Green lasers snapped out from Wheeler's fleet in staccato bursts, raking fire across enemy hulls.

Two capital enemy ships cracked apart in a matter of just a few seconds, drawing a feral grin from Wheeler's lips.

Then the enemy reached range with them and their lasers lanced out in crimson waves—followed by glittering clouds of enemy missiles, slower than lasers, but deadlier by far.

"Flight ops, get our fighter screen to take out those missiles," Wheeler ordered.

"Yes, ma'am," the officer at flight ops replied. She was new, but a necessary addition to the bridge crew now that Wheeler actually had fighters screening her ships.

Waves of Paragon fighters rushed out ahead of the *Gideon,* their twin engines glowing bright blue and winking at her as converging squadrons intermittently occluded each other's engine glows.

Pulse lasers stuttered out from the lead fighters in needle-thin green lines, each bolt flashing out on a slightly different trajectory from the last as they tracked incoming enemy missiles. Explosions pockmarked the void as missiles exploded one after another.

That went on for several seconds while Wheeler's fleet traded fire with the enemy. Then the Faro fighters reached range with Wheeler's and tore into them. Her fighters abandoned their straight-line intercept course with enemy missiles, now juking and jinking furiously to evade enemy fire, while simultaneously firing on the incoming ordnance.

"Our fighters are getting cut to pieces!" Flight ops announced. "Request permission to engage enemy fighters."

"Not yet..." Wheeler replied. Her fleet's fighter screen reached point blank range with the Faros' missiles, and then flew right by them. Wheeler nodded. "Now. All pilots engage enemy fighters at will."

"Aye, ma'am."

"Major Ward, prioritize interception of enemy ordnance with our guns and convey that order to the rest of the fleet. We don't want any of those missiles getting through."

"Switching target priorities..." Ward replied.

"Comms, get me High Praetor Serenity Talos."

"Yes, ma'am."

A moment later, the head and shoulders of the leader of the Paragons appeared. Her usually stoic expression was now grave, and her normally clean white uniform was torn and smeared with dirt. "High praetor, we're clearing a path for you and the council to evacuate. I suggest you get to your shuttles as soon as you can. We'll escort you to safety."

"Your orders were to defend the wormhole," the high praetor said as she coughed into her hand.

"With due respect, ensuring the survival of our leaders is more important than..." Wheeler trailed off as the high praetor's hand dropped to her side revealing a trickle of blood leaking from one corner of her mouth. "You need medical attention, ma'am."

The high praetor waved a dismissive hand. "It is too late to evacuate. Get your ships clear of the *Halcyon,* Admiral."

"But, ma'am—"

"No buts. Follow your orders!" The high praetor's rose-colored eyes glittered with deadly intent. "We've been boarded," she said, speaking more quietly now. "There are thousands of enemy soldiers on board. It won't be long before they find us use us to force a surrender. I refuse to let that happen. Get your ships clear." With that, the high praetor coughed once more, splattering the lens of the holocorder with blood, and then she vanished.

Wheeler gaped at the spot where the high praetor had been a moment ago. Now, in her stead, she saw *Halycon,* gushing fire and atmosphere like blood from hundreds of different puncture wounds in its hull. The Faro fleet encircling them fired mercilessly, heedless of their own troops on board.

"Missiles incoming! Brace for impact!" the sensor operator warned.

Streaking silver bullets appeared out of nowhere, swelling against the black of space as they spiraled in on hot red thrusters. Muffled explosions shivered through the deck one after another, setting Wheeler's teeth on edge.

"Shields falling below fifty percent!" Engineering announced.

"Helm, you heard the praetor! Come about and get us

clear!"

"Aye, ma'am."

More missiles chased them out of the engagement area, explosions booming like peals of thunder. Wheeler turned her control station to face aft, watching as the *Halcyon* shrank into the stars with their retreat.

Then, suddenly, the space around it seemed to shiver and a bright flash of light consumed the facet. It flew apart in a fiery hail of debris that tore through the encircling Faro fleet and ripped it apart. Wheeler winced away from the glare and shielded her eyes.

"They self-destructed..." Major Ward said slowly.

Wheeler nodded quietly, observing a moment of silence for the hundreds of millions who must have just died aboard *Halcyon*.

Another explosion boomed and shuddered through the bridge, interrupting that moment of silence. Damage reports popped up at Wheeler's station, and alarms screamed through the air.

"Engineering! What was that?"

"One of their missiles got through our shields and scored a lucky hit on our reactor! We're losing integrity in the containment field!"

"Lock it down!" Wheeler ordered.

"Here comes another wave!" the sensor operator warned.

Wheeler's eyes skipped down to the grid, and she saw dozens more missiles streaking in. The *Gideon's* laser cannons licked out, tracking them, but those cannons were heavy weapons, and poorly suited for point defenses. They weren't going to get them all.

"Major Ward!" Wheeler boomed. She spun her control station back to face her crew. "Intercept those missiles!"

The Major's hands flew over her holo displays, too absorbed in following that order to acknowledge it.

"Flight ops, get our fighters back here!" Wheeler demanded.

"They're cut off, and the Faro's fighters are faster than ours. They'll never make it."

"Engineering, boost power to shields!"

"Brace for impact!" the sensor operator warned.

Major Ward looked up and turned from her control station, her face drawn and eyes huge.

A muffled roar began, rising quickly in pitch volume as explosions piled on top of each other. "I'm sorry," Major Ward said. "It's been a pleasu—"

Before she could even finish that thought, a burst of white-hot fire boiled through the holo dome and swept them all away.

CHAPTER 33

Captive Aboard the Faro Flagship

Just as Tyra ran into the fray, the surging horde of prisoners suddenly flew backward. Hundreds of people fell in an instant, all piling on top of each other. Tyra stumbled away as the tail-end of that shock-wave rolled into her.

Then three streaking blue blurs flew out over their heads and landed in the midsts of the crowd. Shimmering blades appeared, raised high and poised to strike. The Faros hesitated, waiting for the prisoners around them to regain their footing; then their blades began swinging.

Chilling screams tore from prisoners' lips as they were cut to pieces. People scattered and ran for the open doors of the hangar. Balls of plasma chased after them, exploding with deafening *booms* and scalding blasts of heat. Over all that chaos, Tyra barely registered the sound of the hangar doors rumbling shut.

Abaddon was locking them in with him.

Theola started screaming, terrified by the sounds of battle and death going on around her. Tyra backed away, shrinking from the carnage and shaking her head. She had the presence of mind to cover Theola's eyes just before Abaddon cut a screaming man in half. Somehow, that failed to immediately silence the man's screams. Another prisoner, a woman, was beheaded.

Half a dozen men wrestled with an Elemental, struggling to restrain his arms—then the alien burst into the air, taking three of them with him to the top of the cavernous hangar. Hovering there, he shook them loose like dead leaves from a tree. They tumbled as they fell, their cries lost in the rising tumult, but the sickening *thuds* of their impacts reverberated through the deck, impossible to miss.

A strangled noise escaped Tyra's lips, only audible by the internal vibrations it caused inside of her. They were all going to be slaughtered.

"Stop!" she screamed. "Stop it! Everyone STOP!"

But no one did. People were dying everywhere she looked, the severed pieces of them falling in heaps. Tyra's legs weakened and she fell to the deck. She buried her face in Theola's hair and hugged her to her chest, whispering repetitive reassurances—all of them lies. But Theola believed them and she subsided, her faith in Tyra's ability to keep her safe blinding her to the danger all around.

Eventually the sounds of battle and death grew quiet, and Tyra felt a shiver go coursing down her spine. Someone was watching her. She was almost too afraid to look up, but forced herself to do so anyway—

Only to see Abaddon looming over her. He was dripping with blood, his white teeth smeared with it, and his glowing blue eyes wild with madness. In the background behind him, Tyra glimpsed his two Elementals picking their way through the fallen heaps of prisoners, looking for survivors. Of more than six hundred people, not even one remained standing.

Abaddon followed her gaze over his shoulder and

turned back to her with a smile. "I've saved the best for last. He reached out with one bloodied hand. "Theola... come here, darling," he said in a dulcet tone.

Tyra's entire body went cold and she shook with rage. "If you touch her, I'll kill you!"

"A bold threat under the circumstances," he said, and flourished his shimmering sword by way of explanation.

"You're a coward. I'm unarmed."

Abaddon grinned, and tossed his sword aside. The shimmering shield around it vanished as soon as it left his hand, and it clattered to the deck, now just a dormant hunk of translucent alloy. He spread his arms wide. "Go on. I'll even let you strike first."

Tyra's heart thundered in her chest. She slowly turned and set Theola on the deck behind her. Theola immediately renewed her screams and made a pouty face at Tyra. She raised her chubby arms, demanding to be held again. Tyra felt a sharp stab of dismay, but pushed it aside. She couldn't indulge Theola now.

She climbed to her feet and ran around behind Abaddon, trying to put some distance between them and her baby. Abaddon pivoted on the spot as she ran around him, never letting her out of his sight.

Tyra stopped and studied his stance, trying to decide how best to injure him. Part of her knew that this would only draw things out, but the Mother in her refused to give up.

She decided on an angle of attack and then let loose a feral scream and ran toward the devil standing before her. She leapt up at the last second, using her momentum and weight to deliver a kick to one of his knees. To her surprise, Abaddon's grin vanished in a pained grimace, and he stumbled back a step. Tyra landed hard on her side, but she quickly scrambled to her feet and backpedaled away from her opponent.

Abaddon took a moment to compose himself, and then began limping toward her. "My turn," he said in a strained voice.

Tyra continued backing away, out-pacing the limping alien easily. But after just a few seconds his limp mysteriously vanished, and he rushed toward her in a sudden blur. She caught a glimpse of Abaddon's outstretched arm and felt something solid collide with her chest. She flew backward and landed on her coccyges with a sharp stab of pain.

Tyra sat there on the deck, stunned, her chest aching from the blow. She struggled desperately to suck in a breath, but failed. Had her lungs collapsed from the force of that blow? She reached up to check that her chest wasn't a sunken hollow of broken bones—

To her relief, she found that it was still curving *out* rather than in, but she still couldn't breathe. The edges of her vision darkened steadily, and her thoughts grew fuzzy, as if her head were stuffed with cotton. A ringing began in Tyra's ears, and she barely heard what Abaddon said next.

"The pain's invigorating, isn't it?" He strolled into view and kicked her in the chest, knocking her flat. His boot hovered up, poised to stomp on her face. "Goodbye," he said.

Tyra finally managed to suck in a breath. Her vision and head cleared at once, and she rolled out from under Abaddon with renewed strength. She scrambled to her feet, but he kicked her in the backside, and she went sprawling to the deck once more.

Abaddon's laughter boomed in her ears as she

stumbled to her feet and turned to face him, panting with fury.

"This is all just a game to you!" she screamed at him. "You rail against Etherus, but you're no better than him. You're *nothing* like him. He's a better ruler than you could ever be!" Tyra spat on the deck and a gob of bloody spittle landed at her feet, giving her pause: that blow to her chest might have caused more damage than she thought.

Abaddon's glowing blue eyes glittered coldly, and his mouth twisted into a sneer. "If he's such a good ruler, then where is he now?" Abaddon gestured to the mounds of dead prisoners scattered around the hangar. "Where is he now, when you need him the most?"

Tyra's lips parted for a reply, but her mouth hung open, unable to answer him.

"He's hiding in his Holy City, that's where! And when he had the chance to surrender and save all of you, he did *nothing*. He left you to die, just as your own husband left you to die!"

"Lucien would never sacrifice trillions of lives to save just three, no matter how much he loved them."

"Love!" Abaddon scoffed. "You think your husband loves you? You think Etherus loves you? They abandoned you! It's time for you to wake up, Tyra. Love is the greatest lie of them all. No one really loves anyone. They love what others can do for them, nothing more. In the end we're all motivated by self-interest, even Etherus."

"You're wrong," a new voice declared, and a familiar, dazzling radiance appeared beside Tyra. She turned to see Etherus standing there, and she bounced to her feet and quickly backed away, wincing and shielding her eyes from the glare.

Abaddon's eyes widened and his mouth gaped open in a grin. "So! You've decided to deign us with your presence! Behold—the cost of your refusal to surrender," he declared, and gestured to the hundreds of dead crew in the hangar.

Tyra took the opportunity while Abaddon was distracted to circle back around to where she'd left Theola. She found her daughter wandering in aimless circles, dribbling snot and drool on the deck, and looking dazed. She scooped Theola up and hugged her close. Theola's thumb went straight to her mouth. She tucked her head under Tyra's chin and let out a shuddering sigh.

Behind her, Abaddon was still arguing with Etherus.

"There is no freedom!" Abaddon roared. "Freedom is a lie! Am I free? Is anyone free? None of us could ever do otherwise than that which we do; we're all just slaves to determinism, cause and effect—even you! You know this, and yet you presume to judge us for what we do?"

Tyra frowned, wondering at this new turn of the discussion.

"You're right, you are a slave," Etherus replied calmly. "Because you have no soul—but these people that you killed do have souls. *They* are free. Their lives are precious and meaningful. You and your kind, however, are just vile and hateful *things* created by the original Abaddon."

The clone gave an animal roar and thrust out a hand to his fallen sword. Somehow, the blade skittered off the deck and slapped into his waiting palm. It shimmered to life, and Abaddon rushed Etherus, his sword raised for a decapitating blow.

But Etherus vanished into thin air before Abaddon

could reach him. The Faro king spun around, searching for his quarry, his eyes wild and furious. When he failed to locate Etherus, his gaze fell on Trya and promptly narrowed. "You!" he said, and thrust out his sword, pointing it at her as if it were an extension of his index finger. "We're going to see just how much your god loves you, after all—do you hear me, Etherus?" Abaddon demanded, his gaze searching the farthest corners of the hangar. He threw his arms wide in invitation and spun in a slow circle, taking in the entire hangar. "If you don't come back here and face me, I'll kill her and her baby, and *you'll* be to blame for their deaths!"

But Etherus didn't return. Abaddon's eyes swept back to Tyra, his lips twisted in a chilling smile. "Never was much of a talker, was he?"

Every nerve in Tyra's body came alive with a sparking thrill of adrenaline. This was it. She turned and ran with Theola, but Abaddon's hurried footfalls chased after them, growing nearer and louder with every passing second. She imagined him impaling her from behind, his sword flashing straight through her and Theola at the same time, and a terrified scream burst from her lips. She ran faster still, but Abaddon was *unnaturally* fast. He raced by her in a blur.

And then suddenly he was standing right in front of her, his blade thrust out like a spear, waiting to impale her with her own momentum.

CHAPTER 34

Aboard the Separatist Fleet

"It is time," Abaddon said.

Lucien nodded slowly, his gaze fixed on the holoscreen before him, watching the tail end of the battle. The separatist fleet had the Forge surrounded. They had just forty-one of their massive sphere ships left, but now the Faros' fleet was gone, and the Forge lay utterly exposed to their attacks.

Lucien felt a hand land on his shoulder. "It's not too late to change your mind," Addy whispered.

He turned to her with a wan smile and shook his head. "But it is." By now his family would be dead.

Garek and Brak stood to one side, watching the battle, their faces grim.

Lucien nodded to Abaddon. "Let's get this over with."

The separatist leader rose from the bridge's solitary control station and started toward them. Addy watched his approach with a derisive sneer.

"You're a coward."

Abaddon glanced at her, his glowing blue gaze sharp. "I was clear about the cost of my help." With that, he nodded to Lucien and raised a glowing palm. "Come."

Lucien stepped forward. He wasn't afraid. He was relieved. Death would be a blissful release from the torment he'd endured over the past five days. In all that time he'd barely eaten and hardly slept, haunted by the knowledge that his family was dead and he could have saved them.

Abaddon's glowing palm wrapped around Lucien's face, and he stared into the dazzling light, waiting for his consciousness to seep away as Abaddon's mind invaded his.

Long seconds passed, but nothing happened.

Lucien raged anxiously against the delay. He was about to ask what was wrong when he heard Addy suck in a hurried breath.

Brak hissed in warning, and Garek muttered:

"The frek..."

Abaddon's hand fell away from Lucien's face, but the blinding light didn't diminish—it intensified and swelled to fill the entire bridge.

"Congratulations, Lucien, you passed the test."

Lucien gaped at the luminous being standing before him. His eyes ached from staring into the light, but he ignored that sensation, too shocked to care if he went blind. "Etherus?" he asked. "It was you all of this time?!"

"Yes."

Confusion turned to fury and Lucien felt his blood begin to boil. "You have a lot of explaining to do!"

Etherus inclined his head to that. "I know."

"What test?" Addy asked. "That's what all of this was? Making him sacrifice his family and think that he was giving up his own life, all for... some stupid *test*?"

Before Etherus could answer, the holoscreen began flickering and flashing beside them, drawing their attention to it. Hundreds—no, *thousands*—of ships were jumping in around the Forge. All of them were massive vessels, dwarfing even the giant sphere ships that the separatist fleet employed, and all of them had the trademark mirror-smooth hulls of Etherian ships.

"They came..." Lucien trailed off, confused by this turn of events. The Etherians had arrived too late to the fight.

"Why bother coming after we've already won?" Garek asked, his thoughts mirroring Lucien's.

Glowing white missiles streaked out from the Etherian fleet in shimmering sheets and began colliding with the luminous gold cube that was the Forge. Massive explosions raced over its flat sides, consuming it in fire.

"The separatist fleet cannot lower the Forge's shields," Etherus explained. "And yes, their timing could have been better, but it is the best I could do considering they had to travel for almost nine years to get here from the other side of the universe."

"The other... those are antimatter ships?" Addy asked.

"Yes," Etherus replied.

"How are they not spontaneously exploding?"

"They're all fitted with repulsor shields that repel matter from their hulls," Etherus explained. "As are the missiles they're firing."

"Antimatter missiles," Lucien realized.

"Yes."

"No wonder they're doing so much damage," Addy said.

"They've been traveling for nine years?" Garek murmured. He turned from the holoscreen to face Etherus. "They must have left Etheria before *Astralis* even crossed the Red Line, but we hadn't even met the Faros yet! How did you know to send them? You'd have to be able to predict the future to do that, and if you can predict the future, then..."

"Then it's determined, and no one really has a free will," Addy said, finishing that thought for him.

Before Etherus could reply, an all-consuming flash of light turned the holoscreen white as a sheet. As it faded, the luminous golden cube of the Forge was gone, obliterated by the hail of antimatter missiles the Etherians had fired.

"It is done," Etherus said.

* * *

Captive Aboard the Faro Flagship

Tyra dived for the deck to evade Abaddon's blade, but he followed her down, and Tyra cringed as she fell, her arms forming a rigid cage around Theola to protect her. She waited for the searing heat she imagined would accompany death by Abaddon's sword...

But nothing happened. Tyra struggled to her feet and ran, her boots pounding the deck resoundingly as she went. After a few seconds, she realized no footfalls were chasing after her, and she turned to see Abaddon lying collapsed on his side, his formerly glowing blue eyes now dark and staring.

Tyra's heart pounded relentlessly in her chest. Was this a trick? She searched the hangar for the two Elementals who'd accompanied Abaddon, and a moment later she located one of them lying atop a pile of bodies, not moving.

It took a moment for Tyra's brain to catch up: Lucien, the Forge... they'd won!

Tyra turned in a dizzy circle, not sure whether to laugh or cry. Now what? Would the Faros surrender? They'd cut the head off the snake, but did that mean they'd actually won?

What about all of the Faros' trillions of warships?

And where was Brak? Or Atara? *Atara! I have to find her.*

Tyra's gaze snapped to the hangar doors. They were open a crack, jammed with the bodies of dead prisoners. She picked her way toward those doors to see if she could force them open and escape.

Theola was screaming in her arms, overwrought and miserable, but Tyra barely noticed. She stumbled on in a daze, trying not to step on the dead. When she reached the doors, she had no choice. She was forced to step on them to peer through into the corridor beyond.

There she saw Brak, lying in a colorless pool of his own blood, his head no longer attached to his body. Tyra grimaced and looked away.

That was the last straw. She glared up at the ceiling and gave Etherus an unintelligible blast of pent-up rage. She didn't know if he was listening, or how he even could, but if he really was a god then she was sure that he could have and *should have* prevented this slaughter.

"Etherus!" she roared. "Show yourself!"

CHAPTER 35

Aboard the Separatist Fleet

"Is my family dead?" Lucien demanded, his eyes aching as he stared into the blinding light emanating from Etherus.

"No," Etherus replied, and the light radiating from him dimmed to a more comfortable level. "I managed to distract Abaddon long enough to save them."

With that, a tremendous weight lifted from Lucien's shoulders and the air around him seemed to clear. He took a deep breath and nodded slowly. "Thank you," he whispered as he exhaled.

"What about all the other people who died?" Garek asked. "You lost almost half of the separatist fleet, and I'm sure we didn't fare any better back at the Red Line. By my count that's trillions of people dead."

"The Separatists are all soulless copies of Faro minds," Etherus replied. "They were dead to begin with."

"Assuming I agree with that—which I don't, by the way," Garek said, "Humans all supposedly have souls, so what about *our* dead? You didn't save any of them."

"But I did. I copied the data from New Earth's resurrection centers to The Holy City before the fighting even began. It will take time for you to resurrect everyone who died, but you'll have that time now that the Faros are no longer a threat."

"They're not?" Lucien asked. "They all just stopped fighting?"

"Some of them have surrendered. Others are fighting themselves."

"Why would they surrender?" Garek wondered aloud.

"I have another fleet at the wormhole. I've dropped the interdiction field, and they are under attack by a superior force. They have no defenses against antimatter weapons."

"What about *Astralis?*" Addy put in. "We lost all of our resurrection data when the center was destroyed."

"And the one to blame for that incident saved a copy of the data before he destroyed the center. His goal was to use people's resurrection data to blackmail the living, but instead he used it to resurrect everyone in android bodies. When you find *Astralis,* you'll recover your people's data."

"So that's it?" Lucien murmured. "The Faros are defeated, no one really died, and all of this was just some ridiculous test?"

"No, all of this was a consequence of you wanting to leave the Red Line despite my warnings that you shouldn't. Perhaps next time you will listen."

Lucien saw a flash of anger and indignation flicker across Addy's face. That look was mirrored on Garek's features. "And the test? What was it about?" Garek demanded.

"To see if Lucien would make the ultimate sacrifice. I needed to be sure that he would act selflessly no matter the personal cost."

"Why *me?*" Lucien asked, slowly shaking his head.

"Your mind had all of the same initial conditions that the original Abaddon did, making you among those least likely to act selflessly; that made you a good test subject. The difference between you and Abaddon, of course, lies in your individual experiences and in the souls that you were given. In your case, Lucien, one of your two souls was derived from my own. The influence of that soul is what I was testing."

Lucien was taken aback by that. "*One of* my *two* souls?"

Etherus smiled. "Yes. They've been acting in concert to direct your thoughts and actions. This test was to see if such a symbiotic relationship between two souls could function and produce desirable results. You were the prototype. Now that you've passed the test, I can offer my soul to others and help them become better, too."

"No thanks," Garek muttered.

Etherus spread his hands in invitation. "The choice is yours."

"What's the point?" Addy asked. "In fact, what's the point of souls at all? Back before we left on this quest to destroy the Forge, you said that souls are what give us free will, but now you've admitted that you can predict the future, and that means everything is subject to determinism. You can't have it both ways. If the future can be predicted, then it's fixed, and we're all slaves to our fate. None of us really has a free will."

Etherus's brow lifted at that. "And how do you define *free will?*"

"The freedom to do otherwise," Addy replied. "Our choices can't be pre-destined and the future can't be set. If the future can be predicted, then it *is* set, our choices *are* determined, and we are not free. Rewind the universe, play it back, fast forward... assuming you could do that, everything would happen the exact same way every time."

"You have a good grasp of the concepts," Etherus said, nodding. "But what is the *freedom to do otherwise?* How might such a freedom operate?"

Addy's brow furrowed and she shook her head. "Well, there's quantum indeterminacy..."

"Which only adds random variations to the equation. It makes outcomes somewhat unpredictable, but ultimately fails to produce large-scale unpredictability in people's behavior, and even if it did, you'd be slaves to chance instead of cause and effect. You still wouldn't be free."

"Okay, I give up," Addy said. "You tell me: how is it possible for the future to be set and for us to still be free?"

"There's only one functional model for the *freedom to do otherwise,* and that is the freedom from the dimension of time. You need to be able to go back in time and actually *do otherwise.* Only one being in the universe can have such a power, and it must be used carefully.

"I am that one, and I am free to do otherwise. That is the point of having my soul co-exist with yours. The more you subject yourself to my will, the more you will share in my freedom—true freedom—and the more your lives will begin to follow idealized paths. Even the bad things will turn around for good."

Addy gaped at Etherus. "But that's still not freedom! That's just slavery to you!"

Etherus's expression became sad and wistful with that accusation. "That's what Abaddon said. I tried to give him what he wanted. I allowed him to create a chaotic universe for him and his followers, just to prove that I am not a slave master who forces everyone to do what I want, but Abaddon overstepped his bounds when he invaded Laniakea. Now his followers have all finally seen the horrible consequences of their rebellion.

"Unfortunately, it is still going to take a long time to clean up their mess, and the Etherian fleet will have to remain on this side of the universe for some time in order to help keep the peace."

"So now what?" Garek asked. "You're going to eliminate the chaos by giving everyone your soul so they can behave themselves like perfect little Etherians?"

"Not at all. I said the choice was yours, and it is. If you want to submit to my will, you will know true freedom. You can also choose to what extent you will do so, either following my will, or not.

"You see, there's a middle ground between those who prefer to live in a rigidly perfect paradise like Etheria, and those who wish to live in an unpredictable, chaotic universe like Abaddon wanted. That middle ground is to live in the chaotic universe, but with me subtly influencing your decisions based on what I have seen of the outcomes.

"Through me you will have true freedom, and the future will no longer be set—after all, I cannot predict myself, nor can anyone else, so wherever I choose to intervene, the future will change in ways that no one could ever predict."

Lucien was confused and overwhelmed by all of what he was hearing. He looked to the curving holoscreen on the bridge and gazed off into space. After a moment, he noticed something was missing.

All of the giant, silvery Etherian ships were gone. "Where's your fleet?" he asked, turning back to Etherus.

"They've gone to reinforce the one in Laniakea and to help compel a surrender from the Faros."

"We need to go, too," Lucien replied. "I need to see my family."

Etherus nodded and walked back to the bridge control station. "The separatist ships are slow. It will take us several days to arrive, but I will make sure that your family is safe until then. I am speaking with the Faros now, and the ship that has your wife and daughters on it has just agreed to surrender."

Lucien felt another wave of relief wash over him, and he nodded. "Thank you."

"You are welcome, Lucien. You may all return to your quarters if you like. Alternatively, you'll now have free reign of the ship, so you're welcome to explore. The gardens are a sight to behold."

Garek snorted and shook his head. "Maybe later. Right now I need to go lie down."

"Me, too," Lucien said. Addy came and hooked her arm through his, leading him off the bridge. The doors rumbled open for them as they approached, and she bumped shoulders with him as they walked through. This time the crab-like guards standing outside the bridge didn't turn to follow them.

"I guess this is what they call a happy ending," Addy said.

"I guess..." Lucien replied, trailing off with a frown. It all felt too good to be true. He wasn't sure he believed it yet. Brak trailed behind them, silent as ever, while Garek led the way up ahead.

"Now what?" Addy asked.

"We get some rest," Lucien said.

"I mean after we get back to the Red Line. The war's over... your family is safe."

Lucien knew what she was digging for, but he didn't have an answer for her yet. "All I can think about is giving each of my girls a big hug."

"I don't blame you," Addy said. "What about Atara? Isn't she still infected with Abaddon's mind?"

Lucien's knees snapped suddenly straight as that question stopped him cold. He turned back to the entrance of the bridge, the doors now sealed and shut behind them. That was the one question he hadn't thought to ask Etherus: what about Atara?

* * *

Captive Aboard the Faro Flagship

Tyra sat on the deck facing away from the field of dead bodies, rocking Theola in her arms and trying to get her to calm down, even though she knew it was impossible. Theola was hungry, tired, dirty... and feverish, Tyra realized as she pressed her forehead to her daughter's.

A rumbling noise interrupted Theola's cries, and Tyra twisted around to look. The hangar doors were opening.

Curiosity dragged Tyra to her feet, but caution whispered a warning. She walked over to the doors, but pressed herself to the wall beside them, out of sight.

Etherus walked into the hangar, accompanied by a group of bewildered-looking Faros and—

"Atara!" Tyra screamed and launched herself away

from the wall to greet her other daughter, but Atara greeted her with a sneer. "You think you've won, but you haven't," she said, and Tyra stopped short. Her gaze flicked to Etherus, and then to the Faros picking their way through the carnage. "Abaddon is dead! How is she still infected?"

Etherus met her accusing gaze with a sympathetic expression. "The kill switches were in the bodies of his clones, not in their data."

Tyra shook her head, unable to accept that. "How do we set her free?"

"By finding *Astralis*."

Tyra frowned. "I don't understand."

Etherus went on to explain about Joe Coretti's android empire and the data he'd stolen from the Resurrection Center before it had been destroyed. "Find *Astralis,* and you'll be able to bring Atara back."

Atara smiled smugly up at Etherus. "Over my dead body!"

Etherus stared unblinkingly back. "Precisely."

"What?" Atara blinked and shook her head, confused.

But Tyra wasn't. Her motherly instincts rose up in protest, yet her objections got stuck in her throat. Etherus was proposing that this Atara should die, but that didn't mean that her daughter would be gone—only her more recent memories would be lost, memories of being held a prisoner inside her own mind. Tyra could hardly protest against not salvaging those memories. Having Atara back the way she was before all of this began would be a merciful outcome, and ultimately that's how therapists would have dealt with Atara's trauma anyway—by erasing the memories of it.

Etherus nodded to Tyra, and indicated the Faros still

combing through the hangar. "They are looking for survivors. Go with them. They will treat your injuries and administer to your other needs."

Tyra nodded stiffly. "Thank you," she managed. Then her eyes slid back to Atara. "What about her?"

Etherus gestured to one of the Faros walking about behind her, and gave a slight nod. Before Atara realized what was happening, the alien walked up behind her and injected her neck with a colorless liquid.

"Wait!" Tyra said, but it was too late. Horror stabbed in her veins and twisted in her gut as Atara's body went limp in the Faro's arms. "Is she..."

"Yes, but she is not your daughter," Etherus replied. "I set her soul free of her body as soon as she became infected. Rest-assured, it will return to her as soon as you resurrect her."

Tyra nodded slowly, uncertainly, her eyes never leaving Atara's face. It didn't make any sense. Her emotions screamed against Etherus's logic while her rational mind agreed with him: *who we are lies in the data inside our heads. People are just biological computers. Turn them off and they're dead. Make an identical computer with an identical set of data and turn it on, and they'll come back to life.* Tyra held on to that and forced her emotions aside. She tore her gaze away from Atara, and walked up to the nearest Faro.

"My daughter needs milk," she ground out.

"We do not have any," the Faro replied in halting Versal. Tyra's eyes flashed, and the alien hurried to add, "We can feed her intravenously. Please follow me."

CHAPTER 36

Astralis

—EIGHT WEEKS LATER—

"Joe Coretti, you are under arrest," Lucien declared as the escape pod in front of him popped open, revealing the gangster hunched over inside. His face was completely different from the one that Lucien remembered, but the weaselly look in his eyes was the same. It had taken a little less than a day for the Marines they'd sent from New Earth to occupy *Astralis* and overthrow Joseph Coretti's resurrected empire of androids. They hadn't met with much resistance, since by now everyone was unhappy with the way Coretti was running things. Unfortunately, however, Joseph Coretti had never been found.

Until now.

"Frek you," the android in the escape pod said. "I'm not Coretti. You got the wrong guy."

"We have a lot of witnesses saying otherwise. Seems you got complacent and told everyone who you really were. I guess being infamous isn't as satisfying when your anonymous, huh?"

The gangster sneered at Lucien as he was dragged from his escape pod by two Marine sergeants. "You should be thanking me! Thanks to me, everyone from *Astralis* lived!"

"Thanks to you, we thought they were all dead," Lucien replied. Speaking to one of the Marines, he said, "Take him back to *New Halcyon*. I want to keep an eye on him myself."

"Yes, sir," replied one of the Marine Sergeants while shoving Coretti along. Technically Lucien was a sergeant himself, and he wasn't even a Marine, but everyone was calling him *sir* after he'd returned a conquering hero from destroying the Forge and defeating Abaddon.

Lucien frowned. He didn't feel like a hero. He hadn't actually sacrificed anything, and Etherus was the one who'd actually defeated Abaddon.

Turning to leave the hangar, Lucien found Brak striding in behind him with a squad of Marines. "Back already?" he called out. "Was the data center where Coretti said it would be?"

When they'd found the gangster's escape pod hurtling toward the nearest habitable planet, they'd threatened to destroy it if Coretti didn't immediately tell them where he'd stored everyone's resurrection data.

Brak nodded and bared his black teeth in a grin as he stopped in front of Lucien. "Yes, we find it."

"Is all of the data there?" Lucien asked, his heart suddenly pounding with the fear that Atara's data would be missing.

Brak replied with a nod. "It is being transmitted back to New Earth now."

Relief flooded through Lucien, and he smiled. "Good job, buddy. You should go back to *New Halcyon* with Coretti. I'll meet you at the station."

"Where are you going?" Brak asked.

"To see an old friend," Lucien replied.

* * *

Astralis

After Brak left with Joseph Coretti, Lucien gave Addy a call on his ARCs and asked if he could meet her somewhere so they could talk. She asked him to meet her at her apartment on *Astralis*.

Lucien had been confused by that. What was she doing back on *Astralis?* Wasn't it overrun by androids? He'd tried asking her about that, but Addy had refused to explain anything more over the comms. She wanted to meet in person.

Lucien's hover taxi pulled into a parking lot a few blocks from Addy's apartment complex, and he auto-paid his fare via his ARCs. That done, he got out and walked through the parking lot to a long, busy pedestrian street with shops and cafes lining both sides. A simulated blue sky sprawled overhead. The holoscreen projecting it probably lay just a few feet above the roofs of those stores.

As Lucien walked down the street, he scanned the faces of passersby, trying to pick out some sign that they weren't human, but they all looked perfectly normal to him.

Lucien absently wondered what would happen to these people now. Would they all integrate their memories with their human bodies and power down their mechanical ones?

Lucien reached the end of the street, and his ARCs

indicated that he'd arrived at his destination. A pair of vintage wrought-iron gates barred the entrance to Addy's apartment complex, *Fountain View Villas.* He keyed the holocomm for apartment 401C, and Addy's smiling face appeared in front of the gates just a moment later.

"Come on up!" she said.

A buzzer sounded and the gates swung wide. Lucien walked through a courtyard of soaring trees, hanging flowers, and ornate, bubbling fountains. To either side, at least ten floors of walkways and apartments soared into the simulated blue sky. The courtyard was filled with androids sitting on benches, and children playing in the fountains.

Lucien blinked. *Android children?* Was it even possible for them to grow up?

Dead ahead, a trio of glass elevators raced up and down, carrying residents to and from their apartments. Lucien reached those elevators and punched the call button just as one of them arrived. A man and a woman walked out, holding hands, and Lucien stepped in.

He touched the glowing *four* on the holographic keypad inside the elevator, and watched through the glass walls as the courtyard fell away below. What was Addy doing living with androids instead of her own kind?

The elevator stopped and Lucien stepped out into an open hallway. He walked beside the railing, scanning the glowing numbers on people's front doors as he walked by... *401A, 401B... 401C.*

Lucien stopped there in front of Addy's door. He raised a hand toward the holocomm, taking a deep breath to compose himself. When he was ready, he touched the button. "It's Lucien," he said.

Addy replied a split second later, voice-only. "Be right there!"

"Sure." Lucien nodded and resisted the urge to fidget. Break-ups were never easy, but this one would be harder than most. It wasn't fair to Addy, because he *did* love her, but she was competing with his love for three people, not just one. This wasn't a question of Tyra or Addy. It was about salvaging his family versus ripping it apart.

The door slid open, and Lucien sucked in another breath, about to offer what would be his first of many apologies—

But it got stuck in his throat at the sight of who had come to the door.

"Hey," Addy said.

"Nice to meet you," the man beside her said, and thrust out his hand.

Lucien eyed that hand, an exact replica of his own, and then studied the man's face; it was like staring into a mirror. He belatedly accepted his own handshake and allowed himself to be drawn into Addy's apartment.

"I don't understand," he said, slowly shaking his head. "You and my..." He glanced at the identical copy of himself. "Android?"

Addy grinned and shrugged. "He's got all the right parts in all the right places. All that's missing is blood and guts, but I don't think that really matters, do you?"

"No, I suppose not..." Lucien said slowly.

Addy led the way through a short foyer and into her living room. She and Lucien's android copy sat down on the couch, and she indicated the armchair beside it.

Lucien moved to sit there. He watched Addy holding

his android's hand, smiling freely, their shoulders touching, her head leaning toward his, and he felt his skin begin to crawl. This must be what an out of body experience felt like. He had to look down and check to make sure that wasn't what was happening.

"So what did you come here to talk about?" Addy asked.

"I'm not sure if that matters anymore. Does Etherus know that this copy of me is still around?"

"Yes," Addy said.

"And he's okay with there being two simultaneous versions of me?"

"He's giving all the androids the choice whether to remain as they are or to integrate with their human counterparts. Most of them have chosen to stay androids."

"Really? So he's going to allow people to make simultaneous copies of themselves now?"

"No. He made an exception for everyone who had duplicates made, including me."

Lucien nodded slowly, remembering that Addy had a clone of herself wandering around somewhere, too. All of the surviving crew members from the *Intrepid* did.

But in light of Etherus's explanations regarding souls, there was a problem with that. Lucien warred with himself over what he was about to say next, wondering if it was too insensitive. He decided to risk it. "Doesn't it bother you that he doesn't have a soul?" Lucien asked, jerking his chin to the android.

Addy grinned and shook her head. "Etherus is giving souls to everyone who didn't have them—former Faro slaves and android duplicates alike."

"He is?"

"Haven't you been watching the news?"

Lucien shook his head, and Addy waved the holoscreen in the living room to life. It was already set to ANN. Addy spent a moment rewinding the channel until she found the particular footage she was looking for.

Lucien gaped at the screen, watching as familiar luminous beings with round bodies and hundreds of tentacles descended from the dark indigo sky of some alien world to a waiting crowd of insectoid aliens below.

Then the scene switched to another sky, this one dark with stars. Polypuses were descending from that sky into a shimmering city of domed structures, flying *through* the walls of those buildings to find waiting hosts inside.

"Did you see me—him—get a..." Lucien turned back to face Addy and the android copy of himself. "Did one of the Polypuses descend on him, too?"

"Yes."

"Well, then... I guess all that's left is for me to wish you both the best of luck."

"You decided to stay with your wife," Addy replied. It wasn't a question, and there was a knowing look on her face.

"Yes," Lucien said as he stood up from the armchair. "But you obviously already knew that," he said, his gaze drifting to the android sitting beside her.

"It was a safe bet," Addy replied. "If you were willing to give up your own life and the lives of your family just so you could do the right thing, what chance did I stand of getting you to do otherwise?"

Lucien sighed at that. Addy knew him far too well. "Good point."

"I'll walk you out," Addy said.

She led him back to the door, and he walked out. He stood on the walkway outside Addy's apartment, listening to the sound of fountains bubbling in the courtyard below. "So are you two going to stay here?" he asked. "What about your dream of getting a ship and exploring the universe together?"

Addy smiled. "We've got to save the money to buy that ship somehow. This is as good a place as any to do that."

"That makes sense," Lucien replied. "Well, goodbye, Addy." Just then Lucien's android twin walked up behind her, and he nodded to the machine. "Goodbye..." He trailed off wondering what to call the android.

"You can call me Lucy," the android said with a wink.

Lucien barked a laugh as he remembered his old nickname. "All right, Lucy. See you around."

"See you," Addy said, flashing a broad smile and waving as he turned to leave.

Lucien walked away, and the door slid shut behind him, closing that chapter in his life for good. He remembered the carefree smile on Addy's face, and he carried that image with him back to the elevators and down to the courtyard below.

Suddenly he no longer felt torn between his feelings for her and his feelings for Tyra. Now that Addy had found her happiness, he could fully commit to working on his marriage with Tyra. In time he and Tyra would re-forge their bond, and their happiness would be just as carefree as Addy's was.

Lucien nodded, smiling to himself as he walked back through the courtyard of Fountain View Villas. Etherus had fixed everything for everyone, it seemed. *But not for me, not yet,* he thought. They still had to bring his daughter, Atara, back before his life would be complete.

Now that they had her data, it wouldn't be long. They'd spent the past six weeks growing a clone of her on *New Halcyon.* By now her body had to be almost ready.

Lucien's smile turned to a grin at the thought of seeing Atara again—the old, uninfected version of her.

He couldn't wait.

CHAPTER 37

New Earth

—ANOTHER WEEK LATER—

Tyra stood holding hands with her husband beside Atara's bed in *New Halcyon's* resurrection center. In the room with them was Brak, the surviving copy of him who'd helped find the Forge, as well as Lucien's parents and sister—the in-laws Tyra had never met. Tyra's own parents lived in Etheria and they'd been unable to attend Atara's resurrection on such short notice, but Tyra had made plans to visit them in a few weeks' time.

Lucien's father, Ethan Ortane, glanced at her. Tyra smiled at him, and he nodded, but didn't return that smile. He was still angry about this whole situation.

Tyra supposed she couldn't blame him. Ethan and Alara had just been resurrected to learn that they were grandparents and that they'd missed the first five years of Atara's life and the first eighteen months of Theola's.

Ethan had some choice words for his son when they'd been reunited. He'd looked like he wanted to knock Lucien flat. By contrast, Lucien's mother, Alara had just hugged them all and cried. Now she was smiling from ear to ear as she bounced a giggling Theola on her hip, playing 'got your nose' with her granddaughter. Tyra's sister-in-law, Trinity, stood close making silly faces at Theola and vying for her attention.

Lucien's family had been resurrected before Atara specifically so that they could be here now to welcome her back to life.

Everyone was clustered around Atara's bed, watching her face intently. She was lying on a gurney in a private room of *New Halcyon's* resurrection center. For adults resurrections were conducted in the stasis tanks where their clones were stored, but since that could be traumatic for children, they were brought back in private rooms like this one.

"The transfer is complete," Atara's doctor announced. "I'm going to wake her up now."

Tyra pressed closer to the bed, not even daring to blink for fear that she would miss the moment her daughter woke up.

For a while, nothing happened, and fear crowded Tyra's thoughts. "Nothing's happening... is something wrong?"

Before the doctor could reply, Atara's eyes fluttered open and she sat up with a gasp, her chest rising and falling in quick, shallow breaths.

"Agaga!" Theola said and thrust out a chubby hand toward her sister.

Atara frowned and her brow furrowed in confusion. Her eyes skipped around the room, taking in the sight of Alara, Ethan, and their daughter, Trinity. Atara shook her head and looked to Tyra. "Where am I?"

The last thing she would remember was falling asleep at home in Fallside, the night before the Faros had invaded. She'd lost months of her memories, but in this case that would be a blessing.

Tyra swept Atara into a fierce hug. "We missed you so much!" she said, crying and laughing into Atara's hair.

"You missed me?" she asked. "Where did I go?"

Tyra withdrew and Lucien hugged Atara next.

"Agaga!" Theola reached out again, trying to leap out of her grandmother's arms. Alara obliged by lowering Theola into her sister's lap, and both sisters hugged one another next, but Atara's expression grew more and more bewildered with every passing second. "Who are you?" she asked, her eyes on Alara.

"She's your grandmother, Atty," Lucien said.

"I have a grandmother?"

"And a grandfather," Ethan put in gruffly. He stepped up beside his wife and flashed a crooked smile. Atara looked to Tyra, her eyes seeking confirmation.

Tyra nodded, smiling and wiping the tears from her cheeks.

"How did I get here?" Atara asked.

Lucien turned to the doctor, his eyebrows raised in an unspoken question, and the doctor nodded.

"It's okay. She's old enough to process it. You should tell her."

So they did. By the end of their summary of events, Atara still looked confused, but there was a light of understanding dawning in her eyes.

She began nodding slowly. "I died..." she said. "My friends are never gonna believe this!"

Tyra decided not to point out that most of her friends had probably died, too.

"Do you mind if I give you a hug?" Alara asked,

holding her arms out.

"Okay," Atty said, allowing her grandmother to fold her into an embrace.

"Not without me!" Trinity put in, and wrapped her arms around them both.

"And me," Ethan said, adding another layer to the human sandwich.

After a moment Atara said, "Help! I can't breathe!" And they all withdrew laughing.

"Welcome to the family, kid," Ethan said. He spared a glance at Tyra as he said that, and this time he did smile.

"Thank you," Tyra said.

Half an hour later, they checked Atara out of the resurrection center, and they all walked across the parking lot together. Atara walked between her grandparents, holding their hands and skipping along between them, while Trinity took a turn carrying Theola.

They reached the Ortanes' hover car and all piled in, except for Trinity, who apparently had her own vehicle—a two-seater hover bike. She passed Theola to Alara and took Brak with her. There wasn't enough room in the car for him.

"I drive," Brak said.

"Nice try, muscles," Trinity replied.

Tyra smiled, watching them go. The rest of them took their seats in the back of the hover car. Lucien, Atara, and Tyra sat facing the elder Ortanes and Theola. Once they were all buckled in and the doors were shut, Ethan directed the driver program to take them to his and Alara's new house, where they were all planning to have dinner together.

The hover car shot straight up out of the parking lot and joined a slow stream of slow-moving traffic at 100 meters.

"I hear you're still looking for a place to live," Alara said and nodded out the side window to the scenery below. "Maybe you'd like to consider living near us on *New Halcyon?*"

Theola sucked her thumb noisily from where she lay on Alara's chest. She was already fast asleep by the sound of it.

"We'll probably have to," Lucien replied. "Tyra has a job waiting for her at the New Academy of Science."

"Oh, that's perfect!" Alara said. "That way we can make up for lost time."

Tyra smiled and nodded agreeably as she turned to look out at the rolling green hills and sparkling lakes of *New Halcyon* flowing by beneath them. Stately trees hugged white, sandy beaches and lake shore estates. Families were out on the beaches with colorful umbrellas and beach towels. Here and there barbecues smoked with grilling meat. The distant, muffled strains of music drifted up and reverberated through the car. It was a scene of pure domestic bliss, but somehow it didn't look real to Tyra.

So much had happened that it was hard to imagine a return to normalcy, to jobs and chores and routines, but that's exactly what everyone was doing. Etherus had recommended her personally to head up the New Academy of Science on *New Halcyon*. She also had an offer from *Astralis's* most popular political party to run for chief councilor there, but with most of the androids having chosen to remain as such, she didn't expect any humans to win an election there anytime soon.

Besides, she'd promised Lucien she would get out of politics and start working less. Tyra reached for her husband's hand. He laced his fingers through hers and smiled. Then Atara bounced into his lap and the air left his lungs in an *oomph.* His smile turned to a pained grimace.

Atara pointed down to a lumbering six-legged creature below with three people riding on its back. "What's that? What's that?!"

"I don't know... some kind of hylerocanth, maybe?" Lucien replied.

"What's a *high-ler-o-cath?*" Atara asked, enunciating the word slowly in an attempt to get it right.

"A *hylerocanth,*" Lucien corrected. "I'll take you riding sometime."

"Yay!"

Tyra smiled absently and looked over to where Theola lay on Alara chest, no longer sucking her thumb, and now definitely asleep.

"We're here!" Alara whispered.

"Yippee!" Atara squealed, drawing a sharp look from Lucien.

"Shhh. You'll wake your sister."

Tyra looked out the window to see them hovering down to a landing pad on the roof of a sprawling mansion beside one of *New Halcyon's* lakes. Her eyebrows fluttered up at the sight, and she turned to Lucien.

"You didn't tell me your parents were rich."

Lucien shrugged. "You never asked."

"Angling for a loan already?" Ethan asked darkly. "You'd better start sucking up, girl."

"What? No, I wouldn't—"

"He's joking," Alara whispered.

"No, I'm not," Ethan deadpanned.

"I..." Tyra felt flustered, not sure how to react.

"You'll get used to his sense of humor," Lucien said, bumping shoulders with her. "We all had to."

Ethan arched an eyebrow at his son, but said nothing to that.

The car touched down with a *thud-unk* of landing struts meeting castcrete, and then Ethan waved the doors open and they all piled out.

A warm breeze whipped across the roof, and Atara ran to the railing to look over the edge. Lucien ran after her, saying, "Wait up!" Tyra smiled and glanced back to make sure Theola and Alara were okay. Theola stirred sleepily as Alara climbed out of the car, but her eyes never opened.

"Go on," Alara whispered. "I'll catch up."

Tyra nodded and went to join the rest of her family by the railing. Lucien's hand found hers as they looked down on his parent's sprawling backyard and a sapphire-blue pool. In the near distance was a boat dock and a hover boat bobbing beside it. Beyond that, a hover bike with two riders came speeding over the water toward them.

"Is that Brak?" Tyra asked, pointing to the bike and the broad-shouldered gray alien sitting behind the handlebars. Trinity must have decided to let him drive after all.

Lucien barked a laugh, watching as they sped away, circling back around the lake for another trip. "Yeah, that's him all right."

Tyra nodded, looking around the grounds of the Ortanes' mansion. It was sitting on at least a few acres of lakeside property.

"How did your parents make so much money?" Tyra wondered aloud. "Aren't they Paragons?" If Paragons salaries were that good, everyone would be signing up.

"They made their money as freelance explorers before they joined up. They used to hunt for alien artifacts. Some of them turned out to be pretty valuable."

Tyra nodded slowly. "Interesting."

"Still don't think you need that loan?" Ethan asked.

"Well, if you're offering..." Tyra said. She and Lucien had lost everything when Fallside had been destroyed.

"How do you like the place?" Ethan asked, changing the topic and leaving Tyra to wonder whether or not he really was offering to help them.

"It's really spectral!" Atara burst out before Tyra could say anything.

"What she said," Tyra replied, smiling and tousling Atara's hair.

Alara came to join them at the railing with Theola and flashed a cryptic smile at Tyra.

"Good. I'm glad you like it," Ethan replied, suddenly grinning. "It's yours if you want it."

Tyra blinked, and glanced at Lucien, only to find him wearing a matching grin. "What? You're offering us a... a house?"

Ethan grinned. "Is that a problem?"

Tyra fixed Lucien with a bemused frown. "You knew about this?"

He nodded. "I picked the house."

Tyra blinked, taken aback.

"We haven't bought it yet," he added quickly. "We just rented it for a few days, so we could try it before we buy it. In case you don't like it."

Tyra slowly shook her head. Her eyes found Ethan's

once more. "Are you sure about this?"

He shrugged. "What's the use of having money if you can't spend it on the people you love?"

"But you don't even know me!" Tyra objected.

"I don't need to. You're married to my son, and he loves you. That's good enough for me."

"But..."

"Consider it a late wedding present," Alara said.

Tyra looked away, speechless, back to the pool and the sprawling grounds around the home. The first floor of the house wrapped around the pool in two separate wings, each of them big enough to be a three bedroom home all by itself. Tall green trees waved around the property, their leaves rustling in the wind.

Tyra had worked so hard her whole life to have a place like this, and here it was being handed to her free of charge.

"Lucien explained what happened, how you lost your home on *Astralis*," Ethan said, speaking into the silence. "We wanted to help you get back what you lost. But if you don't like this home, you and Lucien are free to go pick another one together."

Tyra turned back to him and shook her head, blinking tears. "No. This is perfect. I don't know what to say... thank you," she managed.

Ethan grinned and nodded. "Don't mention it."

"We're going to live here?" Atara asked, her eyes huge.

"That's right," Lucien said.

"Yippee! Can I go swimming? Please, please, pleaaase!"

"We can go together," Ethan said before anyone else could reply.

Atara grabbed his hand and dragged her grandfather toward what looked like an elevator or stairwell rising from the center of the roof.

Ethan had to run to keep up with his granddaughter, and everyone laughed at the comical picture of a five-year-old dragging a grown man behind her.

"Wait for us!" Lucien said. He grabbed Tyra's hand, and ran after them. Tyra just smiled, her heart bursting with joy. *Us.* They were an *us* again. Not just her and Lucien, but Atara, Brak, Ethan, Alara... all of them. Everyone was back together; the ones who'd died were all back from the dead, and without even the memory of their deaths to weigh them down. It was a miracle, and they had just one person to thank.

Tyra lifted her eyes skyward, and smiled. *Thank you, Etherus.*

The jury was still out on exactly *what* Etherus was, but at least there could no longer be any doubt about *who* he was: he was definitely good, and that was good enough for her.

GET JASPER'S NEXT BOOK FOR FREE

Worlds Apart: Children of the Future
(A Sci-Fi Mystery)

(Coming December 2017)

Get a Kindle copy for FREE if you post an honest review of this book on Amazon and send it to me here: http://smarturl.it/ds9review

Thank you in advance for your feedback!

I read every review and use your comments to improve my work.

KEEP IN TOUCH

SUBSCRIBE to my Mailing List
and get two FREE Kindle Books!
(http://files.jaspertscott.com/mailinglist.html)

Follow me on Twitter:
@JasperTscott

Look me up on Facebook:
Jasper T. Scott

Check out my website:
www.JasperTscott.com

Or send me an e-mail:
JasperTscott@gmail.com

OTHER BOOKS BY JASPER SCOTT

Suggested reading order

New Frontiers Series
Excelsior (Book 1)
Mindscape (Book 2)
Exodus (Book 3)

Dark Space Series
Dark Space
Dark Space 2: The Invisible War
Dark Space 3: Origin
Dark Space 4: Revenge
Dark Space 5: Avilon
Dark Space 6: Armageddon

Dark Space Universe Series
Dark Space Universe (Book 1)
Dark Space Universe (Book 2)
Dark Space Universe (Book 3)

Worlds Apart
Worlds Apart: Children of the Future
(coming December 2017)

Early Work
Escape
Mrythdom

ABOUT THE AUTHOR

Jasper Scott is a USA TODAY bestselling science fiction author, known for writing intricate plots with unexpected twists.

His books have been translated into Japanese and German and adapted for audio, with collectively over 500,000 copies purchased.

Jasper was born and raised in Canada by South African parents, with a British cultural heritage on his mother's side and German on his father's, to which he has now added Latin culture with his wonderful wife.

After spending years living as a starving artist, he finally quit his various jobs to become a full-time writer. In his spare time he enjoys reading, traveling, going to the gym, and spending time with his family.

Made in the USA
Lexington, KY
14 April 2018